A NEXUS CLASSIC

THE CORRECTION
OF AN ESSEX MAID

Yolanda Celbridge

D1612636

This book is a work of fiction.
In real life, make sure you practise safe sex.

First published in 1995 by
Nexus
Thames Wharf Studios
Rainville Road
London W6 9HA

This Nexus Classic edition 2003

www.nexus-books.co.uk

ISBN 0 352 33780 X

Typeset by TW Typesetting, Plymouth, Devon
Printed and bound by Clays Ltd, St Ives PLC

THE CORRECTION OF AN ESSEX MAID

'You are as sweet as your bottom, maid,' said Miss Duckett and, without warning, delivered another ferocious stroke right across the tender skin of Sophia's stockinged upper thighs, which stung fiercely, brushing her spread furrow, and dangerously close to the lips of her fount.

'Eight,' groaned Sophia. 'Thank you, Miss.'

Miss Duckett laughed serenely. 'I already gave you number eight, maid,' she chided. 'That means we shall have to take the extra stroke.'

'Of course, Miss,' said Sophia at once, conscious of her impropriety. She gasped as her fesses jerked again.

Contents

1

The Sacred Portion

Snowflakes fell on the young woman's head, forming clumps and whorls as it clung to her dirt-encrusted blonde tresses. She had no bonnet, and was too careless of her appearance, or too tired, to brush the snow away. The snow began to shroud her trembling body, hiding the patches on her frayed jacket and skirt, as she shivered in exhaustion and hunger, then slowly sank in a huddle of dejection on the kerbstone. She could be arrested by a Peeler as a vagrant, for it was illegal to sit down anywhere but on a public bench; even there, it was unlawful to sleep, and she had the aspect of a woman longing for sleep even more than food.

Her steps had taken her away from Aldgate and up Commercial Street, towards the Angle, where there was a little park with benches, and the air was healthier than in the alleys of the East End. There were no benches in Commercial Street, a place of gaunt warehouses and the occasional tavern, where a young Lady, had she possessed the twopence for a pot of beer – which this one evidently did not – ventured only for vicious gain, by the lifting of her skirts in feigned passion.

It was afternoon, and on this January day the pale sun was already fading. The only others on Commercial Street were Ladies with beribboned umbrellas, plying their immoral trade by curtseys and winks at the rare carriages which prowled idly past. Occasionally one would stop; a brief discussion would be followed by the clambering of the street Lady into the warm carriage. The huddled woman watched them with dull, frost-glazed eyes. At first, these public women had viewed her arrival with hostility, as an unwanted competitor; then, since she seemed quite uncaring of herself, with scornful indifference. The snowflakes continued to swirl on her, with gentle cruelty, and her blue-tinged face seemed almost to welcome their caress. She was alone in her world of cold and loneliness and fatigue, her very hopelessness a shroud, the cruel emptiness of the street her only world, a friend and comfort: a part of her. She could not have been more than twenty summers.

A large coach-and-four appeared at the top of Commercial Street and made its way at a leisurely pace past the wanton women who, after glancing at its occupants, looked disdainfully away. The coach slowed further as it neared the young woman, and the horses drew to a snorting halt. There was a pause, and silence along the whole ghostly street. The young woman did not look up until she was roused by the click of the door opening. Another young woman descended from the coach; she was equal in age and build to the crouching waif, though her hair was a lustrous raven colour, and she seemed a creature from another world, smartly dressed in dark taffeta and muslin, with flowing skirts, a cashmere cape buckled with a curious silver brooch, and a short silver-tipped cane.

She tapped the crouching woman on the shoulder with her cane, and said a few words to her. The blonde woman looked up in sullen blankness and did not reply, letting her head sink as though even that small effort had exhausted her. The dark-haired woman gently took her by the arm and helped her to stand, then led her to the open door of the coach. She stood in silence, looking at the other occupant of the carriage as though offering her shivering merchandise for inspection.

2

At length a soft female contralto spoke from within. 'I think she might do. Get her in, Miss Duckett, and we'll see what she's made of.'

'Yes, miss.'

The girl found herself inside a plush compartment, with leather banquettes and a little stove which made the perfumed air almost shocking in its sudden warmth. A proud Lady in stern grey tweeds, like a country-woman of the better classes, appraised the new arrival with cool disdain. Her face was strong and handsome, with a curious aura of quiet majesty that suggested her practical, if elegant, costume was a sop to public appearance: that more regal apparel befitted her. Her age was perhaps thirty; the girl could not be sure, and only knew that this being was for the moment her superior.

'Well, High Mistress? said Miss Duckett eagerly. 'Do you think I have chosen correctly?'

'Miss Duckett!' said the High Mistress, gently chiding, 'I know it is your first day out as a Lady. But remember, now you are Miss Duckett, and I plain Miss Brace.'

'Yes, miss,' said the raven woman again, blushing red.

Miss Brace carried a similar cane, this one tipped in gold, and with it she touched the waif under her chin, making her look up. Then she touched the top of her head.

'I think she'll do,' she said at length. 'Good features, and the headbones are well-formed. We must never ignore the phrenological science, Miss Duckett: the indentation of the skull tells us she is no common waif, but has the character of a Lady. What is your name, young Lady?'

The female was speechless with uncertainty and fear.

'Come, come!' said Miss Brace sternly, flexing her cane. 'Don't tell me I shall have to tickle the truth from you, so early in your training!'

The mention of training further bewildered the

3

female, but she managed to stammer that her name was Sophia.

'And your other name? Most people have two.'

'I have no other name, miss,' said Sophia wretchedly. 'I am an orphan, and . . . Oh!'

She began to sob convulsively and Miss Duckett, seated beside her, embraced her with a comforting arm.

'Why, Miss Brace, you'll remember that I myself had no other name when you found me. I think we can deal with the question of Sophia's name in due course. Sophia is a fine name, and one name is better than nothing. Perhaps she needs a jar of hot soup more urgently than another name, and I suggest we stop at the pieman in Whitechapel Road.'

Miss Brace smiled, and said that this was in order, and Sophia repressed a shudder, remembering the pieman's cruel words when she had begged for sustenance not an hour before. The coachman was duly instructed to stop, and soup and a meat pie were duly bought; as Sophia was handed her fare, she noticed to her surprise that the brawny, heavily-muffled coachman was a female. Gratefully, she ate her hot food as the carriage trundled eastwards through the snow, out towards Stratford. Sophia felt glad that she was not returning further near the river, down the Commercial Road towards the house in Arbour Square which had been the cause of so much uncertainty and misfortune.

In truth, Sophia was embarrassed to reveal her name. It was not the name she had been born with, for that was unknown. In her days of upbringing, she had scarcely ever needed to give a family name, and when she did, at first she used the names of the Mistresses of the orphanages, then the workhouse, where she had been so dismally incarcerated; then, at Arbour Square, where her duties as maid had obliged her to venture out into the restricted portion of the world that bordered the Ratcliffe Highway, she had used the name 'Longshanks', mockingly bestowed by her cruel Master, in view of her long legs.

Her 'stepping out' wardrobe being limited to the shabbiest rags and most shapeless dresses, she had never had the opportunity to receive the admiring remarks of any gentleman worth the name, who would have marvelled at her shapely jambs as limbs of wondrous, slender beauty. She was used only to the leering taunts of draymen, dockers and matelots, whose eyes strayed no further than her most obvious and striking feature, which was her large, perfectly-formed croup, two fesses that swelled on her slim body like ripe peaches. She was so inured to the coarseness of their jeers that she was unable to recognise the frustrated desire behind them, so that the subject of her large bottom caused her extreme embarrassment, instead of the flirtatious womanly pride which a more gentle and well-mannered environment might have bestowed.

Yet Miss Brace's words pleased and even thrilled her. She did not know what the phrenological science could be, but Miss Brace thought she had character, that she was that marvellous thing, a Lady! As she ate, her new surroundings and companions began to seem warm and friendly, and she gradually realised that all her life, she had nurtured a flame of hope and a knowledge that, beneath her rags and filth and despite the cruelty and insults which had been her daily lot, she had the spirit of a Lady. It had never occurred to her that her poverty and rags were anything but the just fortune of an orphan, to be which seemed some mysterious sin in itself; nor that there was any injustice in a society which condemned such as her to this wretchedness. There were Lords and Ladies, and a Queen, and there were poor orphans, and Fate had ordained things so. But she had eagerly fed on the stories of young maids rescued by princes, of Cinderella and Rapunzel and the like, and somehow knew that the day would come for the flower of her womanhood to blossom.

5

She looked out of the window and saw that they were crossing a river, smaller than the Thames; then the road began to rise, and they seemed to be leaving the city. Her companions, or rescuers, seemed content to join her in watching the snow-covered landscape through which they passed. Each woman was lost in the thoughts which the startling blankness of snow or desert bring to the soul. After twenty minutes or so, they turned left at quite a busy crossroads, where a signpost pointed to Leytonstone, over a railway bridge. The snow now shrouded isolated buildings, trees and fields. She gazed in wonder, as her sole acquaintance with the countryside had been the occasional outing to the park, or a walk to Islington along the Grand Union Canal. As they proceeded, the trees became more and more numerous, and she was moved to ask where they were.

'You should not ask questions,' said Miss Duckett mildly, startled out of her own reverie. 'To ask questions is unladylike. But this is Whipps Cross, in the county of Essex, and we have a good way to travel before we reach Rodings. That shall be your new situation – your new home.'

Sophia was so accustomed to obedience that the despairing enegy which had led her to flee Arbour Square had now ebbed, and she was happy to acquiesce in her fate, the more so when Miss Brace added lazily, 'Assuming, of course, that you agree to your new situation, Miss Sophia. If you do not, now or at any time in future, you shall be given a shilling and a railway ticket back to London. We do not want any malcontents or recalcitrants at Rodings.'

She pronounced 'recalcitrants' in the tone of a hanging judge. Sophia blurted that she was perfectly content, and very grateful, and would strive to give satisfaction. She began, apologetically, to recount the misfortunes of her life to date, and the cruelties of the master from whom she had fled, but Miss Brace cut her short.

'Your past is a matter of complete indifference to us,' she said sternly. 'I imagine it is no different from that of any other neophyte. Only your future counts. You must not explain nor apologise, in this or any other matter, for a Lady does neither, and you must remember that. So now you have learnt the first lesson of Rodings.'

Sophia wondered what a neophyte could possibly be, and if it had anything to do with phrenology.

'And further – your own person, your own secret desires, do not interest us in the slightest, except insofar as you are successfully trained as a Rodings Lady, and your true womanhood allowed to blossom as a mark of our successful tutelage. Rodings is a charitable foundation: we have no pecuniary interest, and my – our – satisfaction comes solely from seeing my neophytes blossom into correct young Ladies.'

She paused, and frowned thoughtfully. 'I shall not, I repeat, dwell on your sorry past; we must consider today, and your admission to Rodings, as the first real day of your life. But I will ask: at these orphanages –' she curled her lip in distaste '– I suppose you were beaten for your misdemeanours?'

Sophia answered glumly that it was so, and that her petticoats or drawers were no strangers to the strap of various cruel matrons.

'And at this establishment in Arbour Square – why, Limehouse is full of wickedness, and I had always thought of Arbour Square as a haven of respectable folk! – was it the same, with this cruel Master, as you say, this Mr Lee?'

Sophia blushed with remorse, and said that she had run away because she could take it no more. 'It wasn't the pain, miss, but the shame of the beating! Why, my bottom grew used to the strap, as any poor orphan's must, and could take the beatings as nothing. But I could no longer bear the humiliation of it! Mr Lee would not beat me himself, but would watch with an

7

evil smile as his sister Miss Rose did the strapping. Sometimes the servants would watch too, and the instrument of my correction was a flail made from the workmen's belts. Mr Lee would make each of the male drudges unfasten his belt, great heavy things, all torn and filthy and scratched, then knot them together, and give them to Miss Rose for my public chastisement. And the worst thing was that Mr Lee was very frugal in his allowance to servants – our clothes were rarely clean – and I had to take the beating on my dirty shift or knickers, exposing them to the eyes of all. I would not have minded the pain – welcomed it, even – had I felt it was for my own improvement and correction of my sluttish mistakes, and even the hardest beatings given in kindness. But they were not – they were given in . . . in malice, and that was the cruellest part.'

Sophia began to say that there was more to tell, but Miss Brace halted her.

'That is quite distasteful enough, Miss Sophia,' she said, 'and I may assure you that there is nothing of that sort at Rodings. When a neophyte deserves correction, she is punished in a thoroughly ladylike way.'

'You mean that when a young Lady of your institution is naughty or commits an impropriety, she is not beaten?' said Sophia, open-mouthed, as though she had never imagined such a thing. She could not but picture Rodings as an institution like any other, though seemingly kinder.

'I certainly did not mean that,' retorted Miss Brace. 'Improper neophytes, *and* Ladies –' she smiled severely at Miss Duckett '– are punished most soundly if they offend.'

Seeing Sophia's puzzled expression, she added with a friendly smile, 'Rodings is an establishment whose task is to take disadvantaged young women and turn them into Ladies. Or rather, to educate them to understand that they have always been Ladies. Education, from the

8

Latin "to draw out" ... Rodings draws out what is already there. Naturally, in proper education, strict discipline and frequent correction must not be shirked, neither by those entrusted with its application, nor by those who have merited it. An errant Lady will expect and indeed desire her just correction, which she knows will be befitting to a Lady.'

Sophia was sad that the darkness had fallen, but consoled herself that she would have plenty of time to inspect the countryside. The journey was slow and warmly comfortable, broken only on the occasions when Sophia and her two companions variously expressed the desire to stop for commode. Misses Brace and Duckett seemed charmingly unconcerned about squatting openly in the snow, and Sophia followed their example, smiling at the little hissing patterns they made. This was obviously the way things were done in the country.

She was avid to see her new home, and the sternness of her new guardian's words did not prevent her from feeling comforted by her womanly presence; indeed her talk of discipline and correction – in order to make a *Lady* of her! – added curiously to her excitement. She had no doubt that in the course of her education – or servitude? She did not really care – she *would* merit punishment, for she knew herself headstrong and wilful on occasions, and knew that she had frequently deserved the strap. She had spoken the truth: how she wished her beatings had been kindly, and for the amelioration of her character, rather than as a sort of punishment for the very crimes of being an orphan, and a girl.

The idea that chastisement could be administered for her betterment was new and oddly thrilling. But Miss Brace had left the details tantalisingly vague, and Sophia could not imagine what form punishment should take, if not the strap, or even worse, the cane. Would it be solitary confinement, or bread and water, or some other miserable penance? She shivered. The strap would almost be preferable, a swift physical pain rather than a slow spiritual dullness. Sophia had no doubt that young people like her were by nature errant, and that chastisement was a frequent and deserved part of a proper upbringing. But oh, that the smarting pain of chastisement could be kind in its sternness; the offence quickly punished, and quickly forgiven!

Time would tell; in the meantime, Sophia could not but feel awed by the majesty of the great house which their carriage now approached up a winding driveway. At the gatehouse, a simple brass plaque announced 'The Rodings', without mention of the house's charitable purpose. Accustomed to the cramped city streets, Sophia's eye imagined that the wooded grounds and gardens stretched for miles. Under its cover of snow, the house took on the aspect of a castle, with little turrets and battlements which in the melting dawn would no doubt seem more homely. For the moment, it seemed vast, mysterious, and even forbidding.

The front portal was a large oaken door with a shiny brass knocker, and there was ample space for the stationing of coaches on the cobbled square. However, their vehicle proceeded round to the back of the house, where there was a broad court framed by stables and outhouses. Miss Brace said it was time to descend, and they would enter through the rear door, which was more modest than to arrive grandly at the front.

'And I would like to slip in and see if anyone is up to mischief,' she said with a tight fleeting grin.

The ostler who came to take charge of their horses was female, like their driver, and the two women curtseyed solemnly before leaving together. Were there no men here? Sophia longed to ask, but was mindful of impropriety, and did not wish punishment quite so early in her education.

They entered a bright corridor whose stone floor echoed with the patter of feet, and Sophia was at once struck by how extraordinarily clean and polished everything looked. There was a strong smell of soap and disinfectant. She saw a stream of young Ladies, all with grey uniform skirts of thick coarse cotton, with stockings and a sort of cardigan to match, black laced boots and white blouses with a little bow tie at the neck. Their hair was demure and ladylike, and Sophia saw that it was cut short rather than pinned back in customary fashion. Each of them inclined her head deferentially to Miss Brace as their throng parted to allow her passage, on the murmured order of a Lady shepherding them at the rear.

This person was dressed quite differently, and Sophia thought her as beautiful as Miss Duckett. Her hair was a lush mane of auburn curls, pinned back but allowing some tresses to dance impishly on her cheeks; her figure was very full, and encased in a tight white blouse, apparently of silk, with a dark blue robe and blue shoes and stockings. At her open neck, she wore a thin gold chain, and there were gold buckles on her shoes. She carried a curious bundle of green twigs, about a foot long and a dozen in number, bound with golden clasps; it seemed some badge of authority.

'The maids are going for their tea,' said Miss Brace with a benign smile. 'You shall take yours in the kitchen, with the scullery drudges, since you have not yet been admitted to the House. Afterwards, Miss Duckett will take you to Matron for your examinnation, and to the Purser for your uniform, and then to my study, where you shall be admitted, and given your name; I am sure we may have a nice cup of cocoa before you go to your dormitory. Now, you are no doubt curious and a little apprehensive, but you are not to worry. At Rodings, everything is done and every information imparted according to correct procedures. You

11

have been warned already not to ask questions. I know that maids cannot be stopped from tattling, and nor indeed should they, for it is healthy and natural. Nevertheless it is improper, if not actually forbidden, to express too much curiosity about the rooms and fixtures of the House, of the roles and ranks of the various maids and Ladies you shall encounter. You shall be told everything you need to be told, and instructed to do everything you need to do. In a word, Miss Sophia, you shall be looked after.'

The beautiful young Lady with the auburn tresses paused to curtsey as she passed, and Miss Brace suddenly frowned. 'Miss Tunney!' she said sternly. 'What do I see?'

'I . . . I'm sure I don't know, Miss Brace,' said the young Lady, rather flustered.

'I am looking down, miss. When did you last look down? At your shoes, I mean? Buckles unpolished, leather scuffed, and a new maid here to witness! By my ancestors, how could you ever expect to be presented to Mr Bucentaur in such a state? It won't do, will it?'

'N . . . no, High Mistress.'

'Even a Junior Preceptress – no, *especially* a Junior Preceptress – must take care to set the highest standards. Now tell me, what course of action should be taken to correct this matter?'

The young Lady, Miss Tunney, bit her lip. 'I suppose a number three punishment is in order, miss.'

'Tut! Do not exaggerate your iniquity, nor your own importance. I believe a number two shall suffice. You may report to my study at . . . let me see . . . eight o'clock.'

'Yes, miss,' stammered Miss Tunney, curtseying again, and lowering her eyes from Miss Duckett's. 'Thank you, miss.'

Neither Miss Brace nor Miss Duckett spoke again until they entered a kitchen which seemed to Sophia as

vast as the house grounds, though considerably warmer
and busier. Maids in drab grey, with work skirts that
scarcely covered the knee, scurried silently with pans
and cauldrons, amid the fumes of roasting and boiling
food, at the barked directions of a stern, handsome
Lady in a white cook's apron. Sophia was shown to the
bathroom, and told to wash her hands before her tea.
She took the opportunity for a much-needed evacuation
and, having rinsed her face and hands, as well as
scrupulously cleansing her bottom, she was seated at a
rough table in the corner, occupied by a dozen or so
grey-clad drudges who were busy at their meal. She was
surprised and pleased to be greeted with polite nods,
and also that despite the simple meal – tea, slices of
meat, bread and butter, potatoes and cabbage – it was
served and consumed with ladylike decorum. Miss
Brace had a few words with Cook; Miss Duckett said
she would collect Sophia in forty minutes.

There was little conversation, for the meal was evidently a hurried affair, with a new set of drudges ready
to take their place at table; Sophia learned that, after
eating, they were sent to the dining-hall to wait on the
other maids and mistresses. In her first days at Rodings,
she would by turn work as kitchen drudge, or 'slop
skiv', floor-cleaner, or 'scrubber', and bathroom cleaner,
or 'poo-skiv', the nicknames all pronounced with gleeful
derision. After their first weeks at Rodings, the maids
were still detailed to these duties, but at less frequent
intervals, unless as a mild form of punishment.

'I prefer a whacking!' said her straw-blonde neighbour, taking care to empty her mouth before speaking.
'Whap! Ouch! Sore botty! Gets it over with.'

'But I thought . . .' Sophia began, feeling confused.

'Don't think, girl, just obey, and you'll be happy. You
want to be happy, don't you?'

Sophia was unable to argue with that.

'Well then,' said the straw-blonde girl with

triumphant logic, as she prepared to absorb another spoonful of food. 'Got a name?'

'Sophia.'

'I mean a proper name, a Rodings name.'

'Not yet.'

'I hope they give you a nice one. I'm Felicity Straw.'

'What?' exclaimed Sophia.

'Don't laugh. It's rather sweet, really. You see, we all of us maids come here rescued from disadvantage, and most of us had no real name, or didn't know it. While we are neophytes, we get a name that is usually to do with how we look, or our moral demeanour. Straw, for my hair, you see? Or else where you were rescued from disadvantage. That maid is Patience Upminster, that one Clarissa Slim, and Jane Broad, and Emma Shy, and there is Susan Westham, because she was rescued in the village of West Ham. And after we formally become Ladies, then Miss Brace helps us choose a proper name for outside – a Name of Advantage, we call it. Some of us choose to keep our maid's name, if it is nice.'

Sophia mentioned that she had been 'rescued' in Commercial Street.

'Hmm ... Sophia Commercial sounds a bit rum! Well, you'll find out soon enough.'

And with that, Felicity Straw politely cleared her tea-things, adjusted her grey skirt, and took her leave, after wishing Sophia the very best of welcomes. Sophia began to glow with contentment. She could not believe the good fortune that raised her in such a short time from the harshest disadvantage to this benevolent institution. The thought of honest drudgery held no terrors for her: nothing could be worse than all her years of wretched confinement. Miss Duckett came to collect a happy and well-fed young Lady, so polite that Miss Duckett smiled widely and told Sophia that she was already a credit to Rodings – and indirectly to Miss Duckett's own 'advantage record', for her keenness of selection. Sophia was

14

aware of Miss Duckett's newness in her Lady's status, and wanted to please her lovely rescuer.

Felicity Straw's reference to a name 'for outside', given on becoming a fully-fledged Lady – as Miss Duckett seemed to have just done – suggested to Sophia that maids, or neophytes, perhaps did not *go* outside. She dismissed the thought. What if it were true? She could always demand her shilling, and raiway ticket to London, if she wanted to. Every maid and Lady seemed so decorous, and even the stern demeanour of Cook or Miss Brace had a twinkle behind the sternness. Of course there would be discipline – punishments to keep maids on their toes, and help them blossom into Ladies . . . but that was only right and proper, and Sophia felt suddenly that she would feel lost without the knowledge of punishment if she erred. Even on this brief acquaint-ance, the clean, well-ordered friendliness of Rodings made her feel that she would never want to leave . . .

Miss Duckett led Sophia down seemingly endless corri-dors, past rooms in which maids could be seen at school desks, under the supervision of a Preceptress (as Sophia now thought of the immaculately-robed young Ladies), all of them carrying the golden-clasped bundle of rods. Evrywhere was a studious hush, and the smells of young bodies, the sweat and grime of fervent youth, were pleasantly masked by the mild odour of cleansing fluids. Sophia remembered her own hurried experiences of schooling in the orphanages: the stink of the unwashed surrounding her as she struggled to learn her letters from a harrassed mistress, scarcely less miserable than her charges.

Some doors were windowless, and resolutely locked with stern bolts and chains. Sophia knew better than to try and assuage her curiosity.

They ascended steep stairs and the odours of cleaning were joined by a clinical smell as they entered the surgery, and were greeted by a pleasant freckled lass whom Miss Duckett addressed as Miss Crouch. Sophia thought of her as a lass, because her broad Essex vowels and hearty demeanour marked her instantly as a country wench. Miss Duckett said she would attend Sophia's examination and, as they waited, Miss Crouch's merry chatter – she came, apparently, from Burnham-on-Crouch – put Sophia quite at her ease.

Matron herself, when she appeared, was quite the opposite, and Sophia wondered for the first time if all at Rodings might not be as friendly as she thought. Matron was a tall and slim woman in her late twenties, with severe, handsome features and wide, rather cruel lips set in a strongly-boned face. Her lithe movements under her white smock hinted at a musculature more mannish than womanly, as did the tautness of her dainty posterior, and her chestnut hair was cut short, like a kitchen maid's.

This was Miss Lord. Without further ado or any sign of greeting, she fixed Sophia with her piercing dark green eyes, and ordered her into the examining room, which abutted a small bath-chamber. Sophia obeyed, followed by Misses Crouch and Duckett. Miss Lord ordered her to strip. Sophia hesitated, taken aback at the abrupt command.

'I said strip, maid,' rapped Miss Lord. 'Take those filthy things off.'

Numbly, Sophia slipped from her blouse and skirt – they were indeed embarrassingly filthy – and stood shivering nervously in her shift and drawers.

Miss Lord made a face. 'You do stink,' she said. 'I said strip! Are you deaf as well as filthy? The drawers, the shift – off, maid!'

'Do as Matron says, Sophia,' said Miss Duckett anxiously. 'You are to be examined and laved, and you must be naked.'

Although she knew her disrobing was for medical

16

purposes, Sophia felt unaccountably humiliated as she bared herself to the eyes of the three other women, who made no attempt to avert their curious gazes from her body. She was glad to obey when Miss Lord sent her to the small bathing chamber, where there was room only for Matron and herself, alongside a bath, commode, various bassinets, and a large tank from which rubber tubes protruded with an aspect at once comic and sinister.

Sophia shyly asked Miss Lord if she could make commode, after her tea, and Miss Lord said this was perfectly agreeable to her. She stood with hands on hips, waiting, and Sophia realised she was supposed to squat in full view of Matron. There was nothing else for it; she squatted, feeling the porcelain cold on her thighs, and buttocks, and did her business. She felt awfully humiliated, but as she sat under Matron's gaze, she remembered the nonchalance with which she and Misses Brace and Duckett had crouched in the snow, and her humiliation turned to a kind of defiant pride. She was *not* going to be shamed!

She was given a shower-bath, a fierce spray of tepid water which Miss Lord took pleasure in directing at her tenderest places, and then she was ordered to spread herself across the machine with tubes, and bend over. She did so, trembling and ashamed at the naked exposure of her private parts, and was warned by Miss Lord that she was not to resist or squeal, even though there might be a little discomfort.

She looked round to see Miss Lord don rubber gloves, and apply grease to the end of a thick green tube. Taps were opened, and the machine started to hiss and gurgle; Sophia was stunned as she felt rubber-clad fingers spread open her buttocks and prise open her nether hole – her very bum-hole! And then she felt the tube roughly inserted inside her, all the way to her root! Tears of shame and confusion filled her eyes, but she emitted nothing more than a gasp of surprise as hot oily liquid began to pump inside her belly, with an excruciating discomfort that was almost painful, but at the same time almost pleasurable. She was ordered to hold the cleansing liquid inside her until she was told to evacuate, and Sophia strained to obey, panting in her efforts.

'Anyone would think you had never been laved before, miss!' said Miss Lord derisively, and Sophia was too much in distress to admit she had not.

The order came to flush herself and, thankfully, she evacuated the hot fluid, only to have it replaced by a fresh stream, this time ice-cold. The procedure was repeated many times, it seemed, until Sophia began to actually like the tickling, maddening pressure in her bumhole, and even Miss Lord grudgingly admitted that she took it well. Sophia scarcely dared admit to herself or to others that, all in all, she had come to enjoy the laving, nor its pleasant accompaniment by the cool palms of Miss Lord gently stroking the stretched bare skin of her fesses: a stroking which seemed to go beyond the requirements of medical attention into the realm of grudging affection. Miss Lord made little cooing remarks, not entirely unfriendly, about the size of Sophia's 'derrière', as she called it.

'I suppose you have a nickname?' she said. 'Something to do with these –' her hand hesitated and trembled as she stroked Sophia's naked globes '– with these . . . melons?'

Sophia responded that no, she had been called 'Longshanks' after her long legs, and Miss Lord called this information rather scornfully to the other Ladies in her sitting-room, and that she was sure Rodings could do better. Sophia felt uneasy – she wondered how much Matron's influence was, not liking the idea of being called 'Melons'.

Then she was dried in a soft towel, and returned to the sitting-room, still naked, where she was obliged to lie on a table for a thorough examination of her person. It *was* thorough! She had never been prodded and poked like this before, lying helpless as one steel instrument after another explored her most intimate places . . . even her very fount!

'Virgin!' exclaimed Miss Lord, as though bemused, and Miss Duckett's sigh of relief was almost palpable. Sophia felt humiliated anew; yet there was something almost exciting in the helplessness of her situation and, when the examination came to an end, she had actually begun to relish the cold caress of tube and pincer.

'Well then,' said Miss Lord heartily. 'Virgin and clean, and fit for duty. I bid you good evening, Miss Duckett. To you as well, maid,' she added almost tenderly to Sophia, 'and I hope you have a name to your liking.'

Wrapped only in a blanket and wearing cotton slippers, Sophia was taken to the Purser's room, which was a cosy bed-sitting room with a large cupboard. The brisk young Lady in dress similar to Miss Tunney's put down her novel and took Sophia's measurements, and then withdrew a bundle of clothing, which she placed in a canvas kitbag and handed to Sophia, along with a paper for her to sign.

'It's all there, miss, I assure you,' she said, 'so just make your mark, and here is your copy to check. If there is anything amiss, just come back – just now, I simply *must* get on with my book. It is so exciting! The heroine is wearing only her underthings and her wicked Master has tied her with coarse ropes to the railway line, and the Denver Express is due any moment! It is in Colorado,' she added, as if that explained everything. 'I long to visit Colorado.'

Sophia proudly stated that she was able to write her own name, and did so, after which Miss Duckett ordered her to put on her new nightie, dressing-gown and slippers, for after her visit to Miss Brace, she would proceed to her dormitory and well-earnt rest. Sophia obeyed, marvelling at the new, wondrous softness of wool and cotton on her skin. Happiy, she followed Miss Duckett up further stairs, reflecting that if she had drawn a strange pleasure from her lavage and examination, then it was perhaps no less strange that the Purser should long to be tied to railway lines in Colorado.

Sophia and Miss Duckett were a little early, as shown by a red 'busy' sign on the High Mistress's inner sanctum; they sat in comfortable leather chairs in a gaslit ante-room of pleasing simplicity, after Miss Duckett's instruction to wait had pointedly announced their presence. Sophia heard voices from Miss Brace's office, and so did Miss Duckett; it was impossible for either Lady to pretend she did not.

'Well, miss,' came Miss Brace's muffled voice. 'You are most errant. Whatever are we to do with you?'

'You ... you decreed a number two punishment, miss,' answered a Lady's trembling voice. Sophia started: she recognised Miss Tunney, the Lady rebuked in the corridor.

'Yes ... and you are getting off lightly, miss. I am in a good mood, for Miss Duckett has espied a worthy neophyte, a maid whose head promises well, and whose sacred portion is fully advantaged. In fact, I must see her next and give her her Rulebook. So to business, miss. Unclasp your *fasces*, please, and kiss the rods, which are at once the symbol of your power, and of your submission.'

There was a pause.

'Good ... now into submission, please. Bend over, and let us have skirts raised, then touch your toes with your legs wide. Oh, you have knickers. Lower them to your knees, please. The garter straps and stockings may stay, as your sacred parts are well enough exposed. Now ...'

There was a short whistling sound and a sharp, dry impact, which elicited a cry from Miss Tunney. Miss

Brace was heard to tut-tut, and say that she would have to give the stroke again. The fearful sound was heard once more, and this time the Lady in submission was silent. Sophia trembled in awe as she heard the stroke repeated five times more, Miss Tunney taking each one in complete silence. Sophia shuddered: she looked at Miss Duckett, and saw that she too was trembling in agitation, and that her face was flushed. If this was a mild number two punishmnent – six strokes of the rod, or seven, counting the stroke repeated – what could a number three punishment be like?

At last the chastisement seemed over; there was a rustling as Miss Tunney rearranged her skirts, a murmur of, 'Thank you, High Mistress,' and the Lady herself emerged from Miss Brace's study, her face glowing and wreathed in a contented smile, despite the tears that stained her cheeks. She exchanged the most perfunctory of glances with Miss Duckett, and Sophia saw something like triumph in her expression, while Miss Duckett seemed . . . almost envious. Sophia was quite puzzled as she was seated at Miss Brace's rosewood desk, and handed a small book with handwritten vellum pages, and a similar volume whose pages were blank. Miss Brace said that was her rulebook; if she could not manage letters, she must have it read to her, and memorise every word in two weeks, before handing it back; if she could, she must make her own copy in copperplate.

'Everything is explained, Miss Sophia,' she said, 'and Miss Duckett, as your rescuer, will explain the day-to-day details of your routine. This visit is to welcome you formally to Rodings, and have you sign the papers of agreement. We must be brief, so I shall owe you that cup of cocoa I promised. My correction of Miss Tunney, to which I have no doubt you listened –' she smiled tolerantly, and Sophia wondered if it had been staged thus on purpose '– has delayed me somewhat, and I must not get behind in my business, or I myself should be errant – *that* would displease Mr Bucentaur, our Chairman of the Board.'

Sophia said demurely that she had learned to read and write, and was given a short treaty, a document to sign. She looked round the study, its cosy clutter quite different from the bare ante-chamber. It was crammed with antique paintings and statuettes, most of them secure in glass cases, depicting the nude form of various females or goddesses. She was fascinated that in every case, the buttocks and thighs were monstrously exaggerated in size, sometimes the breasts also, and the face was insignificant or even blank. In some, the naked fount was shown, and Sophia thought this immodesty was no doubt excused in the name of art and science.

Her treaty stated simply that the signatory entrusted her person and moral education to the total care and control of the House of Rodings, for as long as the Board should deem it necessary, and that the Board undertook to form her moral education as a Lady to its fullest competence; also that her contract could be terminated at any time at her own request, upon which a shilling would be payable, and a railway ticket to her point of origin.

'Which in your case is London,' said Miss Brace, 'but I am sure, from reading your skull, that there will be no question of recalcitrance in your case, Miss. The name is blank, for we have yet to decide on a maid's name for you. Stand, please, and remove your dressing-gown.'

Sophia did so, and stood in nothing but her thin nightie. Miss Brace rose, and walked round, inspecting her with evident admiration.

'Well!' she said gaily. 'Please gather your nightie, miss, and pull it tight against your sacred portion.'

Her sacred portion? Miss Brace must mean her buttocks. She obeyed, and pulled the cloth tightly against her fesses, until she was exposing them as though naked. She thrilled at the caress of the fine cotton on her bare skin.

'I think there can be no doubt,' said Miss Brace slowly. 'Longshanks indeed! Appropriate enough, for the legs are quite beautiful. But the beauty of legs is that they lead to the sacred portion. Miss Sophia, you have quite the finest derrière it has been my fortune as High Mistress to ... to observe. So you shall henceforth be known as Sophia Derrière. You may mark and sign your treaty thus.'

As Sophia proudly did so, the High Mistress said that while the science of phrenology taught of character through the form of the skull, which reflected the strengths and weaknesses of the brain's personality centres, there was another aspect to the science of character analysis, an older and deeper one.

'In her fesses, a Lady reveals the true wisdom and beauty of her soul. Their smooth dimpled roundness, their orbs approaching true perfection of form, contain and symbolise all the true profundity of Womanhood. Did not the Ancients in their wisdom worship the Female, and in particular the glory of her derrière, her globes the gateway to life and spiritual ecstacy, and the very mirror of the universe? And *your* fesses, Sophia Derrière ... well! That is enough of a lesson for now.'

Sophia wondered if she should err, and ask the one question which was intriguing her, but Miss Brace anticipated it.

'In the coach, Miss Sophia, I expressed disgust at the degrading punishments which you described, and to which no Lady should be subjected. I also advised you that the strict discipline of Rodings always befitted a Lady, but in no way precluded beating of the buttocks. And now you have heard me beating Miss Tunney's sacred portion, which reddened most prettily for me. There is no riddle, Sophia: at Rodings, neophytes and Ladies alike are always punished as befits a Lady. And a Lady always takes her beating on the bare.'

2

Baubo

'Why, what a beautiful po!' cried an excited girl's voice.

Sophia was engaged in neatly laying out the contents of her kitbag on her bed, and checking the garments against her list, before hanging them in her little wardrobe. All around her the dormitory hummed with quiet activity and conversation, as the maids prepared to extinguish their candles on the orders of the Preceptresses. She looked round, and saw a slender girl of about her own height and age, with big hazel eyes that matched her short bobbed tresses, her smile broad on full wide lips, but with breasts and posterior noticeably slimmer than Sophia's.

'I beg your pardon?' Sophia said.

'Your po!' cried the girl, evidently her neighbour, and patted her amicably on her fesses. 'I'm so jealous; you have the best of any maid and I hope I can be your friend. Your derrière is so lovely. Mine is like a boy's – here, touch.'

Without asking permission, she grasped Sophia's fingers and pressed them to her own bottom. The buttocks were hard and muscled ... like Matron's, Sophia thought.

'I ... I'm sure your portion – your, ah, po – is very nice,' she heard herself saying, rather taken aback.

'But your portion is so sumptuous and grand and queeny! If I'm your friend, then perhaps mine will ripen too. You know, under your good aura.'

24

Sophia smiled at the innocent enthusiasm of her neighbour and decided it was better to have friends than enemies, so introduced herself. The maid's name was Bella Frinton, and when she asked if Sophia had been well attended, Sophia answered yes: she had been kindly shown her bed, told of the daily routine, and given a small goodnight kiss by her lovely rescuer, Miss Duckett.

'Ah! Miss Duckett is divine! Her portion ... how I'd love to ... well. Wait till lights out. I can show you some games. Would you like that? All the maids play games; it is such fun. Sometimes po games, with stroking and kissing and ... you know ... and if any maid has taken correction from Miss Brace or a Preceptress, she must show her portion to all the others, quite bare. It is super.'

Sophia looked round, and counted six dozen girls in the long rectangular dormitory. She was not sure if this was the entire complement of Rodings, nor if she relished the idea of having her eventually reddened 'po' inspected by six dozen pairs of eager eyes. But then – there was something rather naughty and pleasing about the idea, especially as it was certainly a minor infraction of the rules ...

'Oh!' cried Bella, 'do let me see your uniform and drill and things. So lovely.'

Sophia pointed out that they were surely standard issue, the same as any other maid's.

'Yes,' said Bella, running her fingers through shifts, stockings, skirts and blouses, 'but there is something so wonderful about *new* new clothes. Almost as if you were becoming a new person. Which, by being admitted, you are.'

The kitbag was tightly packed with clothing and accoutrements of toilet and stationery, offering raiment for every eventuality. The drudge's grey work drill and cardigan would be Sophia's everyday wear, and there were three sets; also a costume much like Miss Tunney's, with a lovely blue skirt and white satin blouse, and this was her stepping out apparel. A formal black suit was there, and she was well supplied with a variety of surprisingly fashionable shoes as well as work boots and drudge's aprons. But to her delight, the kit contained a bountiful supply of underthings: petticoats, corsets, bustiers, camisoles, garters, stockings and panties, most in white or beautiful pastel shades, but with some flame-red or sky blue, and all were in the softest silk! Sophia remarked on this, and Bella said that white knickers and undies were worn with normal grey drill, but that Miss Brace – and thus Mr Bucentaur and the Board – believed that a humble maid, even a neophyte, must be constantly reminded that she was a Lady. Thus, the garments that touched her most intimately, and especially her sacred portion, must be of the softest and most ladylike cloth.

'Isn't it lovely when you pull your knickers – you know – all the way up?' murmured Bella. 'I mean, really tight? It is so naughty and sweet and gives you such a funny tickly feeling, doesn't it?'

'Yes, I suppose it does,' said Sophia uncertainly. Her heart swelled. For the first time in her life, she felt herself possessed of a proper wardrobe, a Lady's wardrobe!

The central gas jets were extinguished, plunging the dormitory into the twinkling glow of bedside candles. These would be extinguished in half an hour, on order of the Preceptress, giving the maids a short time in which to read or attend to letters. Although the dormitory was open, and every bed visible to every other, each maid had a measure of privacy, in that her wardrobe and writing-desk were arranged to form a sort of compartment, affording partial privacy. Sophia felt that already she had her own little study.

She decided that although questioning was discouraged, she might as well use Bella's obvious enthusiasm as a short cut to gain information. In the meanwhile she excused herself and said she would pass the time until lights out in the study of her rulebook. In truth, she was avid to open the pages: the hardships of her previous life had been visited on her without rhyme nor reason, seemingly at the whim of various tyrants, of which Mr Lee had been the worst. Now she was to have proper rules to obey. So if she was punished, she would at least know why . . .

She began to peruse the rules, and rapidly became confused – not at their complexity, for they were sternly clear and simple: a list of peremptory requirements, dos and don'ts that brooked no excuse and no exemption. Her confusion came from the seemingly arbitrary nature of the rules. She could understand the obligation to maintain neat and clean dress at all times, or to show politeness to superiors; when to bow, or curtsey, or lower the eyes. But it was not clear why a drudge was forbidden to button up her cardigan, nor why certain rooms and corridors could only be visited on the authority or in the company of a Preceptress; why on some days it was obligatory to wear panties and petticoat, on others only panties, and on others a corset – subject to inspection to see that it was tightly laced – and no panties at all!

Similarly, there were Submission Days, when drudges were obliged to have ladders in their stockings, and have torn or dirty knickers, and forbidden to comb their hair, and before addressing a Preceptress had to first make submission, by turning round, lifting skirts and bending down to show the upturned knickered derrière. Sophia's spirit at first rebelled against such petty restrictions, but with equal force her female good sense imposed itself, and she determined that the best way to deal with rules was to obey them more thoroughly than anyone else, and thus became Mistress of them. One thing puzzled

27

her: each rule had a prescribed penalty for its transgression, being a punishment ranging from one to ten, the greater number for the more heinous offence. Yet these punishments were not detailed.

Bella was obviously itching to converse, and when they put their candles out and lay bathed in the faint starlight, she burst into excited chatter. Where did Sophia come from, where was she rescued, how did she come to have such a magnificent croup, were her bubbies just as splendid, didn't she think it a bore to have to wear silk knickers *all* the time, weren't garter straps an awful nuisance to do up, and so on. Sophia did not mention that she had never found garter straps a nuisance, never having possessed them, and was thrilled to have them for the first time, but interrupted with the kindly observation that the rules forbade talking after lights out: to which Bella Frinton predictably replied with a 'Pooh!' – that rules were made to be broken, and maids would be maids.

Sophia did not know how to explain that she wanted to obey the rules, never before having had any to obey; that the presence of rules conferred a dignity on the obedient, even when they sometimes erred, because they did so in full knowledge of their error; that rules were preferable to the tyranny of no rules. Then, she reflected, perhaps the comradeship of maids was just as much a rule, though unwritten; that the custom of the dormitory expressed itself in soft whispers and laughter; and thus satisfied, joined the conversation. Bella added unexpectedly that Sophia was quite right, but that some of the rules were reasonable: for example, every maid got rips in her stockings or knickers, and normally this was unseemly, but a Submission Day had the function of putting these items to proper use.

'What happens if a clean and orderly maid has no such rips?' asked Sophia.

'Why, then she must make some!' cried Bella in delight.

She added that breaking rules was not really a crime in itself, rather a sort of forfeit that had to be paid. Sometimes a maid would err deliberately, and in the knowledge of a Preceptress who did nothing to stop her, knowing that she accepted to pay the price of the prescribed punishment. A maid who broke the rules flagrantly, and to flaunt herself improperly without the intention of owning up, would frequently incur unofficial punishment from a court of the maids themselves. The only real crime was informing on another maid, and it was the worst crime. In such cases, the maids would join in cleansing any errant Lady of their number with the utmost strictness.

Sophia expressed her disquiet at not knowing what the variously numbered punishments actually were. Was there no book of punishments?

Bella laughed nervously. 'The only book of punishments is the one in which all your transgressions and penalties are entered, to be kept for all eternity,' she said portentously. 'There *is* a list of numbered punishments, but only Miss Brace is allowed to see it. It changes, you see.'

'Miss Brace is *allowed*?' said Sophia in disbelief. 'But she is High Mistress. Who is to *allow* her?'

'Why, the Board, of course.'

'Meaning this Mr Bucentaur?'

'Well, yes.'

Sophia asked about Mr Bucentaur: his age, appearance, demeanour, to be told that Bella had never seen him, and nor had any maid. To be presented to Mr Bucentaur was a privilege rare for a Lady, and even for a Preceptress, and *even*, she whispered, for the High Mistress herself.

'As for punishments, well, you get to know them as you go along. It is part of our training, you know, and there is not a Lady's bottom here unfamiliar with the kiss of the cane or the slap of bare on bare. For example, a Preceptress can give a number two, that's a whipping with the rods of the *fasces*, but if she gives more than seven strokes there must be a friend of the errant, as witness, to see that she can take it. You can get up to thirteen strokes, you know. I've had that, and gosh, it hurts so! Then a number one – well, that is humiliating more than anything, for it is a spanking with a baubo, at assembly, in front of the whole House. The maid has to bend over and take off her knickers, then hand them to the Mistress – sometimes the High Mistress herself – and that is the shaming part of the punishment! A dozen with a baubo doesn't hurt much, but it makes you jump, and in a way that is shaming too, for you've no chance for theatricals, you know, gritting your teeth and taking it. The baubo makes your bottom red all right, but not terribly *red* enough to be worth a dorm show.'

Sophia enquired what a baubo was, and learned it was a brightly painted statuette of the eponymous goddess, with whom she was unfamiliar, and it was very much like a policeman's truncheon, though a lot jollier to look at.

'A number three,' continued Bella, 'well, that is thirteen with the cane, not the *fasces*, and though it is only one rod, it hurts more, for the rod is much springier and heavier. I've had that, from High Mistress – oooh, I remember it still! But I was very proud on dorm parade, with all the other maids touching and admiring my crimson bottom. A number four – two canes are used; a number five, three bound canes, and the errant maid is tied by ankles and wrists. Number six is the same, only the number of strokes is greater – imagine twenty-one, on the bare derrière, with three canes at once! – and the offender has to "kiss the gunner's daughter". That is a punishment they have in the Royal Navy – Mr Bucentaur is very keen on things maritime – and the offender is strapped over the barrel of a cannon, the punishment to be witnessed by the whole House. We have such a cannon here,' she added proudly, 'a massive, lovely thing, that Mr Bucentaur had brought from the Naval School at Shoeburyness. But I do hope *you* never have to kiss her.'

Sophia found herself unaccountably excited at the thought of a number six punishment, and asked eagerly about numbers seven to ten.

There was a pause. 'Number seven is the birch,' said Bella hesitantly and in a soft, sad voice. 'That is the most I've had. You may think of a birch as fluffy and tickly, making a lot of swishy noise but not really hurting that much. Sound and fury, mostly. Well, there are such birches, but a birch can be all things . . . a Rodings birch hurts. I wasn't able to take it very well. I don't know about the other numbers, but something in me wants to take the number seven again, and the others, to show I can stand it, that I *am* a Lady.'

Sophia felt the most profound confusion. These punishments were harsh, there was no doubt. But then a Lady should keep to the rules, which were clearly set out. Sophia, so glad of her rulebook, wanted desperately to be a model maid, and obedient in every respect. Yet something told her that she could not become truly of Rodings *unless* she erred, and incurred punishment; that Miss Brace somehow would not respect her as a Lady unless she had frequent occasion to chastise Sophia's naked buttocks. Sophia, despite her mind's chill revulsion from the prospect of such punishment, found that her belly warmed and quivered at the thought of baring her derrière thus. Could it be that the unknown founder of Rodings, and the creator of her rules, had seen deeply into the mind of every young maid, more deeply than she herself knew?

This reverie was interrupted by the arrival of another maid, her soft padding on bare feet taking Sophia quite by surprise. Suddenly her bedclothes were pulled away, and she stifled a cry of surprise. By the pale starlight, she saw a maid's face inspecting her with a rather disquieting smile.

'Well, a new drudge, eh?' said the new arrival.

'Oh, leave her alone, Ransome,' said Bella, 'it is her first night.'

'You were mounted on your first night, Bella Frinton, as I recall,' said Ransome, a handsome, heavily-built maid whose nightie clung quite beguilingly to the full curves of her body.

'That is different,' protested Bella. 'My bottom's all hard and muscly, I could take it easily. Sophia has a . . . a soft bottom – not soft exactly, but awfully sweet and . . .'

'Oh, so you've made her acquaintance, you minx?' snapped Ransome, and Sophia was glad the darkness concealed her fiery blush.

'You know the rules. If a maid wants to be mounted as a Rodings Rider, she has to take her tickling.'

Mounted? Rider? Sophia began to stammer her quite understandable questions, and was told that the Rodings Riders were a group of the very *best* maids, and they showed a Lady's superiority by mounting and riding males! Sophia had never heard of such an unnatural thing, and said so, daring to add that she hadn't seen any males at Rodings to be mounted.

'Well, we *shall* mount them, when there are some to ride,' said Ransome rather lamely. 'But that's not the point. Do you want to be a Rider or not? You have to take a tickling for five whole minutes without giggling, you see.'

She held up a large white goose-feather, and Sophia laughed. So that was all! She had thought a tickling meant something far more ominous – a spanking . . . or caning! – but she was ready even for that. And – she gulped – willing . . .

'I'll take a tickling, Miss Ransome,' she exclaimed, not without irony. 'I do so want to be a Rodings Rider.'

32

She heard Bella snort derisively, then was ordered to crouch on her bed, with her nightie lifted and her naked derrière exposed. She did so, and buried her face in her pillow. Then Ransome told her to clutch each fesse with her hands and spread them apart so that her skin was taut. She thought this rather immodest but did as she was told. The tickling began, making her shiver at its delicate touch on the soft skin of her bare fesses. Ransome was quite expert, tickling her first with the tip, now stroking her with the feather's thorny flat, and straying deep into her furrow, making her gasp as a quite unfamiliar pleasure seemed to creep up her spine, and the feather's tip played at the small of her back, at the very top of her cleft.

'Yes,' said Ransome, 'the very softest Essex goose-feather, my maid; one day, if you pass the test, you will be riding young Essex men, and tickling their bare bottoms with more than a feather. We will teach men their lesson!'

Sophia thought the mention of a male posterior naked was shockingly improper, but did not dare say so, for fear that she should burst into a giggle. The tickling was not as harmless as she had imagined, and its pleasure was rapidly becoming a sort of ecstatic pain. She wanted the tickling to stop – she panted at the feather's caress – yet with all her heart, she wanted it never to stop. All sorts of strange new sensations flooded her body, and she felt curiously warm and light and moist in her very belly and fount. These were redoubled when she gasped at the feather's penetration of her most private place, her bum-hole itself! Her shock knew no bounds ... Ransome's tickling of her tight little bud, well-stretched by her trembling fingers, was positively indecent! And yet now more than ever, she wanted her ordeal to continue, and felt her hips begin to writhe as Ransome concentrated her tickling on that most sensitive little puckered spot. Five minutes must be up – but she did not want her tickling to stop!

Suddenly it did. Sophia stayed in position shivering, and ready for more – what, a harsher ordeal? A hand-spanking, or the cane? She did not care, she wanted it, wanted to prove herself a Rodings Rider! She heard a flurry as Ransome disappeared into the darkness, with a muttering of annoyance, and then through her dizzied pleasure she recognised a stern voice, both sad and angry.

'Sophia!' cried Miss Duckett. 'Out of bed, and inde-cent! I make my Preceptress's rounds, I come to you, mindful of your welfare, and I see this shameless, no, shameful, display! Don't waste time and tell me you were making commode; I can see your chamberpot and it is still clean. I know all about the tickling ritual, and all that nonsense! And I know that as a neophyte you are not to blame. You must tell me who did this.'

Sophia replaced her nightie and righted herself to sit on the bed. She felt as if the whole world was observing her shame. She stammered that she did not know who tickled her, that she had been told simply to bare her nates and submit.

'Come, come, maid; I was not born yesterday. By whom were you told to submit? You must know.'

Sophia suddenly realised that she had not in fact been told – that the word submit came from her own imagin-ation. She repeated that she did not know. Suddenly Bella emerged from her bedclothes and said loudly that she was to blame, whereupon Miss Duckett drew back her blankets and said scornfully that she saw no feather hidden.

'Laudable, Bella, but untrue. I shall overlook that particular offence, for it was a white lie rather than a red one. But Sophia is in a different pickle. Speak, Sophia, and you shall avoid punishment. How I had hoped my duties as Preceptress, and as your rescuer, should not lead me to this! But you have let it come to pass. The name, Sophia!'

Sophia shook her bowed head.

'Very well,' sighed Miss Duckett, stroking the rods of her *fasces* rather ominously. 'I shall have to place your name on report, Sophia Derrière, and High Mistress shall read out your decreed punishment at assembly tomorrow morning.'

She gently touched Sophia's thigh. 'It should only be a number one punishment,' she said soothingly, 'and I am sure that croup of yours can take it with ease. Afterwards, I must take you to the hairdresser for your maid's coiffure . . . I hope you won't mind. And, Sophia, I am pleased you are going to be beaten, for I am glad, really, you did not break the greater and unwritten rule against sneaking on another Lady.'

Sleep did not come easily to Sophia, and she tossed herself fretfully, excited both by the strangeness of her new home and by the knowledge that already she had earned herself a chastisement – a bare spanking in front of her new friends! Yet after a while her unease turned to a glow, almost of satisfaction: she had earnt her punishment honourably, by refusing to be a sneak. She would take it like a Lady, and earn respect. Thus eagerly anticipating the morning, she drifted into a contented and dreamless slumber.

Rodings no longer seemed vast to Sophia's morning-fresh eyes. Now, the corridors, refectory, and assembly hall had a pleasing cosiness and even intimacy. The dormitory was Rodings in its entirety, and the masses of strange maids of Sophia's imagination proved not to exist. It was as though every maid, far from being a waif rescued at random, was somehow hand-picked according to a mysterious plan.

After the gentle waking bell, the maids rushed from dormitory to the washroom. They queued for their places at commode, or to empty their chamberpots, and then for the icy caress of a cold shower-bath, which they took together under the Preceptresses' watchful eyes, the maids naked together and without regard for feminine modesty. Sophia thought wryly that the howls of exuberant anguish at the scald of icy water were a splendid method of sending air and blood coursing healthily through sleepy young bodies.

The drudges went through this process first, for they had to be ready for the others' breakfast. After bathing, she dressed in her grey drill, and accompanied the dozen or so other drudges, including Miss Felicity Straw, down to the kitchen, where half of them were put to work while the others gulped tea and porridge and boiled eggs; then the situations were reversed, and finally they busied themselves serving their sister-maids, and the Mistresses at High Table, in the surprisingly comfortable refectory. Like much of the house, it seemed cosily English and historic, although Sophia's untutored eye could not distinguish sixteenth from seventeenth century. They cleared and swept the refectory, then ferried the dirty dishes back to the kitchen, and only when the kitchen was once again spotless, under the stern gaze of Miss Stavanger the cook, could they join their sisters, who had enjoyed half an hour of leisure after their meal, for morning assembly.

Sophia supposed that the cramped assembly hall looked like a chapel, although her acquaintance with chapels had been limited to the noisome huts in her orphanages. The chamber was of pleasant burnished oak panelling, with a polished parquet floor; Sophia had no doubt she would in due course be on her hands and knees, attending to its cleaning, and as she sat waiting, allowed her imagination to drift, seeing herself kneeling as a scrubber, with her panties thrust up for strokes of encouragement from a Preceptress's – let it be Miss Duckett's! – rod . . .

There were benches for the maids, a dais and a lectern, with chairs at the back for the Mistresses; the Preceptresses were stationed at the rear of the maids' benches, and those maids who had become Ladies but were not yet Preceptresses, sat at the front. Sophia found herself with the other drudges in the row directly before the Preceptresses. There were seven Preceptresses and seven Mistresses, in addition to Cook, Purser, and Matron, who had Preceptress rank. Sophia knew from her rulebook that Mistresses were higher in rank, and could administer or order a Preceptress to administer punishment for most offences that did not require a visit to the High Mistress; and only Mistresses were allowed to chastise full Ladies.

A Preceptress's authority was more limited, beating maids for everyday improprieties, and for major ones sending miscreants either to a Mistress or to the High Mistress herself. However, Sophia was to learn that because of their intimate daily contact with their maids – from whose ranks they had been so recently elevated – Preceptresses had great latitude in deciding what was or was not a minor offence, and busy Mistresses were frequently content to delegate their disciplinary obligations.

The position of Ladies who were not Preceptresses was somewhat in between: they, too, were empowered to impose and administer chastisement to maids, by a system known as ticketing. A maid apprehended in wrongdoing could elect to take summary justice from a Lady, which punishment was not formally entered in the punishment book. Instead, the maid was given a ticket to show that her error had been corrected, so that if it were later discovered by a Preceptress or Mistress, she could prove she had already paid the just penalty. Sophia guessed from her rulebook that this system was open to a certain abuse, and was duly proved correct, although this was known as toleration.

A maid who intended to err, for example absenting herself from House in order to visit the village of Leaden Roding without permission, could confess her error in

37

advance to an understanding Lady, and receive her ticket and punishment before she had even committed the offence. This removed from her the fear of apprehension which might mar whatever pleasure she was seeking. It also meant that obliging Ladies could in theory establish a clique of favourites, and so a ticketed punishment was required to be sterner than the miscreant might normally expect from Mistress or Preceptress: any beating had to include extra strokes.

Although not entered formally in the eternal punishment record, copies of tickets had to be lodged with the Purser, and were regularly inspected. Any Lady found to be administering lenient punishments or 'soft tickets' was errant herself, and had to take punishment from High Mistress: for every short beating she had given, the proper strokes were calculated, and if she was found to have given, say, only seven for a thirteen-stroke offence, then she had to take double the short strokes herself.

On any ticket inspection, an errant Lady might thus find herself owed forty or fifty cane-strokes. She could elect to spread these over separate days, in batches of thirteen or twenty-one, although some hardy derrières proudly elected to take them all at once. Oddly, this did not affect her status and privileges as Lady, and she could still give tickets: like the maids whose fesses she flogged, she had paid for her offence with her own ticket, and squirming under her own cane. Maids, as Bella had asserted, would be maids, and the Board in its kindness seemed to recognise this.

Ladies were allowed to keep canes in their quarters, but not to carry them. The Preceptresses carried their bound rods as both symbol and practical implement of authority; the Ladies carried baubos, short thin cudgels in bright colours, which could be used as a spanking instrument, but were more for decoration. Sophia peered at these tools, but could not see quite clearly. Felicity Straw noted her curiosity and whispered that they were quite immodest.

'But you'll find out soon enough, Sophia. I gather you're for a tanning.'

Embarrassed, Sophia admitted this was so.

'Don't expect mercy just because you're a neophyte,' said Felicity with unjust glee. 'Your neophyte's bum will really smart under the great baubo, my maid! I know mine did.'

Sophia retorted that at least she was now a Rodings Rider. But with Felicity's warning uneasily in her thoughts, she paid only scant attention to the proceedings. Miss Brace in her red High Mistress's gown read various notices concerning everyday or classroom arrangements, and assembly seemed no more than that. Sophia had expected some kind of dreary prayers or religious observance and such things seemed mercifully absent from the culture of Rodings. Sophia had experienced religion, of course, hurled at her by various orphanage staff, but she had taken little of it in.

The lectern at which Miss Brace stood was veiled in a flowing semi-transparent cloth, like a Lady's gown, and it was of strange design, more a statuette than a simple lectern. But the statuete had two – no, three – legs, the central one thinner and slightly shorter than the two flowing curved trunks which framed it: these swelled at the top into two large and beautifully contoured globes, which tapered at the top to carry the tablette of the lectern. Sophia craned to see: they looked just like – no, it couldn't be – like a Lady's buttocks! And right at the top, where the spine should begin, sat two open eyes.

This, then, was a baubo, or indeed Baubo herself. The third shaft, between the beautiful curved legs, was a smaller version, the legs not parted, and the swelling of the buttocks growing from, or attached to, the goddess's furrow. Sophia wondered what the obverse of the statuette's fesses looked like, and surmised that it must be immodest: the swelling of the fount. She became aware that Miss Brace was now speaking sternly. She spoke of her noble disciplinary duty, of the beauty of just chastisement, and that no neophyte could use foolishness as an excuse. Her words and eyes were directed at Sophia herself.

'I know of the tickling ritual, Miss Derrière,' she said, plainly identifying her intended victim. 'It is honourable that you refuse to inform on the true culprit; less honourable that you participated in a foolish ceremony which makes light of a Lady's sacred portion. Step forward to bare your beauty, Miss Sophia Derrière.'

Sophia obeyed and, once on the dais, was instructed to bend over, lift her skirts and remove her panties completely, handing them to Miss Brace who placed them reverently on the lectern. Then she had to bend over and touch her toes, with her feet well apart, and her nates facing the assembly. Her bottom was now bare for her beating; Miss Brace adjusted her garter straps so as to reveal the maximum amount of trembling buttock-flesh.

Then she reached under the filmy gauze covering the lectern, and detached the third shaft from between the legs. This was no ordinary baubo, as Ladies wore at their waists, but a fearsome cane full three feet in length, two inches wide, and solid as an oak. Her movement made the veil sway, and revealed the lectern's plinth, on which there was a word deeply etched. Sophia's eyes widened; then the veil swirled back, and it was covered, and her thoughts were arrested by the first stroke of her bare.

She had to steady herself on her fingertips, so hard was the impact of the first lash. To her surprise, this was the signal for applause, as the whole House clapped their hands in a steady and unceasing rhythm. This was evidently a prescribed part of a number one punishment, and she could not tell if the hand-clapping was in applause, sympathy, or dismay. The pain lanced stinging across her naked fesses, to be followed by another, even more agonising. She gritted her teeth; she knew she must not cry, but it was very difficult.

Miss Brace was putting all her considerable strength into each stroke, and her aim made sure that not an inch of Sophia's bare backside was left unblushed. Sophia shuddered as expert strokes found the soft inside of her spread bare thighs, or the tender flesh at the very tops of her fesses. The pain changed from single hot strokes into a sheet of searing flame that seemed to blanket her entire naked bottom; by the seventh, Sophia had lost count, and was fighting back her tears. She was quite alone in agony, but gradually a strange, fierce exultation suffused her. The pain filled her so completely that she now felt it to be a part of her, her fiery red bottom a mark of pride and ladylike prowess. She took the pain into her, and let it comfort her, making her spirit sing. The hand-clapping grew: she was taking it nobly, like a Lady. When the beating was finally over, the whole House cheered.

Assembly was over; the House departed to their various tasks and classes, while Miss Duckett took charge of Sophia, to lead her to the Purser for her first haircut. Sophia replaced her panties, then gravely thanked Miss Brace for her beating.

'It is pointless to say that it must not happen again, Sophia,' said the High Mistress softly, 'for I know it shall, and you are wise enough to know it too. And,' she added in afterthought, 'it shall happen to Miss Ransome, as soon as she is wise enough to own up to her error.' She smiled.

'Yes, High Mistress,' gulped Sophia, remembering to curtsey correctly.

On her way to the Purser's she frowned as she remembered the inscription etched on the base of the baubo, the sculpted glorious derrière which had watched over her chastisement. It had been one word, in stark letters: SOPHIA.

3

Wet Spanking

'So here you are again, Sophia!' trilled the pretty little
Purser, whose name it appeared was Miss Sassi. 'Sometimes it seems I have to do everything here. So I'm a
coiffeuse as well. I like it, there is something terribly
exciting about cutting a maid's hair.' She blushed.
'Oops! Perhaps I shouldn't have said that.'

'We all must enjoy our work, miss,' said Miss
Duckett.

'I hope you enjoyed your meeting with Baubo,' said
the Purser. 'Or is your bottom too sore to sit down?
You may take your cut standing up, if you like. Oops
again! Too suggestive a phrase, perhaps. I am a cau-
tion!'

They entered a little boudoir adjoining the Purser's
bed-sitting room. Sophia said she was happy to sit,
although her bottom *did* smart awfully. She sat before a
glass, and observed herself as Miss Sassi began to comb
her hair, scratching quite sharply at her roots and
peering intently. Sophia was disturbed and asked if
there was anything wrong.

'Nooo . . .' said Miss Sassi slowly. 'I'm glad to say
you are free of lice.'

Lice! Sophia shuddered at the repugnant word, far
more than when her buttocks had been lashed with the
baubo. Then Miss Sassi knelt and lifted up Sophia's
skirt, causing her to tremble even more, and especially

42

as she felt a cool hand remove her knickers from her bare skin, for the second time that morning. She stammered in confusion, as she felt Miss Sassi's fingers on the very swelling of her fount.

'Any itching down there, at your Lady's place?'

'Why, no. Of course not! Whatever can you mean, miss?'

Miss Sassi chuckled, feeling and scratching within the lush curly hairs of Sophia's mink. 'The crabs down here are sisters of the ones on the head,' she said. 'They like a cosy life, nice and warm with all the girly smells and moisture. And very sly – sometimes a maid doesn't even know she has them. But you are OK.'

'OK?' said Sophia. 'I don't understand.'

'OK ... "Orl Korrect". It is what they say in America.'

'Are you American, then, miss?' said Sophia. 'It is just that you have a slight accent, and your name ... Oh, I do beg your pardon. I sound awfully improper.'

Miss Sassi laughed, and said rather wistfully that she was not American, but Finnish, and her name was Miss Kutti Sassi, it being the only thing her father had the grace to leave behind him when his ship sailed from Tilbury. 'But crabs, like rats, are international,' she added gravely. 'The intrepid "forty-niners", the gold miners of California, suffer terribly, as detailed in *Sourdoughs of Sacramento* by Mr E. R. Calhoun. Have you read it?'

Sophia admitted that she had not.

'I wish I were a gold-miner,' sighed Miss Sassi. 'There are women who dress as men, and become gold-miners, you know. I must lend you some books. Anyway you have no crabs.'

Sophia said she was pleased, though mystified and a little hurt. She said that she was a clean maid and always had been, taking care to wash her Lady's parts every day, and Miss Sassi's voice murmured agreement from beneath her skirt. She was taking a long time to replace Sophia's panties, and finally did so after commenting that Sophia was graced with a particularly fine and thick forest between her legs, and that she could have it trimmed if she cared.

Had any of these mysterious crabs been found, Miss Sassi would have no choice but to shave her fount completely bare, and repeat the operation every day for a whole month! Sophia did not know what to say, especially as she felt Miss Sassi's fingers accidentally brush her closed fount-lips before replacing the knicker-cloth, which she patted reassuringly. The touch of her hand on the fount swelling sent a little tingle through Sophia's belly. And to her surprise the thought of having a naked fount, even as a mark of shame and uncleanliness, was rather bewitching.

Miss Sassi wrapped her in a sheet, and said she had a privilege in store, as she was going to be the first wearer of 'Maid's Curls', which was a new creation of Miss Sassi's very own, or at least she had read about it in a Parisian illustrated paper.

'It is called a permanent,' she said, 'and it makes your hair curly. Isn't that nice? Although it isn't really permanent. Some maids are grumpy about losing their locks, although it is for their own benefit. And if you were so foolish as to merit a number nine punishment – *well* then!'

Sophia's soft knickers were doing little to soothe the hearty stinging of her skin, so she was just yet in no mood to find out what a number nine was. Miss Sassi said she would be more comfortable if she loosened her blouse and pulled it down to leave her shoulders bare, to avoid itchy hairs clinging to the cloth. Then, bare-shouldered, Sophia tensed as Miss Sassi's combs and scissors began their work, and looked sadly in the glass as her golden tresses fell forlornly to her shoulders.

Yet there was something oddly sensuous in the caress

44

of the hair on her naked skin, almost like kisses from tiny cherubs' lips, and she looked to see that Miss Sassi's face was slightly flushed, and her breath rather hoarse, as though the act of cutting Sophia's hair pleased and excited her in some way. Sophia felt a rush of pleasure herself, remembering the gentle touch of Miss Sassi's fingers on her fount. Miss Duckett watched the proceedings impassively, her arms folded with one hand clasping her bundle of rods.

Sophia cheered with anticipation as the washing and curling of the 'permanent' began. It was nice to be pampered and the centre of attention, even such stern attention. And the permanent was not brutal after all, for when it was finished, she gave a little cry of delight at her reflection. Her hair was short, but bobbed and standing up from her skull in a lovely meadow of pouting little kiss-curls, like a frilly bonnet. She wondered what Miss Brace would think of her phrenology now!

'How wonderful! At first I was fearful, miss,' she said to Miss Duckett. 'I thought of all the times I had caught a swift glance of my lovely hair, in a window or whatever would serve as a glass; of all the times I stroked it, and thought my hair was my only friend in the world. It seemed strange that at last I find myself in a place of joy and freedom, and I must lose my friend. But Miss Sassi has done marvels; my new hair is still my friend.'

'I am glad,' said Miss Duckett softly, and began to stroke Sophia's bottom quite openly and even voluptuously.

'And at Rodings, you have discovered another and better friend, Sophia: I mean your derrière.'

Miss Sassi pronounced herself pleased, too, and began to sweep up the fallen hairs, but Sophia, on impulse, stopped her, and begged to be allowed to keep her own hair. Miss Sassi smiled and said she was a foolish goose, but that she might do so, and Sophia scooped up her locks – her own property – knotting them in her kerchief as though she had won a precious trophy. Teasingly, Miss Sassi kept a little handful of the locks from her.

'These are for my show collction,' she said coyly. 'Professional mementos, you might say. My other collection is not for show.' Mischievously, she put her hand quite firmly on Sophia's fount, clasping her swelling young bulge with her fingers firmly squeezing the lips. 'The hairs come from there,' she whispered. 'I am very naughty! But the secret collection is just as big as the open one.'

Sophia smiled nervously; the pressure from Miss Duckett's hand on her fesses, and Miss Sassi's on her Lady's place, gave her a feeling of comfort and submission. She was not helpless, but she felt as though she were, and the feeling was quite beautiful.

'Well,' said Miss Duckett briskly, and removed her hand. 'To your duties, maid!'

Sophia was led through a bewildering labyrinth of winding narrow corridors, where her new hair-look attracted glances from other maids; she was not sure if they were mocking, or envious, or both. Some of the maids trudged rather than scampered, for they carried sponges, cloths and buckets, and, curiously, wore little lanyards from which hung wooden things like clothing-pegs.

'Scrubbers!' said Miss Duckett cheerfully. 'You'll be joining them, Sophia, I am sure. It is tiring and indeed humiliating work but, like all work, a job well done gives satisfaction. And then you may be put to chamber duties, or perhaps the garden. You'll still be a slop-skiv – I mean, kitchen drudge – at mealtimes, though, and after your apprenticeship as scrubber and drudge, you will be permitted to attend classes. That way, you see, maids understand that classwork – training in deportment and manners, and of course good discipline – is a privilege and not a penance.'

46

They came to the Housekeeper's office, which was more like a military quartermaster's, containing a distinguished Lady of mature years, yet surprisingly slim in figure, and dressed in fetching satin blouse and pleated full skirts of grey twill. She sat at a large wrought-iron desk well provided with stationery, candlesticks and even one or two little pin-cushions and cameos as decoration. From this homely alcove she surveyed an acridly scented empire of buckets, sponges, soaps, cloths and cleaning fluids.

'The new drudge, Miss Wragge,' said Miss Duckett with a curtsey. 'Sophia Derrière, to be assigned her duties.'

Miss Wragge peered at the nervous maid, with a twinkling eye and a reassuring, pretty smile on her lips.

'A fine strong one I hear,' she said, 'and aptly named. Well, maid, you shall work hard in your first month – and forever after! But your first month is mine.'

'I . . . I am not afraid of hard work,' stammered Sophia, feeling obliged to say something.

'Good!' said Miss Wragge briskly, standing to reveal herself not only slim but possessed of a well-rounded figure, the bosom full, the waist evidently corseted, and the derrière a sweet pear-shape.

Sophia was beginning to understand that staff and maids alike exhibited the same philosophy of Rodings, and were chosen with an eye to their posterior quality, quite possibly with an eye to nothing else.

Already Sophia's smarting bottom was reminding her to feel proud of herself, and glad that her fullness of figure was at last receiving recognition rather than mockery. Her joy was augmented when Miss Wragge paid her a nice compliment on her new hair, proceeding to issue her with two pails, containing sponges, cloths, soap and liquid, together with a small dustpan and brush. As she arranged these about her person, Miss Wragge hung a lanyard on her neck, saying that she had

47

her pegs and pads, and her kit was complete. Sophia looked puzzled by the latter items.

'Why, a cleaner does her work on all fours, maid!' said Miss Wragge brightly, 'and a Lady must not spoil the perfection of her body – hence the pads for your elbows and knees. The pegs are to hold your skirts up – to this purpose, there is a flap under the armpit of your blouse.'

Sophia still looked puzzled.

'A scrubber kneels,' explained Miss Wragge. 'It is a position of just humiliation, my dear maid. That is why there are no brooms or long-handled brushes, to be used standing. That, and the shape of the long handles, might give a maid ... ideas. But we won't go into that. Part of the submissive posture is that the knickered fesses are always displayed by lifted skirts, and furthermore, they must always be pegged tightly at your front so that the cloth is well stretched over your globes.'

She gestured towards her clothes rack, which as well as a voluminous rubber cape, umbrellas, boots and hats, contained a selection of walking sticks and canes, some of which were so thin and supple that their purpose could only be disciplinary.

'You see,' she said, 'from time to time I or a Preceptress have occasion to inspect the scrubbers at work, and if a maid is idling, why a swift reminder of her duty is easily and cleanly applied to the tight knickers, without any interruption to her labours. Mr Bucentaur believes in efficiency at all times. May I ask what you have there, in your kerchief?'

Sophia bashfully showed Miss Wragge her locks of shorn hair, and to her surprise Miss Wragge put her fingers into the golden silky mass of hair, after first politely asking, 'May I?'

She let the hair cascade between her fingers as though kneading string pearls or silk, and her face became a little pink in her evident pleasure. 'Such beautiful tresses!' she sighed, and reached out to touch Sophia's permed curls. Again she asked permission; Sophia did not mind, and in fact was curiously flattered and excited herself, as she felt the Housekeeper's gentle fingers stroking her scalp.

'Of course it will grow again,' sighed Miss Wragge, 'you lucky girl. Did you know that in China, some maids make a living out of selling their tresses for wigs? Black hair is coarser and not so valuable as fine blonde hair like yours. It seems in the Orient, ladies wear wigs in the most unlikely parts! But you must go to work.'

Sophia was given a hand-drawn map, to show her the routes she was to take, after Miss Duckett's preliminary escort to her first workplace. She was grateful for this, as she felt she would never fully learn to negotiate the intricacies of Rodings, as though it had been deliberately planned as a maze. A charming one, but a maze nonetheless.

She was to spend one hour cleaning Miss Letchford's classroom, then pause at the kitchen for three minutes to claim a cup of tea, then one hour cleaning the Lower Washroom, before returning to the kitchen for her lunchtime duties as kitchen drudge, and her own meal. After that, Miss Duckett would instruct her on the rest of the day. Miss Wragge said that while she was to look after her kit, she must not be frightened of wearing out the cloths and other things, as a drudge who presented a well-used item for replacement was obviously a hard worker.

Her maps were curious, in that they contained only the bare essentials of her direction, with instructions as to turnings and landmarks, and the locations of sinks and bathrooms. They were not complete maps at all. Sophia, having reached her various destinations, would have no idea where she was in relation to the rest of Rodings. Miss Wragge concluded the interview by reminding her to keep precisely to the map's instructions, not deviating or satisfying any improper curiosity about any chamber adjoining her route and, above all, she was not to ask questions of anyone, including herself.

Miss Letchford's classroom was empty save for one drudge on hands and knees, busy swabbing the floorboards. Flecks of dust swam lazily in the beam of sunlight that illuminated her upturned bottom, which was all that Sophia could see of her. It was as Miss Wragge had ordained: the maids skirts were pinned up and her knickers tight over a firm round derrière, whose twin globes looked most beguiling to Sophia, with their furrow vividly shaded by the sun's ray.

Miss Duckett lifted her rods and tapped the maid gently but firmly across her twin globes, and the maid shivered ever so slightly, tensing the buttocks under the thin cloth.

'Ooh! Mmm!' she said softly, but Sophia could not tell if her discomfort was at all real.

'Come on, Chaste,' she said, 'let us see some work!'

Chaste protested that she was working as hard as she could, and Miss Duckett said she was a born fibber; it seemed some friendly game both women were content to play – and had, Sophia suspected, played often before. She felt a sudden pang of annoyance, not at the kneeling maid, but at herself, for feeling left out of this harmless banter. That was soppy. There would be plenty of time later to be chided by Miss Duckett and her like.

Briskly, Sophia selected a place to kneel, and positioned herself, unbidden, beside the blackboard, where the floor was strewn with chalk dust and scraps of pencil sharpenings.

'Shall I start here, miss?' she said to Miss Duckett as she fastened her elbow and knee-pads.

'Start!' snorted the kneeling Chaste. 'Why, there is precious little to do, you late maid. And you don't even know how to pad yourself, or pin your skirts, I'll be bound. May I rise, miss?'

Miss Duckett nodded, and said she would leave the

maids to their tasks; the lock was to be their governess, and she departed, but not without administering a further warning tap to Chaste's wobbling buttocks, slightly harder than playful. Chaste made a funny frown and began to help Sophia to kit herself, chattering gaily as she did so.

'The Duck's a new Pre, so she'll cane hard and a lot. You'll feel it soon enough, maid. New Pres always want to let you know they are in charge. Did she rescue you? Have you got a pash for her? New maids always have a pash for their rescuers, but it won't stop her lacing your bum. You'll probably want her to! And the Duck's a fearful good caner – I know from experience!'

'But . . . if she is a new Pre, how do you know? How can she have caned already?' asked Sophia, mystified.

'Ha! Do you think we maids keep our games till we become Pres? You learn to be a Lady – *everything* – from your first day at Rodings! And with a bum like that, you'll probably learn quicker than anybody.'

Deftly, Chaste fixed on the pads and without ceremony lifted Sophia's skirts to reveal her knickers. With one hand, she pegged the skirt hem up under Sophia's arms and, with the other, tightened the waistband of her knickers and drew the cloth into a bundle, which she pegged so that Sophia felt the knickers drawn very tightly across her fesses. This rapid operation was concluded by a friendly pat on Sophia's buttocks, now wobbling themselves against their encasing silk.

'There,' said Chaste brightly, now you can get to work, maid.'

Her hand strayed across Sophia's fesses once more, this time to linger in a pat that became the subtlest of caresses, and Sophia distinctly felt a finger brush her furrow. 'My, you *are* well portioned!' said Chaste in admiration. 'Does it still smart – from that drubbing you took from Bracey?'

Sophia was taken aback at such familiarity

51

concerning the High Mistress, but said that it did indeed smart there, and she was proud to have taken it like a Lady.

'It is good that you protected Ransome,' said Chaste. 'I hear she owned up to that tickling, and is in for her own tickling! Probably eleven, with a splayed tip, and an extra one *there* and *there*.' Mischievously, she touched Sophia right underneath her furrow, at the very tops of her thighs, a hair's breadth from the lips of her fount, which Sophia felt were clearly visible against the stretched knicker.

'That must hurt awfully!' she blurted, her face reddening.

'It certainly does. Still, she's stupid, that Ransome. A show-off in front of the dorm. We scrubbers, why, here on our own, we can do all the tickling we want.'

Chaste showed Sophia to the washroom, or 'fluvium, where she filled her bucket, and then both women knelt and applied themselves to their scrubbing; Sophia's initial feeling of foolishness at the exposure of her bottom dissolved in her application to her work. Conscientiously she divided her patch into little squares, and began to clean each one thoroughly before wringing out her cloth, polishing it dry, and moving to the next. A tap on the bottom interrupted her.

'No, silly!' said Chaste. 'You brush all the dirt first into one pile, and leave it. Then you swab the floor, and after that you plunge all your cloths and sponges into the dirt, then shovel it into the bucket and rinse it down the 'fluvium. And, hey presto, you can go back to the Ragger with nice dirty cloths to show how hard you've worked.'

'But isn't it wasteful to dirty cloths on purpose?'

No sooner had she spoken than she felt foolish. Chaste giggled with mischief-bright eyes, her tall frame trembled in her amusement, and her tight, thrusting bosom trembled in her amusement, as though joining in

52

the amusement of her lovely rosebud lips. She brushed a non-existent auburn hair from her brow, and said to Sophia that cleaning was as easy as pissing, and Sophia tried to conceal her shock at these crude words, uttered so merrily. She had much to learn!

'Go back with a dirty kit, and the Ragger thinks you've been hard at it, see, my girl?'

Rather unwillingly, Sophia agreed to go along with Chaste's policy, although she thought it rather unfair, both to Rodings and to herself. She *wanted* to work hard, and become a Lady! After a while, Chaste began to whistle, and Sophia felt bold enough to ask her how she got her name.

'Why, I chose it!' said Chaste merrily. 'Nice one, ain't it? Chaste Marsh, that's me, because they rescued me in Hackney Marshes. And you?'

Sophia introduced herself, and then returned the conversation to the mischievous Ransome and the Rodings Riders. Chaste laughed raucously and said almost everyone was in the Rodings Riders but it meant little, as there were no men to ride.

'But we play maids' games on our own,' she said mysteriously. 'As for riding men, I've had enough of it! I've ridden men, been ridden by them, spanked and been spanked, diddled them, queened them ... I've had enough of men to last me a lifetime. Ladies are nicer and sweeter; we know each other in ways that men cannot and, frankly, there isn't much worth knowing about men except what money they have in their pocket-book.'

Much of Chaste's language was lost on Sophia, but she gathered with a slight shivery thrill that Chaste was a maid with a murky past, and whispered that she was ignorant of men and boys, except as cruel masters.

'You mean ... You're virgin?' said Chaste in awe.

Sophia nodded dumbly, not sure why she blushed.

Chaste took her hand tenderly, and kissed her cheek.

'Keep it that way for as long as you can, maid,' she said earnestly. 'Stay sweet and innocent. When you still have your cherry, you don't know how precious it is, and long to lose it, to be made a Lady by a kind gentleman. And when you have lost it, and know that there is no such thing as a kind gentleman, you weep bitter tears, for now you do know what you are missing – your precious innocence, lost forever.'

Sophia stammered that she could not believe there was no kind gentleman for her – somewhere in this world. She thought of the dreadful Mr Lee: surely not all men could be like him. Even though he had never threatened her precious virginity, his cruelty had been worse, in its disdain.

'Ha!' retorted Chaste, 'how do you think I came to be called Marsh? Because I was plying my vicious trade on a nice summer's evening on Hackney Marshes. And Chaste – I chose that name for mischief, for I was anything but!'

Suddenly, she put her hand quite blatantly on Sophia's bottom, and slipped her fingers inside the waistband, to stroke the bare skin, still stinging from the morning's beating. She asked if she could feel her hot fesses. Sophia thrilled at the gentle caress of cool fingers, and nodded, saying that it did hurt, but that Chaste's fingers were wonderful ointment. Chaste began to stroke her hair, and said she was jealous of her new curls, and might spank her again for making her so, and Sophia warmly said that Chaste was most welcome to spank her if she deserved it. She thought she made it sound a joke, but Chaste looked at her and she blushed, for they both knew to their secret pleasure that it was not a joke.

'We maids know how to delight each other better than any male can,' whispered Chaste, allowing her finger to descend into Sophia's furrow and tickle her tender skin right at the wrinkle of her bum-hole. 'Baubo is our Mistress, our arses our souls and beauty, Sophia; we don't need males nor their false gods.'

Sophia shivered, not knowing what was happening, nor why her body tingled with warmth and excitement, which were increased when she felt Chaste's other hand begin to stroke her bubbies, squeezing the ripe plum nipples through the cloth which bound them, and they tingled too as Sophia felt them strangely hardening to her friend's touch. Chaste bent to brush her lips, and Sophia felt the sweetest, softest kiss imaginable, when suddenly there was the rattling of keys, and the door opened.

'Well! You are a pair of pretty maids, and no mistake!' boomed a Lady's voice. Chaste withdrew her lips, not, it seemed, in any great hurry; shocked, Sophia looked round to see a tall young woman in boots and a tweed skirt and rubber cape, like Miss Wragge's. Her cheeks glowed red under her stern, thick blonde tresses, evidently from the invigorating winter sunshine, and Sophia felt herself blush no less redly. Unconsciously, she smoothed her hair and clothing as if to lessen her embarrassment.

'We were working hard, Miss Flye,' said Chaste rather unctuously, 'I promise.'

'I saw no work!' thundered Miss Flye. 'Quite the opposite! You were . . . you were *diddling*, admit it! I saw your hand under the maid's knickers, Chaste. It is very serious – a number four or five for you both!'

'Diddling!' cried Chaste in genuine indignation. 'I was soothing Sophia's nates after her cruel beating with the baubo this morning. Honestly, on my honour as a Lady. And anyway, did *you* never diddle, when you were a maid?'

'Insolence is of no avail. You are not yet Ladies,' sneered Miss Flye, 'you are both maids, and maids have no honour until it is beaten into them. Is shameless kissing part of soothing hot fesses?'

'Why, yes, miss, I believe it is,' said Chaste defiantly.
'And you are early, miss. We expected Miss Letchford.'

'My class begins in five minutes, and I have work to
prepare. Oh, Baubo! I'll have to beat you myself, rather
than write a report. We'll call it a ticketing offence, as
it is such a nice day – none of your smoky London fog,
but bright snow and blue sky. There, you see, I can be
good-tempered, even to diddlers like you two. You are
a London girl, are you not?' she said, peering at Sophia,
or, more precisely, Sophia's displayed derrière. Sophia
nodded.

'Well-formed for a London filly. All right, then,
knickers down, and hurry. I'm going to cane you both.'

Miss Flye unfastened the heavy crook-handled cane,
pink in colour, which adorned her waist. Sophia obediently lowered her knickers, and noted the sharp intake
of breath from her would-be chastiser as she saw the
splendour of Sophia's naked globes. But Chaste did not
bare herself; instead she asked whether it were seemly to
reduce their offences to mere ticketing, that surely they
should report to Miss Brace and tell her why *Miss Flye*
had sent them.

'No,' said Miss Flye uncertainly, 'I shall attend to it.'

'But if Miss Letchford were here, she would do things
thus,' said Chaste with the smugness of one who knew
her law, 'and no doubt Miss Letchford is sadly indisposed, so that your substitution is duly noted in the
book.'

'No!' cried Miss Flye. 'I mean yes! I mean ... Oh,
why are you maids so wicked and confusing? I shall
cane you, and hard, for your insolence. Now, bottom
bare, Chaste Marsh!'

Sophia wondered if Miss Flye's substitution was
indeed authorised, or if Miss Letchford had taken
unofficial absence on some secret errand.

Chaste would not give up her teasing – for, Sophia
saw clearly, teasing it was. Her knickers were halfway to

her thighs, tantalising both Sophia and Miss Flye with the twin lush globes of her bottom, when suddenly she stopped. 'Oh, miss!' she cried in an attenpt at piteousness. 'You have excited me so! I must make commode.'

Miss Flye was furious. 'Enough of your games, Chaste Marsh!' she exclaimed. 'Approach at once, on your knees, and fesses bare for me.' To emphasise her words, she swished her pink cane alarmingly in the air.

Chaste moaned long and high. 'Oooh,' she squealed. 'It is too late. See what you have made me do!'

Sophia looked: there was no mistaking the wet patch that dampened, indeed flooded, the silk of Chaste's knickers. And to her discomfiture, she found that she was suddenly desperate to make commode, both in her agitation at the approaching punishment, and in the strange stimulus she felt as she watched the delicious arse-globes of her new friend clearly outlined and clinging to the soaked silk of the wet panties. Sophia felt an insistent pressure in her own belly; she tried to hold herself as Miss Flye erupted in passionate anger, but it was no use.

She was suffused by an awful tickling, a feeling of blessed relief mixed with utter shame as, helpless, she felt her cascade flow hot and steaming down the stretched knicker-silk and stockings, and pool on the newly-cleaned floorboards.

Miss Flye's anger now knew no bounds. She hissed in a steely voice that she would not dirty her cane on such filthy maids, that they should take their tickets all right, but that they should sully their own hands with the shame of chastising each other. Sophia and Chaste were ordered to spank each other's bare, glistening bottoms.

Sophia was to be spanked first.

'Go hard on her, mind!' snapped Miss Flye, busy writing their tickets. 'And hurry; my class will be here soon.'

Chaste raised herself and knelt on the floorboards,

her calves tucked under her, and Sophia bent across her thighs, which were moist from her soiling. Her hands and feet balanced her on the floorboards, and her knickers were pulled down to her knees, leaving her naked wet fesses high and exposed for her spanking. Chaste put her fingers in her furrow and spread her cheeks uncomfortably and immodestly wide, ordering her to hold the position. Sophia felt utterly defenceless and helpless, her most intimate places exposed to the two women's gaze – and, to her shocked surprise, her belly warmed at the thrill of her exposure.

'Yes, miss,' said Chaste, 'I shall go hard on her.'

And she did. Although the slaps from her stern palm were nothing to the weight of the baubo, nevertheless the rapidity of her stinging blows, and the subtlety with which her rigid fingers found and tormented every secret crevice of Sophia's naked Lady's place, soon had the maid's reddened bare bottom smarting anew with a fire that made her squirm in pain and humiliation. She tried to count the slaps that spanked her so furiously, but they seemed to follow each other so fast and hard that she could not: her whole derrière seemed washed by a searing shower of hot stinging raindrops. And, in horror mingled with awed delight, Sophia realised that she did not want her beating to stop! That the contact with Chaste's cruel palm was a desired and tender form of intimacy between the two maids, a communion more profound than words or even kisses.

She had no need of Miss Flye's reluctant order that her own chastisement should cease, and Chaste's should commence. Neither did Chaste need any encouragement to lower her knickers and spread the cheeks of her beautiful bottom to their fullest extent. Sophia trembled as she lifted her hand above the smooth pale skin, shining with warm droplets; the tender bud of the bum-hole and the thick fount-lips were like fruit for the plucking. She brought her hand down on Chaste's bottom with all her might, and was pleased to see her friend tense her nates and her body stiffen. A few more slaps in rapid succession, and the globes began to glow. Sophia's hand was sticky with Chaste's unseemly wetness, but she did not care, taking this as benison rather than shame.

With each slap, Chaste's tensing and squirming became more and more frantic, and Sophia suspected she was putting on a show, for her or Miss Flye's benefit. She did not care! Exultantly she rained spanks on Chaste's quivering naked bottom, spurred on by the fervent smarting in her own globes which still roasted from Chaste's slaps. She heard Chaste groaning deep in her throat, an felt her own belly flutter in a warm tingling thrill that both alarmed and excited her. On and on she spanked, reaching, she thought, at least a hundred slaps, and her fingers probed every crevice of Chaste's bottom, which was now a fiery crimson, blushing from furrow to thigh and all around the defiant wrinkled hillock of the arse-bud; sometimes Sophia allowed her fingertips to catch Chaste there, on that very spot, and was rewarded with agonised writhing and muffled squeals.

When noises and shuffling were heard outside the door, Miss Flye finally told Sophia she could stop. Chaste's bottom glowed a beautiful crimson, and Miss Flye's face was reddened too, her breathing curious and harsh, and her hands trembling. She seemed embarrassed and even resentful to be revealed thus. As Chaste and Sophia completed their cleaning, making sure their cloths were well soaked and begrimed, she gave them their tickets and told them that they had not heard the last of this disgrace, for their names would be entered in the Long Punishment book.

They left the classroom to be greeted by a throng of maids scarcely able to restrain their giggles. They had been listening! Bella Frinton was there, and grinned at

Sophia, who blushed violently, but Chaste greeted the other maids with a cheeky and even triumphant grin. The maid Ransome was there too, looking pained and sullen in Sophia's direction, and grimacing as she rubbed her bottom. When the two maids rounded the corner, Chaste kissed Sophia again.

'Did I hurt you, Sophia?' she murmured.

'Yes, you beast! Two beatings on my very first day. My bottom stings awfully.'

Chaste touched Sophia's bottom gently, and Sophia flinched at the touch of her hand on raw skin. 'Didn't you enjoy it?' said Chaste. '*I* did.'

'*Enjoy* it? Oh, you are wicked!'

But suddenly Sophia gasped. She *had* enjoyed it! Then she fixed Chaste with an accusing stare. '*You* . . . you arranged things so that we should spank each other's bare! You wet yourself on purpose.'

'And what if I did?' retorted Chaste. 'Didn't *you*?'

Sophia was silent, numbed by her shock that Chaste spoke the truth. It was not until they reached the kitchen for their cup of tea that she asked Chaste about the Long Punishment book. Chaste replied scornfully that she thought it an invention of the Mistresses, to cow the maids.

'You see, if a maid or Lady wants to leave Rodings, all her past crimes are read to her from the Long Book, and she may elect to take punishment for them all at once! It is supposed to be quite fierce . . . a number eleven punishment.'

Sophia saw Chaste tremble slightly.

'But it's never been done, to my knowledge. No maid or Lady has ever chosen to leave Rodings. It is unimaginable.'

'You mean we all stay here for ever and ever?' asked Sophia, quite perplexed.

'No, no,' said Chaste patiently, as though to a child. 'We go out into the world – we *go out*, to pursue the work of Rodings, but we never *leave*. Only a most improper wanton would do such a thing.'

'But if she did choose to leave, if she did, why ever would she elect to take punishment?' Sophia persisted.

'Why,' said Chaste solemnly, 'because otherwise, she would cease to be a true Essex Lady. She would incur the Board's displeasure.'

4

A Queen Scourged

Sophia drank her tea quickly and gratefully, before her visit to the Lower Washroom, which she considered with a mixture of curiosity and distaste. Still, she thought, my panties and skirts are still wet from my impropriety, and I shall at least have a chance to refresh myself.

'Miss Letchford is a sly bitch,' burbled Chaste, and Sophia protested she could not help being indisposed.

'Indisposed,' snorted Chaste. 'She is off in High Roding with some young man, or in a haystack on the way. Ha!'

Sophia could not imagine what a Mistress might be doing in a haystack, but it was time to go. Chaste was due to visit another classroom; together, they returned to the Housekeeper's office, where another drudge took their dirtied cloths and gave them new things, and then they went their separate ways. Guided by her curious map, Sophia found her new workplace without too many wrong turnings.

The Lower Washroom was a cavernous, gurgling chamber in an L shape, whose rough slab floor was awash with fluid. Curiously, in this secretive place, it had no door, no doubt deliberately, so that maids could be observed about their most intimate business, in order to instil correct humility. One wall was lined by wash-basins with single taps, the other by a row of commodes,

62

or rather one single commode, a long porcelain channel with a ceaseless flow of drainage water, and rough seats perched at intervals. In the L-shaped alcove were two giant baths, or sluices, like horse-troughs, also with taps, and buckets.

Sophia grimaced. Her task, alone it seemed, was going to be arduous. She must wipe the floor dry, and clean the basins and commode as well. This washroom was for maids alone, and hence the commode afforded no privacy. Sophia knew she would easily accustom herself to nudity with other maids, but the idea of making commode in the presence of others still unnerved her. But she told herself cheerfully that was the way of Rodings.

She decided to begin with the muckiest part, the commode trough, and leave the floor until last. She took care to pin her skirts up correctly, and draw her knickers up tightly, remembering Bella Frinton's remark that doing so was a pleasant thing. It *was* pleasant! She pulled the knickers up as tightly as she could, blushing although she was alone, for the hard caress of the thin silk strand in her furrow and the crevice of her Lady's place gave her a satisfaction and a tingling joy that was not all to do with her work. When she was properly pegged and exposed, she almost hoped that a preceptress would come and tickle her helpless fesses with her bundle of rods.

Then, with a sigh, she bent over, raising each of the wooden seats and began to mop and scrub, wincing a little as the icy sluice chilled her fingers. But she did a good and conscientious job, forcing herself not to mind the occasional speck of ingrained soil in the fissured porcelain. Water cascaded plentifully over the floor, and she was glad of her solitude – glad too of the pads that protected her knees and elbows when she knelt to mop. Bells sounded in the distance; although she was unaware of the exact hour, her brain nevertheless kept its own clock, and she was aware of the approaching luncheon hour.

With the floor dried and sparkling, she rose and stretched, then proceeded into the alcove to the 'horse troughs'. Here the work would be lighter, as the alcove floor had its own separate drain and in any case needed drying rather than actual mopping. When she was busy with this final task, well begrimed and lathered in sweat, she promised herself a quick cleansing shower-bath as her reward.

The washroom was still empty; feeling slightly daring, she turned the spigot to fill one of the troughs, and looked forward to stripping for her bath. She thought of herself naked, and experienced a sudden and curious new thrill as she imagined herself scrubbing and mopping in a state of complete nudity: not just a drudge, but a naked drudge – a slave! – her bareness adding a delicious piquancy to her humility. If anyone were to see ... And then she understood that she longed to be seen, and inspected, thus. To be dismissed contemptuously, a mere naked poo-skiv, her bare buttocks rewarded with stinging slaps and cane-strokes as she laboured in her helpless submission under Miss Brace's, or sweet, raven-haired Miss Duckett's stern eyes. She giggled to herself, and then froze. The sound of voices rang as two maids entered, desiring to make commode.

'I do declare, this is my favourite 'fluvium!' cried one. 'The seats are so rough and grainy and tickle the bum so! And the trough's nice and clean, the slop skiv must have already seen to it.'

'It doesn't smell as nice as the Upper Cloaca, though.'

'When have *you* been there?'

'The Ragger sent me to clean; I was poo-skiv. And I helped myself to some Pre perfume and things. It was lovely! Such soft sponges.'

'That's a number three, you minx!' cried the second unseen voice playfully. 'I should bum you here and now!'

'Ooh! Get off!' cried the first, not very convincingly. Sophia heard the sound of slaps on bare flesh, then giggling.

'*You're* the minx,' said the first. 'You spank most wickedly. But,' she added in a haughty tone, '*that's* not a bumming, you know. A bumming is . . . is what boys do.'

'With each other?'

'Yes, sometimes. In their bum-holes, you know, with the baubo that dangles between their legs. It gets all stiff when they are excited, and hard, just like a real baubo.'

'The beasts!'

'But sometimes with maids – in our Lady's place. They spurt cream, all hot and sticky, and spurting it gives them pleasure, and they moan as if they were taking spank.'

'But does it give *us* pleasure?'

'Oh, yes! *Oodles!*'

Sophia recognised the voice: it was Felicity Straw.

There was silence as both maids, attending to their ablution, pondered the enormity of this assertion. Sophia noticed that her tap was still running, and stealthily moved to turn it off. Then she heard more giggles, muted and coy this time.

'Let's wipe each other,' said Felicity.

'Oh . . . yes, all right. Mmm . . .'

'And now . . . we've time before luncheon duty.'

'Oh, no, Felicity! We daren't.'

'Yes we do. *I* do. You spanked me; you have made me all hot and wet and soppy.'

'Spank me, then! It is only fair. But I don't dare.'

'Yes, you do,' said Felicity. There was the sound of more spanks, the slapping of a stern hand on a bare and evidently moist croup, accompanied by sighs and little muted squeals.

'*Now* do you dare?' said Felicity softly.

'Oh . . . no! I mean, yes! Oh, damn you, Felicity. All

right, diddle me. Let's do each other. I . . . Oh, don't stop.'

There was silence, punctuated only by the sweetest and most tender of moans from the two maids' breasts. Sophia was aflame with curiosity, and could not restrain herself; cautiously she moved to peek around the wall of the alcove. Felicity Straw was squatting beside the buxom and red-headed maid she recognised as Susan Westham. Their skirts were up and their knickers round their knees, and each maid had her hand firmly clamped between the other's thighs, on her Lady's place. They made only the slightest of rubbing motions, yet each caress seemed to send shuddering thrills through their bodies, and their faces were well flushed.

'Tell me what you see, Susie dear,' said Felicity, her eyes tightly shut, 'and I'll tell you what I see.'

'Oh,' said Susan Westham, 'you'll think me naughty. I see a young man, so handsome, with a waxed moustache, and wearing a cape, and – and he kisses me on the lips, and his moustache tickles me so, and then . . . Oh! He opens his cape and folds me in it, holding me to him, and . . . Oh! I can't!'

'Go on,' Susie,' whispered Felicity, 'or I'll stop diddling your lovely stiff clitty.'

'That is a very naughty thing to say . . . but my dream is naughtier, for when my young man opens his cape, he has nothing on, and his baubo is standing up, and I feel him against me, all hot and stiff and throbbing.'

'And what happens then, Susie?'

'I . . . I'm not sure. His cream spurts all over my tummy, I suppose. Oh, gosh, Felicity, I'm all quivering and hot, and my Lady's place is all wet for your fingers. I feel so trembly and strange! Do *you* like it?'

'You know I do,' said Felicity. 'And I'm wet for you, too. But my dream is different. It is a young man, but with no moustache, and he is quite naked for me.'

'Oh!'

'Yes, and bending over for chastisement. We are at the Naval College at Shoeburyness, you see, and he is a cadet, a beautiful young man with golden silky locks that I pin up over his brow, like a maid's. He *is* my maid, for I am his governess, and must punish him for ... for some boyish crime. Eleven of the best – no, thirteen, for I am governess – with my stoutest cane, on his bare buttocks! First I dress him in my petticoats and pinafore, like a maid, for he is my maid and I tell him he will be punished like a maid, on the bare! A tear comes to his manly eye, and my lips brush it away and I tell him to be brave. Then he must strip himself quite bare for me, and bend over to touch his toes ...

'I see his baubo, dangling between his legs, all soft and floppy, and I touch him there, and feel him quicken! Now I am excited ... Oh, yes, sweet Susan, keep diddling me; I know I am coming to my joy ... My dream is so lovely ... Yes, there is another maid, and he is dark jet, an African prince, as in the picture books, a proud warrior! Only here he is, bending over for my cane – I am to drub two at once. His baubo is lovely silky chocolate, and he stiffens too as I touch him. Two bottoms so trim and bare for my lash, and as I begin to cane them in turn, very very hard, the stripes quite cruel and crimson across their naked fesses, their baubos begin to stand until hard, like the masts of beautiful ships.

'And then they have each taken their thirteen and I have watched their naked bums squirm and flinch at each of my merciless strokes. They long to scream, but they mustn't, they mustn't move. Their helpless bums are dancing under the lash of their stern governess, whose every order they must obey. You want the male to wrap you in his cloak, Susan, but *I* want to see their bottoms writhe sweetly for me, their muscles rippling as they tremble at each stroke. Those two beautiful knickerless bottoms, the squirming young men all bare

67

for me alone, as I punish them for their crime of male pride. Their croups are a mass of sweet crimson, and I touch their stiff baubos and they both spurt their cream . . . Oh! Oh! Susan! I have reached my joy! Ooooh . . .'

Felicity's long moan of pain and pleasure was joined by Susan Westham's, and Sophia watched as the two maids embraced each other with little sobs of mewling pleasure. Sophia felt a wetness in her own Lady's place, and a tingling warmth in her belly. So that was joy! Just the merest touch, the merest rubbing of that curious little nubbin between the folds of her fount-lips! Her curious and lustful hand involuntarily crept to touch herself there – she had forgotten about her task, and the luncheon duty – when Felicity observed that the room was strangely silent, that the tap in the trough had been dripping and now someone must have turned it off. The two maids looked up to see Sophia, who was not quick enough to regain concealment.

'You!' cried Felicity, not without a twinkle of merriment in her eye, while Susan Westham seemed mortified by her discovery, and hurriedly adjusted her clothing. Felicity Straw did so as well, but took her time, almost flaunting the lush blonde hairs of her mink before slowly drawing up her knickers to cover herself. Then she smoothed her dress and rose to approach the trembling Sophia.

'Well, well, a poo-skiv with mischievous eye,' drawled Felicity. 'I suppose you are going to blab to the Duck, or Bracey, and get us into trouble.'

'I would never dream of sneaking,' replied Sophia hotly.

'But you were spying. That's just as bad.'

'Worse!' cried Susan.

Felicity stood with hands on hips, eyeing the nervous maid with a rather cruel smile. 'Saw your tanning this morning,' she said. 'A good bum, and your strokes well taken. I suppose a few more wouldn't go amiss, as a spy's punishment. And something about you, my friend, puts me in a mood for spanking. I'd like to tan your croup, miss – a maid's ticket we call it. Then you won't remember the naughty things you overheard.'

'They mean nothing to me!' retorted Sophia. 'I don't care what lewd things you have done, with boys and . . . their baubos. You *have* done them, haven't you, Felicity?'

'Well, no,' said Felicity, now blushing. 'I am virgin.'

'I know a thing or two,' said Sophia, regaining her self-assurance. 'I know about riding and queening and spanking, and about the men's baubos and cream and everything. Chaste Marsh told me.'

'She would!' cried Susan Westham. 'The slut!'

'But she knows,' insisted Sophia. 'And we *don't*.'

Felicity interrupted to say that there was still her chastisement to attend to, and that she wasn't going to weasel out of it by confusing them with talk of lewdness. She began to stroke Sophia's body; trembling in anticipation of what she knew was to come, Sophia did not resist.

'You are nicely pegged,' said Felicity. 'And the knickers are well tightened. They'll have to come down, of course, for a sensible bare spanking, Sophia. Look, Susan. Her bum's still red from the baubo. That *must* have been hard.'

Hesitantly, Sophia blurted out that she had taken a second chastisement, and explained what had happened with Chaste Marsh.

Susan snorted derisively. 'A maid soiling herself! That will never do! I think she needs to be taught commode manners, don't you, Felicity?'

Felicity Straw nodded assent, and with exaggerated politeness invited Sophia to stand by the commode sluice. She did so and felt a firm hand grasp her neck, and push her not ungently down towards the rushing water, while another hand expertly thumbed the waistband of her tight knickers and prised the silk from her skin, lowering the garment until her bottom was quite bare.

Sophia gave a squeal of dismay as she found her face pushed nose-deep into the cold water. She wrinkled her nose to stop the water getting in, and breathed through her mouth, overcome with the shame of having her face in the commode. A bucket of water was poured over her naked fesses, soaking her skin and knickers too. Felicity laughed and explained that this was called the ducking stool, and that though there was a real pond and ducking stool, for the discipline of chatterbox maids in the olden days, it was not now used.

'You're horrid!' spluttered Sophia.

But her protests were of no use, and she moaned as she felt the first spanks descend on her bare wet bottom. They made a sinister cracking noise, like wet fish striking a slab, and despite the coldness of both bum-skin and hands – both maids seemed to delight in spanking her at once, each to a fesse! – she felt the biting warmth of a sound chastisement. There was nothing playful about the hot pain that seared her croup, and she felt herself wriggle and flinch in protest.

'If we are so horrid, why don't you use those long shanks of yours to run away?' sneered Susan. 'We shan't stop you.'

Tears of rage flowed in Sophia's eyes. Damn these cruel maids! She, and they, knew very well why she did not choose to run away. And as the spanking became a pounding, stern rhythm, like a solemn drumbeat, her squirming fesses accommodated to its fiery caress, and danced now in a sinuous motion, almost in chorus to the rain of slaps.

'Felicity,' she gasped, 'your fantasy – about being a governess at the young men's academy – is it true? I mean, can a Rodings Lady aspire to such a thing?'

Gasping with her exertion, Felicity told her that a

Rodings Lady who excelled and pleased the Board, and proved herself *really, really* adept at the arts of discipline, might – just might – be rewarded with the rank of Governess, and that a Rodings Governess was a jewel of the highest esteem to the noblest families of the land. Water cascaded over Sophia's face and now, as the spanks lashed her bare, she imagined herself bathed in a fragrant brook, the waters of heaven raining down to inflame and purify her smarting nates.

'You see, Sophia,' she panted, 'they say – *gosh*, you can take it, maid, your bum is *so* red! – they say great leaders are made by their mannish discipline at school, and that may be so. But they are silent as to the real discipline behind great men – their Governesses! One lash from a Governess's cane on a male's bare smarts a thousand times more than a dozen from the cat in his brutal male schoolroom. Especially when she accompanies it with a stern and tender word. That's what I think, anyway. There! You've had enough, maid, and we must get to the kitchen for our drudgery.'

Sophia rose, rubbing her reddened bottom before pulling up her knickers, and feeling even the gossamer silk smarting against her bare skin. She knew, from Felicity's wise words, that she would one day – that she must be! – a Governess – a Governess of males. And she knew also that to achieve this, she must first purify herself by utterly submitting to her role as maid, to being thoroughly and implacably governed as a humiliated female. If that meant her fesses were to smart in unending crimson, then so be it . . .

'I suppose I should say thank you for my chastisement, maids,' she said in quiet mockery, with a litle curtsey. 'I think I am well on my way to becoming a Lady, and a Governess: my derrière has blushed with three beatings on my very first morning.'

Felicity and Susan smiled.

'Perhaps so, maid,' said Felicity. 'But there is more to

discipline than flogging, you know . . . and now we must hurry to the kitchen. We'll take a short cut through the yard.'

Felicity said that Sophia should keep her cleaning things for her afternoon duties, whatever they should be, and the three young women hurried from the wash-room, their clothes properly adjusted. They took a passage unfamiliar to Sophia, and emerged into the yard across from the doorway to the kitchen. The sun was bright in the blue sky, and just beginning to melt the crisp white snow into slush; Sophia suppressed a sudden desire to gambol and make snowballs. Instead, Felicity told them to keep to the covered arcade skirting the stables, as she did not want them to be seen crossing the deserted yard, or leaving footprints.

'Is it then improper?' asked Sophia nervously.

'Of course!' crowed Felicity. 'Maids will be maids.'

'Felicity,' said Sophia after a while, 'is it true what you were saying, about . . . young men, and their baubos, and what they do to maids, and to . . . each other? Bumming? I mean, Chaste Marsh told me almost everything,' she added hurriedly, 'but not *quite* everything.'

'Yes, it is true,' said Felicity seriously. 'You see, when the male's baubo is rubbed, it gives pleasure, and we get pleasure *from* his pleasure, but a sensible male will also know how to give us pleasure. Having our Lady's place filled by a big hot thing shall be so wonderful. Especially if he knows how to tweak our clitties at the same time, and diddle us.'

'But the bum-hole?' persisted Sophia. 'What pleasure can there be in that? It must hurt awfully.'

Felicity laughed mysteriously. 'Not at all. It is quite beautiful, if done tenderly. Oh, you have much to find out. And bumming is no crime, for you remain virgin. Perhaps that is why boys do it to each other. With them, it is a question of power, you see, of expressing proper

72

humility. A male can beat another male, and make him submit in that way, but a far more effective way, and one which frequently accompanies a beating, is for a sound bumming to take place to the agreement and satisfaction of both parties, the one in dominance, the other in humility. Males rub and stroke their baubos with their fingers too, just as we maids rub our clitties, and that is just as nice for them, I believe, although not really the same. They have to spurt cream, you see.'

'How I wish I had a baubo,' sighed Sophia, thrilling suddenly at the thought of a naked male croup red and squirming after she had lashed it, then *really* squirming as she plunged her stiff hot baubo inside his bum-hole, to his yelps of reluctant ecstacy, and . . . spurted her cream!

'Why, when we are full Ladies, Sophia, we shall,' Felicity replied with a deeper smile, 'and then, we can do to maids what Ladies do to us.'

'You mean . . .?'

'Why, yes, maid! Don't be soppy. There's nothing more wonderful than to be rewarded for taking your cane well; than to have a Lady pleasure you – and herself – with her own baubo, pushed deep inside your bum, and moved in and out, to teach proper joyful humility. It is so lovely and tickly and filling . . . and I think the Ladies diddle themselves when they do it, although they never allow you to look, and that is *their* pleasure.'

'I have heard,' added Susan portentously, 'that there is even a double baubo, so that a Lady can pleasure herself and her maid at the same time, or a many-pronged device by which both holes can be filled, for each celebrant of the rite.'

'Even . . . Miss Duckett would do such a thing?' asked Sophia, her breast and belly trembling.

'Especially Miss Duckett.'

As Sophia wonderingly digested this information,

they scurried past carriages and carriage-horses munching quietly in their stables, and after that the stables were empty of beasts, although Sophia glimpsed a wondrous array of harnesses, yokes, little dogcarts with dangling chains, silver-handled horsewhips, and even what appeared to be sinister shackles. She had not time to take in all the sights, but as they gained the door to the kitchen, she remarked that the Rodings estate must be truly vast, to require such a variety of farm animals and implements for their direction.

'It is vast,' said Susan. 'We feed ourselves, you know.'

'But be aware, Sophia,' added Felicity, 'that there are no farm animals kept at Rodings.'

Sophia pondered these strange words as she went about the rest of her day's tasks. She was pleased that on her very first day at Rodings, she already fitted into the establishment's routine, and was treated by the other maids with the respect due to one who had been so nobly thrashed. The afternoon was spent cleaning other classrooms, and sweeping corridors on her hands and knees, pegged as always, and in the corridor she was rewarded from time to time with an idle stroke to her knicker-tight buttocks as a stern Preceptress passed; she even felt the kindly thud of a baubo from a mischievous Lady or two.

At tea, her kitchen drudgery was repeated, and then the maids had a period of free time, when they could amuse themselves by wholesome games, or feminine accomplishments such as sewing and needlework. Sophia said to Miss Duckett that she preferred reading to such things, and Miss Duckett smiled, then accorded her a library privilege, which meant that she was permitted to browse in the library under supervision of a Preceptress willing to make free time – in this case, Miss Duckett, of course.

They passed through the winding corridors, up two

flights of corkscrew stairs, and came to the door of the library, which Miss Duckett solemnly unlocked, and opened with a portentous creaking of hinges. Sophia was admitted to a small dark chamber, whose oaken shelves were positively crammed with books, and whose musty air thrilled her with its perfume of paper and leather. She gasped – Miss Duckett noticed that her face suddenly flushed with a pleasure that was more than scholarly. In wonder, Sophia reached a trembling hand to touch one of the leather-bound spines. She saw that many of the gold-embossed titles were in foreign languages, and remarked on this.

'They are not in foreign languages, maid,' said Miss Duckett drily. 'They are in Greek and Latin, which Mr Bucentaur would be displeased to hear described as foreign languages. But what is it? You seem perturbed.'

'No . . . no,' said Sophia, the shadowy light from the narrow window hiding her blushes. Dare she tell? 'You know something of my history. Of my imprisonment in the house of Mr Lee, at Arbour Square.'

'Yes. Go on.'

'It is just that sometimes, for a beating, Mr Lee would bring me to his library, which was very much like this, and I would bend over a chair, to be whipped by his sister, on my knickers, while he read one of his books. And from time to time, if I squealed or jumped at her whip-stroke, he would grunt as though he had found something pleasant in his book. But I knew it was not the book that gave him pleasure, it was my squirming helpless bottom. Or perhaps the two pleasures were as one.'

'So, being in a library gives you a curious sort of nostalgia?' said Miss Duckett thoughtfully. 'Perhaps the pleasures of reading are akin to those of the lash, my dear. In both cases, the enjoyment is accompanied by a slow, rhythmic crackling noise, whether the rustling of pages or the lacing of bare skin.'

'You seem to know a lot about me already, miss,' said Sophia, her voice trembling with tender longing.

'I know that you disgraced yourself before Miss Flye,' said Miss Duckett slowly, wreathed in shadows. 'You made pond – you wet your knickers, soiling yourself.'

'Yes, miss,' said Sophia. 'And I was well punished.'

'Your disgrace is my own, as your rescuer,' said Miss Duckett with a sigh that was not all anger. 'I should punish you further, had I cause. Well, choose your book, maid.'

Although there were plenty of books in English – all, Sophia noted, works of history, art, and geography, with no fiction or other light reading – she felt drawn to the sumptuous leather tomes in the ancient languages, and began to peruse them. Miss Duckett warned her to take care, as they were antique and valuable. Sophia found herself thrilling at the very ripeness of the books' smell, the feel of the crackling paper, and the sonorous titles, whose meaning she could only guess at. She picked and opened one at random.

The book dealt with Boudicca's punishment, further defiance, and subsequent heroic rebellion against her oppressors; but the greater part of the pictures dealt in loving detail with the humiliation she was forced to undergo, and which, far from subduing her, inspired her to rebellion. Miss Duckett whispered that the tract was intended to be patriotic, and justify such unlawful rebellion against ordained authority, by showing the hideous provocation by which authority had overstepped its bounds. But Sophia sensed that these depictions had a purpose more than moral – even a lewdly inspired one, judging from her belly's tremors as her eyes feasted.

The whipping was the culmination of subtle barbarities by which the Romans hoped to make the queen submit. They were shrewd, not marking her body until, their temper evidently exhausted, they decided on the fearsome spectacle of her final whipping. Before that, her torments were silent ones, the greatest shame of the English queen that her submission was supervised and orchestrated by another *woman* – a raven-haired, beautiful Roman, evidently some concubine of General Suetonius. She gave gloating orders to the centurion, and his soldiers covered Boudicca's shameful nudity with a girdle made of horsehair, a sort of knicker that was strapped tightly in her crevice and, Sophia thought, must have stung abominably.

Then her generous breasts, with nipples intriguingly depicted as very full and high, like plums, were encased in a similar garment, a type of painful bustier. Her ankles were bound with metal cuffs, and her waist with another girdle or corselet, this apparently of leather, which was fastened very tightly, and then attached to her bound ankles by a chain, drawn up so that her legs were bent with her feet almost touching her taut fesses. In this position she was made to lie on her side, and rolled around the floor like a toy, while the soldiers spat on her. At first she was blindfolded. Later, her torment was increased by a leather hood, which replaced the blindfold and covered her entire head except for her mouth and nose.

At the raven-haired woman's direction, the centurion took a small baubo from Boudicca's discarded robes, evidently her sacred amulet, and gestured obscenely with his fingers, to the amusement of his soldiery and the Roman woman. Then the gestures were put into practice. Plate after plate showed the most intimate details of the queen's body, as her hempen girdle was pulled tight into her furrow, to reveal her anus bud and Lady's lips, and then the baubo was pushed deep inside both her orifices in turn, while the centurion himself released his massive *membrum virile*, quite naked, and plunged it into Boudicca's open mouth between the lips of her leather hood. Sophia was shocked, as she had never seen the male organ before, even depicted.

The raven-haired Roman woman watched, her eyes and lips glistening with bright pleasure. Sophia saw in her the features of Miss Duckett, and she herself was the trussed Boudicca. She thought she had never seen as beautiful a Lady as this dark Roman.

She supposed that the antiquity of the volume and its moral purpose gave such graphic candour its respectablity; yet she was more shocked at her own reaction to these cruel tableaux. There was a warm fluttering in her belly, and she could feel her fount begin to seep with warm oil. Could it be that in her repulsion from these scenes, she was secretly attracted by them? That she longed for such torments to happen to her, to be the plaything of such a cruel Lady and her virile servants, and helpless in her maid's humiliation? She thought back to her ordeals at the hands of Mr Lee: what had been so distressing in her punishments was precisely that he had not been cruel, for cruelty at least shows interest – his cruelty was in his very indifference to her, reading a book while she was flogged, as if she were of no more importance than a rag doll.

She looked more closely at the posture of Queen Boudicca. Whether the artist had intended it or not – and Sophia knew well enough that true intentions are often unconsciously expressed – there was a definite agreement in the twisting of her body, as though she were aiding the soldiers in their humiliation of her. Her mouth did not reject the massive and terrifying shaft which was plunged into her throat; rather, she seemed to be savouring the male flesh. She could submit at any time, make obeisance and be released from her torment; she must *know* that her position faced with Roman might was quite hopeless. Yet she did not. It was as though she rejoiced in her humiliation and the fierce destiny to which it drove her. No doubt, Sophia imagined, the centurion was spurting his cream into her, and she was swallowing the hot torrent, making him for a moment *her* prisoner. She felt giddy, and suddenly longed to taste a male's secret essence, watched by a cruel, beautiful Governess.

Finally, she was released from her bonds, only to be subject to fresh humiliation. Her hood was removed and the centurion interrogated her anew, thrusting a parchment for her to sign – evidently her deed of abdication. She had only to sign it, to accept the inevitable. She spat in his face. At this, his fury reached its peak. Now, her girdles of penitence were once more removed and she was entirely naked. Sophia could not help admiring her fiery mink of lush red curls, and the mane of red hair on her crown: these, together with her superb buttocks, breasts and thighs, reminded her unaccountably of the maid Susan Westham. The cuffs on her ankles were replaced by loose shackles which permitted her to hobble; her arms were stretched and bound to a heavy wooden pole across her shoulders, forcing her to walk with her head bowed.

Most cruelly, her nipples and the very lips of her fount were clamped by pegs, just like those that held up a maid's dress to reveal her knickers. These pegs were attached to a stout rope, and with this she was led like an animal into the light of day, where her sullen tribe awaited the spectacle of their Queen's chastisement. Her shoulder-yoke was bound to the flogging-post, and this was not all. With a dry razor, her lush mink of pubic hair was roughly shorn, and the hairs cast to the wind like the petals of a tender flower; her mane of head-hair was cut to a ragged fringe, and strewn likewise.

Then her whipping began. The centurion held a *flagrum* of thin metal rods, about seven, and his flogging was expert, under the gloating eyes – and, Sophia noticed, the scarcely-concealed lustful embraces! – of General Suetonius and his concubine. The plates dwelt in horrified, or horrifying, detail on the reddening of her back, her fesses, and her thighs, and left the reader in no doubt of the length of the chastisement, for its end was illuminated by a lurid sunset whose rays were matched in crimson by the punished naked flesh of the Iceni Queen. She was left there for her tribesmen, the deed of abdication scornfully pinned to her ragged hair. Yet at the last, her head lifted under its yoke, and there was almost a smile of patient glory on her radiant, serene face. Was this the *joy* of which Susan and Felicity had cried, in their playful diddling?

What followed was enthralling – the rebellion, the burning of London and Colchester, the final defeat by Suetonius and his troops, and Boudicca's tragic end by her own hand, but Sophia skipped through it quickly, her mind concentrating on those terrible yet thrilling images of the Queen's torment. She found herself wondering a little mischievously if Boudicca had acted properly. Would it not have been better to demand abasement before Suetonius himself? To take his whip, and swallow *his* cream? To approach things sensibly, a Lady's way, and become his Governess, so that it would be the proud Roman who eventually begged the privilege of baring *his* buttocks – *and* the naked fesses of his lush concubine – to the English Queen, for their beating in just humiliation?

Her thoughts were interrupted by Miss Duckett, who advised her that she must hurry.

'May I take this book, miss?' said Sophia.

'If you are careful,' replied Miss Duckett, looking at her with amused yet searching eyes. 'But you know no Latin.'

'Oh, I shall learn. I mean to educate myself, miss.'

As they proceeded away from the library, Sophia could no longer contain herself. She took a deep breath and said, 'Miss – you said that it should be your duty, or your pleasure, to punish me further, were I guilty of any other impropriety than those already paid for.'

'I did say that, and it is true. I should take great

delight in whipping you bare, Sophia, and I make no secret of it, for I think you have been chastised too leniently.'

'Well, miss, I *am* guilty of further impropriety,' blurted Sophia, 'for in the Lower Washroom, I sloppily neglected to empty the bathing-trough, and left it full of dirty water.'

Miss Duckett stopped, and brushed a silky raven hair from her brow. A quizzical smile played on her lips as she looked deep into Sophia's eyes, melting the young maid. 'That *is* serious,' she said gravely. 'You shall certainly be punished for it.'

'What do I deserve, miss? A number two? Or a three?' said Sophia with nervous joy.

'Why, I must give the matter some serious thought, Sophia,' said the Preceptress. 'I shall speak to you a week from today. Try and take care not to commit error before then, otherwise your poor bum will be too tender for my whip's just ministrations – and I want her to be tender from *my* whipping. A week of trembling contemplation will add to the piquancy of your chastisement.'

Sophia's heart leapt with joy. Miss Duckett *wanted* to punish her . . . *wanted* her!

'As for the severity of your punishment,' said Miss Duckett dreamily, 'you have a week to study your book. No doubt Queen Boudicca will give you some ideas.'

5

Rare and Firm Punishment

That night, and every night in the week before her punishment, Sophia's sleep was made richer by strange dreams, following her avid and secret perusal of her book. She was Boudicca, squirming under the rods, wielded by the mysterious Roman lady, whose raven hair seemed to have metamorphosed into Miss Duckett's. The saturnine eye of Miss Brace looked upon her chastisement, but she was arrayed as General Suetonius, and caressed a giant baubo held between her legs, most lasciviously; she rubbed the swollen tip, the carved fesses of the goddess, at each whipstroke to Sophia's naked buttocks and back ... Now, it was Sophia herself who administered the flail, scourging Miss Duckett; then Chaste Marsh, Felicity Straw, Susan Westham, all together, their naked fesses spread like an array of succulent bare fruits joyful in their acceptance of her biting. Miss Brace, as General Suetonius, murmured that Caesar would be pleased, and flexed a whip on whose silver handle – another baubo – was inscribed *Bucentaur Sophia* ...

Under the lash, Sophia's body joined her comrades in a helpless squirming of pain so acute that their bared fesses assumed a frenzied power and life of their own, and were liberated by their torment to take wings and fly. Sophia would awaken from her dream sweating and puzzled, yet somehow content. Her belly was warm and tingly, and her Lady's place unaccountably wet. At first she thought she had made pond and soiled herself, but on closer inspection it was not the case: her fluid was oily and secret. Bella Frinton looked at her once or twice with a strange secret smile, but said nothing, except to repeat her gentle compliments on the fullness of Sophia's derrière, and playfully suggest that one day, as a Preceptress, she would show Sophia what a *real* thrashing was.

As she smoothly adapted to the rhythm of Rodings, Sophia became more self-assured, and knew that her physical beauty could be turned to her advantage. She had learnt her rulebook almost by heart; her manner towards her comrades became no less decorous and reserved, but there was a quiet assertiveness in her very reserve. She looked with envy on the maids who had been accorded the privilege of class-study, and worked ostentatiously hard at her skiv tasks, to prove herself worthy of the same; at least, to make sure that Miss Duckett and Miss Brace had no excuse to hinder her from studying. Felicity Straw said darkly that she should save some of her energy for the spring sowing, but refused to elaborate, grinning rather cruelly. Sophia once said she loved Felicity dearly, but sometimes she could be a right madam – an expression she had learned from Chaste Marsh.

A look of pain came over Felicity's face, much to Sophia's surprise: not from the friendly insult but because, Sophia realised, it was a word of Chaste's. Obviously the question of Chaste Marsh was a painful one for Felicity, as shown by her suddenly moist eyes and bitter words.

'That cow! That's what *she* says, the dirty cow.'

'Oh, Felicity, I didn't mean to hurt you,' said Sophia, embracing her friend.

'*You* didn't hurt me, Sophia,' murmured Felicity, and suddenly emitted a sob. Sophia cradled her to her breast.

83

'Oh, Sophia,' exclaimed Felicity, 'we are not supposed to form attachments, we maids, but we *do*. And if you have any sense, you'll understand why it is forbidden. Don't cuddle me any more, I beg you, it is too sweet, and I don't want to form an attachment to *you* – you would only break my heart.'

Sophia protested that she would never break anyone's heart, and Felicity told her primly but sadly that it was not within her power, and that it was precisely the sweetness and gentleness of a heart-breaker that made her so.

'Chaste is the opposite: she is vicious and cruel, and doesn't care nor pretend to. That is what makes her so devilish attractive, one longs to tame her. But you, Sophia – you are already tamed. You are submissive, and in your very powerlessness lies your power. You work harder than any other skiv, you obey unquestioningly, and your obedience spurs the Pres and the Mistresses to give you stricter and stricter orders, to test you. Always, you take it without complaint! And that is what is so infuriating about a submissive, she may transfer her affections at any time, in the pure goodness of her heart, sensing another's need. I should be terrified of having a pash for you, sweet, for a submissive is the cruellest slut.'

Sophia's head whirled in confusion. 'Submissive?' she cried. 'Why, I have never thought of myself as such! For you, Felicity, I should be the most domineering of maids – of Mistresses – if it would please you, and make your eye smile instead of glisten!'

'You see?' exclaimed Felicity. 'You *are* submissive, even agreeing to make yourself a Mistress for me.'

'If I am submissive, Felicity,' she said quietly, 'it is because my life has been drudgery and whiplashes, and I have never had the choice of being anything else.'

Sophia was astonished by Felicity's retort. 'Sophia, perhaps your life has been thus, and you have never been offered any other choices, precisely *because* you are submissive. You have not adapted to your circumstances; they have adapted to you. And now you find yourself at Rodings, where your submission to date is nothing to what you must endure in the future. Yet, do you take your train ticket and go back to London? Do you protest? No! You submit to your utmost, and I'm sure you fret because you cannot submit even more. Am I right or wrong?'

Sophia was silent: she knew Felicity was not wrong. She was spared a reply by the arrival of Miss Duckett who said sternly that the skivs should see to their tasks, and not spend time billing and cooing, otherwise a mischievous Preceptress might get the wrong impression and think she saw a pash.

Miss Duckett swished her rods with vigour. 'And we know what happens to the bums of naughty maids with a pash, don't we?' she cried gleefully. 'Much the same as your derrière will experience tomorrow morning, Sophia. Or had you forgotten?'

Sophia trembled. 'No, miss, I had not forgotten.'

'Good. It shall be quite a treat. Miss Brace has authorised a number – but I shan't say it, to keep you in delicious suspense, my maid. Harder than you might expect, that is all! I am the cruellest of Preceptresses, am I not?'

Miss Duckett's face glowed with pleasure, which was increased when Sophia humbly nodded her assent. 'Well, Sophia, you asked for it, by your own admission of guilt. You have the joy of submitting to your own honesty.'

When Miss Duckett had departed, Felicity pressed Sophia for details.

'You mean you admitted . . . you *asked* for punishment?' she said incredulously, when Sophia had told her of her impropriety – the unemptied bathwater. 'Why, there you are, a pure submissive! *And* I shouldn't be surprised if *you* had a pash for Miss Duckett.'

Fiercely, and turning to hide her hot blushes, Sophia returned to her scrubbing, and decided to change the subject.

She asked Felicity – the thought came to her quite out of the blue – about Ransome and her gang, the Rodings Riders. Ransome had not spoken to her, although she had been favoured with a curt nod of greeting on occasions. She seemed a charming maid, despite her airs, and Sophia wondered if she should try and make friends. Felicity scornfully said that Ransome was a nice cow, but a soppy one – all lip and no knickers – and that the Rodings Riders were really a figment of her heated imagination.

'We'd all like to ride men, I suppose,' she said wistfully, 'and that is why we must work hard to become Governesses. A Governess can do anything she pleases with her males. But we have no males to practise on.'

'There are males in the villages,' said Sophia firmly. 'Miss Letchford has a pash for one, Chaste told me.'

'One or several,' replied Felicity drily. 'But what male wants to be ridden? And whacked with a crop, and disciplined? It is because they are intractable and *don't* want to be disciplined that they *must* be, don't you see?'

'Surely there must be males who submit to the whip as readily as a female?' insisted Sophia.

'Then it mightn't be as much fun,' mused Feliity.

'We could practise on each other,' said Sophia eagerly.

'You mean ride each other, and spank each other's bare, and ... well, other things? Even ... diddle? Mmm.'

'Whatever gave us pleasure and instruction,' said Sophia.

'I'll have a word with Ransome,' said Felicity, affecting indifference. 'I'll tell her there is a maid who is longing to be ridden and spanked. You *do*, don't you?'

'*I*? Well, *no*! I mean ...'

'Does a rider control her horse, or the horse its rider?' asked Felicity, smiling.

Sophia set herself with greater zeal to her tasks, her face aflame. Why, she wondered, does every woman know my heart except *me*?

The morning of Sophia's caning arrived and, as she rose from her bed, she apprehensively stroked her bottom; suddenly she was reminded that her fesses had gone unpunished and unlaced for a full week, and wondered if the forgotten smarting of cane or lash would be bearable, the only swishing she was now used to was the delicious caress of silken drawers. Miss Duckett appeared and smiled, stroking her *fasces*. She said that Sophia should report to her study after her breakfast duies had been completed, and that Miss Brace had excused her further skiv duties before luncheon.

'So we have all morning, maid,' she said very civilly, and with a faint, enchanting curl of her lips, 'and I can skin that lovely bare bum *nice* and slowly.'

At breakfast, Felicity urged her, 'Keep your chin up, and show a good pair of melons,' with the promise that there was a treat in store: she had spoken with Ransome, and said gravely that if Sophia was well reported from her thrashing by Duckett, she could expect some stout training as a Rodings Rider, at a special secret gathering.

With some trepidation, Sophia mounted the narrow twisting staircase to Miss Duckett's study, guided by a hand-drawn map to what seemed the remotest eyrie of the House of Rodings. She was pegged with her knickers tight around her fesses, and being obliged to walk through the corridors thus, all the while keeping her face calm, was, she knew, an exquisite and humiliating part of her punishment. She knew too that in a short time those knickers would be stripped from her, to leave her buttocks naked and unprotected from Miss Duckett's cane.

87

Her heart fluttered; Miss Duckett had promised her a punishment harsher than customary, and had kept the number from her. Would it be only *one* cane . . . perhaps two, or even more? Sophia shuddered; the thought of three rods lacing her naked skin at a single stroke seemed somehow more than she could take without blubbing. Trembling, she knocked, and was admitted to the raven-haired Preceptress's study.

Sophia had not known what to expect: a cosy nook, perhaps, like Miss Sassi's, or some artistic, pompous chamber like Miss Brace's. Instead, Miss Duckett's room was astounding in its simplicity: bare white walls, a simple wooden cot, table and chairs, with a worn leather armchair, and the only element of luxury a rich astrakhan carpet which colourfully adorned the brightly-polished floorboards. There was one painting on the wall above the bed: a sumptuous antique oil depicting a naked goddess – Baubo, it seemed, but with long, raven hair and a gleaming olive skin. The goddess was bound by waist, wrists and ankle to a whipping-frame set amidst an olive grove, under a sunny Greek sky, and a magnificent but fearful centaur was applying a scourge of rods to her whip-flamed naked buttocks, while a group of naked young men and maids, garlanded with flowers, looked on with laughing enthusiasm.

Sophia could see the young women's Lady's places, all plump and shaven, and the men's baubos, shaven too, and curiously soft and pretty, which seemed at odds with their well-sculpted virile musculatures. Miss Duckett said it was Baubo in the guise of her sister goddess Demeter, and it was her custom to visit the earth thus, to be ritually flogged for the spring festivals of Sparta, Corinth, and other Greek cities. The fertile benison of Baubo's fesses was greater than that of any other goddess, even the Goddess of Fertility herself.

In the corner stood a cabinet of gleaming rosewood, curiously and deliciously embossed with a large golden baubo on each of the twin door-panels. Accustomed to meekness, Sophia nevertheless retained her Lady's curiosity, and Miss Duckett saw her eyes fix on the cabinet.

'You admire it?' she said. Sophia nodded.

'It is a gift . . . a very special gift. No one has ever looked before. But you are the first, so I suppose . . .' Miss Duckett's face was flushed with excitement, try as she would to maintain a Preceptress's haughtiness.

'You mean, miss, that I am the first maid you are to punish here? In your own chamber?'

'Yes, Sophia. You may consider yourself honoured.' She took Sophia's hand, and added softly, 'As I do.' Then her manner became brisk and cheerful. 'Well!' she said. 'I said I was going to give you a good skinning, maid, and you shall have it. Are you ready?'

'I am ready, miss. I shall take your punishment.'

'Promise not to squeal, or blub, or anything? You know you'll take it on the bare, but . . . there is more to it.'

'I promise.'

'Very well. Miss Brace, as you know, authorised a special punishment. She feels that you are wilful and strong, and must be tamed perhaps more than the other maids. She senses power in you, Sophia, power that must be broken – or harnessed to good ends.'

'I, wilful, miss? Oh . . .' Sophia felt tears well. She so wanted to please, and told Miss Duckett that the thought of wilfulness was quite horrid.

'There, there,' said Miss Duckett, brushing her forehead with cool lips, 'we said no blubbing, didn't we? There is nothing unnatural about being wilful. Mr Bucentaur understands. Why, even Queen Boudicca was quite wilful.'

With a flourish, she opened the cabinet, and Sophia gasped. Inside was an array of implements of correction of an artifice and variety which she could never have imagined. There were whips and canes and baubos of giant dimensions, shackles and hoods, garments of constriction in leather and rubber. She trembled at the treasures of Miss Duckett's cabinet, and unconsciously reached out to stroke the artefacts shining in their silent, terrible beauty.

'A gift?' she murmured.

'The cabinet, and everything in it. Do not ask from whom. Do not ask anything, Sophia, but prepare for your chastisement. Sophia, *it is to be a number six*.' She glanced anxiously up and seemed to be looking at the centaur's buttocks, in his furrow beneath the uplifted tail. 'Yes – a number six.'

'Three canes?' Sophia gasped.

'You may proceed to make your choice,' said Miss Duckett gravely. 'Take your time – when you have chosen three of my virgin rods, you will bind them with a thong to make my scourge. And then, according to the rules, I must bind you. First, though, you must denude yourself entirely. The knickers off, the underthings and blouse and skirt.'

'Mayn't I even keep my shoes and stockings?' asked Sophia, with the vague idea that even this useless minimum of clothing would ensure some scrap of dignity and aloofness still adhered to her.

Miss Duckett looked up again. 'The stockings – very well,' she said. 'And the garter belt, of course. But the cane will touch your bare, anyway.'

'I know, miss,' said Sophia as, shivering, she began to strip herself under the watchful eye of her Preceptress and, it seemed, of the flogged goddess Baubo and her virile tormentor. When she was naked but for her stockings and belt, she felt her flesh tighten in little shiver-bumps, and saw that her nipples had stiffened into hard fruits surrounded by a sea of goose-flesh, which in other circumstances she would have found quite beguiling. She saw the taut downy skin of her belly shiver and, inside her, fear was mingled with a moist and expectant pleasure.

She was horrified at what awaited – a number six, for such a trifling offence! – yet knew that it was ordained, was therefore just, and she must be wholehearted in her submission. And at this thought the tingling warmth in her belly became joined with a seeping wetness at her Lady's place, the same moisture that soiled her nightie every dream-filled morning, and that she knew to be evidence of her lewd and improper excitement! She was about to confess this to Miss Duckett, but she looked deep into her eyes, and the Preceptress smiled, revealing pearl-white teeth and wet pink tongue. She knew.

Not another word was necessary. Numbly, Sophia touched the implements of chastisement, a willing accomplice in her own torment – her own guilty pleasure. Miss Duckett saw the trembling of her fingers as she stroked the supple, whippy cane-wood, and whispered that it was not wrong to take pleasure in just chastisement and corrective pain. At length Sophia selected three of the strongest rods, about three feet each, and stroked them gingerly as Miss Duckett handed her a leather cord to bind them and make a handle for her. This Sophia did with deft fingers, using a tight reef knot that would keep her scourge safely intact through the impact of her flogging. When she had finished, on impulse, she kissed the rods, and, kneeling before her Preceptress, handed them to her.

'There is more,' whispered Miss Duckett. 'You must be bound, maid.'

With that, she approached her bed, bent over with a delicious rustle of her blue skirts swirling around her own buttocks, and pressed a lever. To Sophia's surprise, the limbs of the bed slowly and gracefully slid apart, then up, until the bed was transformed into a frame, which Sophia saw was to be her flogging-bed. It was like the skeleton of a table: four short vertical posts linked by horizontal bars, with a neckrest and grooves for wrists and ankles, together with a pad at the centre for her belly. Had an observer lain beneath the frame, her nudity would have been apparent, with her stockinged thighs cruelly stretched and bare breasts swelling ripe and unsheathed.

Sophia needed no order: she positioned herself on the frame, and felt the tight leather cords knotted around her extremities, then a strap binding her waist to the belly-pad. When this was done, and she was helpless and immobile, Miss Duckett worked a foot-lever which cranked the belly-rest upward, painfully so until Sophia thought herself stretched to bursting!

The result was that her splayed buttocks were higher than her head and feet, and thus her derrière stood like two smooth taut hillocks, naked and alone, proudly awaiting the kiss of the lash in their helpless nudity. She had never felt as helpless in her life, and this thought caused a wickedly moist sensation in her Lady's place; the feeling of utter helplessness made her not just seep, but flow abundantly with the oily fluid of her womanhood. Her nipples were stiff now, and not from the shock of nakedness; she felt her damsel, the secret nubbin within her Lady's flaps, tingle and stiffen in sweet harmony with her naked breast-flesh. Her whole body seemed to tingle with sensation and vitality, and the caress of the silk stockings, her only adornment, was like the breath of petals. She was ready for her chastisement.

Suddenly words began to flow from her in a torrent. She told Miss Duckett of her dream, of the whip handle with the strange words *Sophia Bucentaur*, of seeing the word *Sophia*, her own name, incribed on the base of the baubo with which Miss Brace had delivered her first beating at Rodings. Miss Duckett listened indulgently, all the while stroking Sophia's naked bottom, and her silken stocking-tops, with little cooing noises that were half-lustful, half-regretful.

'Such a shame to redden such glorious fesses, Sophia,'

she murmured. 'And you will dance very red indeed before the end of your punishment. It shall be twenty-one strokes, you know. Twenty-one with the tricorn cane ... Afterwards, you may be quite proud of yourself as you play your silly games with the Rodings Riders. No, say nothing. I know more than you think; it is a Preceptress's job to know.'

'Then you must know what my dream meant, miss,' gasped Sophia, her Lady's place now flowing copiously with oily fluid at the cool touch of her Preceptress's fingers. 'And what the inscription on the baubo meant, too.'

Miss Duckett checked, finally, that Sophia's bonds were as tight as could be, then lifted her fearsome cane, which made a dry crackling noise in the still air. Sophia tensed and shuddered.

'You know who Mr Bucentaur is, of course,' said Miss Duckett, 'and it is a quaint thing that *Bucentaur* was the magnificent state ship of the Doge of Venice, the seagirt island nation of mysterious lakes and canals and palaces; the name comes from the Greek, "bous", an ox, and "centaur" ... Well, you can see from the painting of flogged Baubo. The *Bucentaur* had a prow that was a centaur, a man-headed ox. Venice was called "Bride of the Sea" and every springtime the Doge would cast a golden wedding ring into the lagoon, to assert the City's mastery over the waters. It is quaint that it was the bride herself who bestowed the ring to symbolise *mastery*. As for "Sophia", you ought to know that it is simply the Greek word for *wisdom*.'

Sophia's face twisted in terrible shock, as the cane whistled in the air and the three rods struck her full and hard across the quivering skin of her stretched bare buttocks.

'You will please clearly count each stroke as it is safely delivered, maid,' said Miss Duckett, 'and thank me.'

Sophia felt her body writhe uncontrollably in her bonds, her buttocks frantically clenching and squirming in the searing hot agony of that first cane-stroke ... only the first! Her throat caught a scream – she must *not* blub, must *not* cry out! She must take it like a Lady.

Sophia looked up at the centaur in the painting, his magnificent muscled buttocks seeming to grin at her, as he gleefully whipped the goddess's full bare nates. Sophia wondered what Baubo felt, and if her own fesses should glow so red and piteously after Miss Duckett's chastisement.

'One,' gasped Sophia through clenched teeth. 'Thank you, miss.'

'So, only twenty more to go,' murmured Miss Duckett impassively. Sophia shut her eyes. Her flogging had begun.

The strokes came at very long intervals, perhaps of two minutes, and each one seemed harder than its predecessor. The wait between strokes was welcome as it allowed time for Sophia's pain to dissipate, and her squirming to die down, but fearful in that as her fesses relaxed, her heart pounded in dread of the next stroke of the tricorn canes. Sophia was glad she had to keep count, and concentrate, although her hoarse breath scarcely let her form the words.

'Two. Thank you, Miss. Oooh! Three! Th-thank you, miss . . .'

The intervals between strokes became longer until, after the fifth or sixth, Miss Duckett seemed to be panting as hard as her tethered maid, whether from her exertions or from some secret emotion, Sophia could only guess.

'Well,' said Miss Duckett softly, after a while, 'you are holding up quite nicely, maid. You're squirming quite a bit, but that is only natural. Are my strokes hard?'

'Oh, yes, miss!' cried Sophia quite sincerely. 'My poor

bum has never smarted so novel! Every stroke is like a flame right through me – not just my bum, but all of me. I never thought it possible to feel such pain.'

It was as though talking of her discomfort brought Sophia joyful relief; her chastiser seemed to feel the same, and her strokes slowed to intervals of perhaps three minutes. Sophia did not care, for she found that after the sixth stroke, her agony had reached a plateau of habitude: she was accustomed to it, had incorporated the pain into herself, so that each further stroke seemed merely an addition to the wash of white-hot torment which had become normality.

'I've never been beaten so hard!' she added, thinking this would please Miss Duckett.

It did. 'You really mean that?' she asked, in delight. 'You don't want me to stop? For I shall if you wish, you know.'

'No, miss!' cried Sophia in genuine alarm. Truly, the thought of demanding a halt had never occurred to her. Nor, she realised with a guilty thrill, to her Lady's place, whose torrent of soft love-oil continued unabated even under this fearful thrashing! And guiltily too, she wondered if Miss Duckett experienced the same. She *knew* it must be so.

Again, she felt her Preceptress's – her rescuer's – cool hands stroke the naked inflamed skin of her derrière.

'You poor thing,' said Miss Duckett. 'You are flushing quite beautifully. The tricorn cane is a very special instrument. Boudica's own fesses were no strangers to it.'

'I should take anything from you, miss,' Sophia blurted. 'I have one-and-twenty, but twice that if *you* wished.'

'You are as sweet as your bottom, maid,' said Miss Duckett and, without warning, delivered another ferocious stroke right across the tender skin of Sophia's stockinged upper thighs. It stung fiercely, brushing her spread furrow, and dangerously close to the lips of her fount.

'Eight,' groaned Sophia. 'Thank you, miss.'

Miss Duckett laughed serenely. 'I already gave you number eight, maid,' she chided. 'That means we shall have to take the extra stroke.'

'Of course, miss,' said Sophia at once, conscious of her impropriety. She gasped as her fesses jerked again.

And then she heard a soft 'Oooh' escape from Miss Duckett's own throat, accompanied by breath harsher than from mere exertion. Miss Duckett asked her if she thought she could go to twenty-one, and Sophia murmured yes.

'Even if it means I can't sit down for a week, miss.'

Miss Duckett laughed and gave her another stroke, right at the top of her croup this time; it was excruciatingly painful, the blow unshielded by the firm buttock-mass. Sophia counted off correctly, and Miss Duckett asked her if she felt vengeful, and wished to punish her in her stead.

'It would be quite normal,' she added. 'A number six is a rare and firm punishment for such an offence, and you would have reason to resent me for insisting on it.'

'Oh, miss! I should never want to do anything to hurt you!' exclaimed Sophia through her tears.

Miss Duckett flogged her again.

'And what . . . what if it didn't hurt me?' she said softly. 'What if it gave me pleasure, as I am now giving you your strange submissive pleasure, maid? Don't deny it.'

Sophia sobbed that she would do anything to give Miss Duckett pleasure. She would strip her, and bind her, and flog her naked bottom until she pleaded for mercy. Miss Duckett came to Sophia's head and lifted it by the cropped curly hair, which hurt her more.

'And *would* you show me mercy?' she asked quietly.

Her eyes pierced Sophia's, and Sophia answered, 'N . . . no, miss, I should not. I should make you whimper.'

At this, Miss Duckett's nostrils flared and her eyelids narrowed, shutting for a moment as though she were lost in her own far-off world. Sophia's head was relinquished and as her eyes sank once more, Sophia saw a vivid moist patch on Miss Duckett's skirts, above her Lady's place.

'How many strokes have you left to take?' she asked.

'Eight, miss.'

'Then you shall take them hooded, maid. I shall deliver them from here, by your head, and you shall be hooded with my own skirts. It is proper that you should be covered for what is about to take place. What you know, Sophia, fate has decreed.'

With these portentous words, she suddenly lifted her skirts and shrouded Sophia's head. Inside the warm dark tent of skirts and petticoats, Sophia breathed deeply of the woman-scented air, and found her face and lips pressed firmly on to the swelling of Miss Duckett's fount.

She wore no knickers, and her naked fount was shaven bare. Sophia could not control her own flow of moisture, and felt her copious gush hot and tickly, wetting her stockinged thighs. What must she look like? She did not care. Eagerly, as though driven, her tongue found the swollen lips of Miss Duckett's gash, licked and licked the hot salty oils, then penetrated to her little damsel, the erect shivering nubbin standing ready for the maid's embrace. Sophia fastened her lips gently on the stiff bud and began to lick her tenderly, whereupon Miss Duckett made a moan.

'Oh! Don't stop, maid,' she whispered, 'it is so sweet.'

Sophia was powerless to stop: the flow of hot oil from Miss Duckett, as copious as her own, intoxicated her, as she drank the very essence of this most beautiful of all Ladies!

'I shall count now,' gasped Miss Duckett, recovering some of her composure, and laid an unsteady but still

burning stroke crossways across Sophia's upper buttocks.

'Fourteen,' she said unsteadily, then, 'Thank you,
miss.'

The strokes followed in rapid succession, Miss
Duckett artfully lacing Sophia's croup with alternate
cross-strokes, and sometimes reaching down so that the
cane-tips stroked the middle of her thighs, which hurt
awfully, and had the effect of redoubling the intensity of
Sophia's tonguing. Her own nubbin throbbed, and she
burned with desire to touch herself there. Or . . . to feel
Miss Duckett's own tongue between her oily hot thighs.

The beating was finally concluded, with a stentorian
cry of, 'Twenty-one!' and Sophia realised that her body
had been jerking and wriggling in time with her probing
tongue; as Miss Duckett threw aside her worn canes, she
grasped Sophia's head and pressed her fervently against
her belly, which started to quiver, then shudder alarmingly, as though some demon had taken hold of the
Preceptress. Sophia redoubled the force of her tonguing,
and now Miss Duckett's moans turned to veritable
squeals of pain, or ecstacy, and her love juices flowed so
copiously that Sophia had to fight to swallow every
drop of the delicious liquor, though swallow she did.

Her bare bum was a fire of glowing coals, yet she was
sad that her beating was over. All, however, was not.
She felt the skirts lifted from her face, and Miss
Duckett, still mewling, slide on to her back, beneath the
open flogging-frame. A few touches to the levers, and
Sophia's middle was lowered, so that her naked fount
was poised directly over Miss Duckett's lips, and Miss
Duckett's bared belly over her own glistening mouth.
Sophia wondered at the awesome flowing beauty of a
naked Lady's place, like the petals of some undreamt-of
rose, and vowed that she too would be shaven there –
Miss Sassi would be happy to oblige.

Thus cheered, she plunged her lips and tongue anew

between Miss Duckett's thighs, and her body leapt with joy as she felt Miss Duckett's lips on her own gash, her mouth eagerly drinking the copious liquor which gushed from her. And then Sophia too moaned as Miss Duckett's probing tongue-tip found her hard lttle damsel, sending electric thrills coursing through her flogged body. It seemed she had never known such a warmth and fullness of sensation before, had never dreamt of such a thing and, as she licked and drank, and felt a Lady worshipping her own fount thus, a strange fire grew in her belly, that was neither pain nor pleasure, but pure tingling joy, and then Sophia Derrière too cried out uncontrollably as her body was washed in the hot waves of her first spend. Sophia had come to joy.

Time seemed to stop. Dimly, Sophia heard a bell for luncheon in the distance, as though from another world. And then, shaking, Miss Duckett was on her feet, smoothing her dress and releasing her victim from her tight bonds. Sophia rubbed herself until the sensation came back to her limbs, and, her naked body still glowing from the caress of whip and tongue, began sadly to dress herself.

'Oh, miss,' she cried, 'I wish I could be naked with you forever. To kiss your bosoms, your fesses – all of you!'

Miss Duckett sobbed, and kissed her full on the lips.

'Sophia, my love . . . You must come at the same time next week. In the meantime, you will think of some impropriety to commit of your own, to justify your visit, or else suspicions would be aroused. You shall be punished again, Sophia, but this time by visiting the same punishment on *my* person. You shall flog my buttocks as naked and as red as your own, maid, for my own wickedness. And more . . . You will see the uses to which a stern baubo can be put, you will make me your slave, your Queen Boudicca. Oh! I knew it from the first moment I saw you, huddled so sweet and pure in that cold street. What Lady can resist her heart?'

Sophia said, puzzled, that she did not understand. What impropriety could Miss Duckett have committed? Miss Duckett turned away from the wall, and lowered her voice to whisper in Sophia's ear.

'Oh, Sophia, I have been guilty of the worst impropriety! *I have formed an attachment to you!*'

Above them, the glistening dark fruit that was the anus bud nestling in the furrow of the centaur's massive buttocks, seemed to wink in complicity.

6

Miss Letchford's Itch

Sophia pondered long on her astounding session of chastisement with Miss Duckett. Partly, she contemplated how she could profit from her new, attached, situation. As well, she had questions about Miss Duckett herself: who had given her the secluded room, with its eyrie view; her artful cabinet, and the painting of Baubo with her centaur, the virile beast whose buttocks had seemed alive, with the bum-hole bud winking at her like the very eye of the goddess – an obscene representation, no doubt, in the eyes of many. But then, Sophia understood that the eyes of Rodings were not the eyes of the many, and felt herself privileged.

She was newly filled with the knowledge of her awakened womanhood – of her joy, as Miss Duckett's tongue on her stiff damsel had brought her to a rush of ecstacy, her birthright as a Lady. Now she knew what diddling was – a thing so simple, yet so beautiful! All the years of ignorance seemed to dissipate like a stormcloud at the sun's rays. How could Sophia ever have thought that it was naughty to touch her damsel, even to think about down there? She understood, too, the beauty of the goddess Baubo and her ingenious representations, the size of this now not-so-mysterious male appendage. She knew that acquaintance with that fleshy delight would duly come to her – as governess of males, she would *make* it come to her.

In the meantime, Sophia embarked upon a journey of self-discovery, centred on her Lady's place. Before entrusting her person to the fingers of other maids, she wished to be sure of herself, of the correct stroking, pleasures and responses her body needed. Night after night, under her bedclothes, she thoughtfully diddled her nubbin, bringing herself to pleasing wetness – how could she ever have thought her delicious hot liquor soiling! – and did not care if she kept Bella Frinton awake with her little squeals of pleasure as she moved beneath her bedcovers.

One night, without a sound, Bella slipped between Sophia's sheets, and lifted her nightie right up to her neck, then lifted Sophia's nightie too, and pressed her bare body against her. Their soft naked breasts and founts met.

'Ooh ... You make me all itchy, you do!' Bella giggled.

'You're shaved,' whispered Sophia, feeling the smooth silk of Bella's fount rubbing against her.

'Yes. Sold it to Miss Sassi,' murmured Bella, and then her voice was stifled as she pressed her head to Sophia's breast and began to flick her bare nipples playfully, one after the other, until they stood hard and trembling. All the time the motions of her hips grew stronger, and Sophia felt tingles of excitement as Bella's bone brushed against her damsel. To her willing satisfaction, Bella's finger penetrated her Lady's lips, which were already moist, and her thumb found the damsel herself. Sophia shuddered, and groaned in pleasure.

'Well, come *on*,' said Bella. 'Don't make me do all the work. You know how to find a damsel, don't you? She's all stiff for you already!' Bella's palms clasped Sophia's naked derrière. 'Oh, you are beautiful!' moaned Bella. 'Such lovely globes. Oh, yes!'

Sophia's finger had found Bella's throbbing wet nubbin, and with her other hand she pressed Bella's own buttocks, letting her fingers stray up and down the furrow and caress the wrinkled little anus bud.

'*That*'s nice!' moaned Bella. 'Naughty, though. Miss Duckett must have taught you a thing or too, with her number six punishment. Don't pretend she didn't! Everyone gets to know everything round here. Are your fesses still red?'

'Yes,' said sophia proudly, 'and still smarting beautifully. Miss Duckett treated me with royal severity!'

They fell silent, each maid working thoughtfully at her friend's pleasure, until Bella whispered that Sophia was very good at diddling, and must have practised a lot. 'You've been doing it for years and years!' she said.

In the darkness, Sophia blushed. Shyly, she confessed that until now, she had been ignorant of the simplest and most rewarding Lady's joy.

'Well!' exclaimed Bella mischievously. 'The Duck is certainly a good Mistress. Oh! Don't stop, I love it . . . Oh, yes, sweet Sophia, I'm going to spend, oodles and oodles of joy. Can't you feel how wet you make me! Your smell, such lovely perfume, and those gorgeous fesses, so smooth and tender . . . I'd like you to sit on my face and squash me with them! Don't tell me you haven't learnt about queening from Chaste Marsh, the expert. Oh Sophia, your bum is born to be queen . . . Oh, yes! There! My spend . . . Oh!'

Bella's fingers became pistons as they slid in and out of Sophia's dripping wet slit and flicked her stiff damsel, which sent shudders of joy through Sophia's tingling spine, until she too melted in a gorgeous warm spend.

'What do you think of when you spend, Sophia?' said Bella somewhat coyly. 'I think of young men, you know, all hot and bare, with that lovely stiff baubo between their legs . . . you know, inside me! I wonder if the young men at Shoeburyness and places, in their dorms like this, think of *us* when they diddle each other, and spurt? I suppose they do. I've never had a real male baubo inside me, I mean one that spurts lovely cream, not like Chaste Marsh has. Have you?'

Sophia answered that she was virgin, and Bella said that a polished wooden baubo was super, but male flesh must be better. Sophia replied that she was virgin in every way.

'You mean – a wooden baubo – you don't . . .?'

'Never.'

There was a silence as Bella digested this information. Then Sophia pointedly suggested that their diddling, and the joy they took from caressing their nubbins, surely made them less than virgin.

'Oh, no,' cried Bella. 'Why, I've diddled scores of maids! Well, more than a few, anyway,' she added rather sedately. 'Diddling is *fun*. See, even as our fingers go so smoothly in and out of each other's slits, we never pass . . . there . . . the sacred barrier of our purity. And as for going all the way inside, with a baubo in the nether hole, why there is nothing at *all* wrong in that. I suppose in an attachment, a pash, it might be different, and a maid led into error, and that's why special attachments are forbidden.'

Sophia debated for a moment whether to reveal Miss Duckett's confessed attachment to her own person, and decided against it. Even as she wriggled in pleasure as Bella's fingers probed her lush wet Lady's folds, her mind was aware of the need to press her advantage with Miss Duckett. Though inexperienced, she reasoned shrewdly that Miss Duckett would expect no less, that she would *want* to be used and to suffer for her desire, like a true lover. Subtly, she planned to punish Sophia by forcing on her the responsibility of chastisement, so that by submitting to Sophia's lash, Miss Duckett would make Sophia *wish* to dominate her, hence want her . . .

On a practical level, it seemed wise to begin demanding favours from Miss Duckett, to indulge her lover's desire to sigh and be used; a first step would be to secure

104

permission to use the library at any time. Sophia was drawn to the shelves of musty books, which she was sure contained treasures little-known, perhaps unknown, for centuries. In the meantime, she must keep Miss Duckett's pash a secret, just as she must not blurt out to Miss Duckett the forthcoming session of the Rodings Riders, which a strangely subdued Ransome had whispered to her at teatime. Already, being a Lady was becoming quite complicated.

'It is odd,' said Sophia, 'that here we are, embracing, and you are dreaming of the young men at their lonely Naval College, and yet they are out there diddling each other and thinking of *our* naked bodies, I suppose. Wouldn't it be nice if we were all together, males and maids, so that we could diddle each other and not have to dream?'

'But that would be rather improper,' exclaimed Bella.

'When *I* spend,' Sophia continued, 'I don't really think of baubos. I think of young men, yes, but their bottoms, Bella. Their lovely naked bottoms, all red and quivering and glowing hot under my cane! And when I am Governess . . .'

'Aren't you getting ahead of yourself?' Bella said sympathetically. 'Only a few Ladies become Governesses.'

'When I am Governesss,' Sophia continued firmly, 'those young males shall be governed as never before! Now –' she patted her friend lovingly on her bottom '– off to bed with you, maid, for I've been told to start classes tomorrow. Yes, I shall be with you to learn all the things a Lady must know. It is Miss Letchford's class after breakfast and assembly, and I don't want to be a sleepy-head.'

Sophia drifted into a warm sleep of contentment, her drowsing fantasy a giant croup, two golden pear-shaped fesses ringing as they were lashed with a golden whip, and crying, 'Sophia,' at each stroke.

'No,' her voice murmured to her in her half-sleep, 'you are not one of the few. You are Sophia – the *one*.'

The next morning, Miss Duckett led her to Miss Letchford's classroom, although by now Sophia was sure of the way. She had cleaned it on several occasions, including the previous day, each time alone. However it was part of the Rodings ceremony that she was to be delivered by her rescuer. As they walked through the corridors, lined with chattering maids by their classrooms, Miss Duckett said nothing of Sophia's next visit to her study, and Sophia felt herself excited at the studied normality, or even indifference, of her manner. Fleetingly, she wondered if Miss Duckett had other visitors, if she were indiscriminate in her attachments. After all, Sophia reasoned, if Miss Duckett could have a pash for her, she could conceive one for others. But the thought of Miss Duckett touching another maid suddenly became horrid to her, and she warned herself against this sign of attachment. It was one thing for a Pre to be attached to her, and quite another for her to let go a Lady's reserve. To put the matter to the test, she decided that disdainful attack, not wheedling, was the best policy.

'I'll want the key to the library, miss,' she announced without looking at her companion. 'I have a thirst for books and knowledge, more than can be gained from the prattle of girls. I dare say you can have your key copied.'

'But only Preceptresses, Mistresses and Ladies may have such a key!' exclaimed Miss Duckett. 'It is impossible.'

'Is not every maid a Lady?' replied Sophia scornfully. 'You might find that this Lady's arm is indisposed at our next meeting, Miss Duckett. Or that she commits no impropriety to warrant a visit to your little art gallery.'

'Sophia!' cried Miss Duckett. 'Look at me!'

Slowly, with a curled lip, Sophia did so impassively.

'You must obey me!' said Miss Duckett. 'I am Preceptress . . . I am your rescuer.'

'I must bare my bottom to you, miss, if I merit chastisement,' said Sophia, 'and I do so with the sweetest forbearance. But the atrocious punishment you have promised me – the anguish of having to beat the bare of my own rescuer – that is quite another matter and, I suspect, quite beyond the bounds of normal rules and relations.'

Miss Duckett blushed and gulped, and shook her head, and hesitated most delightfully, but when Sophia sniffed that it was all the same to her, the Preceptress gave in. She enjoined Sophia to secrecy – Sophia insisted haughtily that a Lady never *swore* – and promised her a key of her own, and that she should say she was in the library on Preceptress's orders. Sophia nodded coldly, then broke into a wide smile that quite melted Miss Duckett's reserve, so that when they came to Miss Letchford's classroom, the Preceptress was ablush with renewed fire.

The line of maids in the corridor was quite silent, unlike the rowdy queues elsewhere, and when Miss Letchford approached, Sophia sensed why. She had seen Miss Letchford at assembly, of course, but never near; and only close up was the size and powerful aura of the Mistress apparent. Her very smell exuded authority and disdain, and a lesser spirit might have quailed at the contemptuous scrutiny of those piercing pale eyes. Sophia met her gaze as Miss Duckett made her formal delivery, then trooped into the classroom with the other maids, to be seated right at the front.

Miss Letchford was noticeable firstly by her height. She towered over the maids, even well over Sophia, herself generously proportioned. Sophia reckoned she must stand at least six feet in her stockinged feet. Not that it was possible to imagine Miss Letchford – 'the

107

Letch', in the maids' furtive appellation – in stockinged feet: she was distinguished by gleaming black leather boots, with sharp pointed toes and equally pointed heels, a quite regal – and not at all English – six inches in height. Endowed with dominant physical presence, Miss Letchford seemed to delight in and emphasise it, rather than seek to shrink her appearance to more 'ladylike' proportions.

And in truth, she was superb, as Sophia noted, chiding herself for her swift pang of envy. She had a perfect hour-glass figure, in harmony with her height, so that her bosom was an overpowering thrust of proud, firm flesh, under the tightest white satin blouse which showed her torso's only undergarment to be a flimsy camisole: that magnificent flat belly had no need of corsetry. And above her broad hips, the waist narrowed to an almost impossible taper, almost as though it might be cupped by two hands. Surely there must be a corset beneath the camisole, a waspie or tight girdle!

Yet it was impossible to discern any outline, and the camisole was so flimsy that the faint outlines of her wide strawberry nipples could be seen perched atop firm, almost conical teats. Her legs were long and rippling with powerful muscles, her skirt daringly slit to just above her knee, but revealing no flesh, rather the shiny leather of her boots which evidently proceeded well up her thighs. The derrière was neatly sheathed by the smooth satin skirt, provocatively unpleated so as to hug thighs and fesses, and these globes were – Sophia hoped desperately! – not quite as gloriously proportioned as her own, though larger, and, she thought with a little shiver, begging for a bare spanking.

Not that it was easy to imagine Miss Letchford as a maid, bared for punishment, or as anything other than a vengeful goddess. She carried on a white leather belt, with curious golden studs, a flail of three bound canes, like the ones which had flogged Sophia, but of wood so pale as to be almost white. Beside this was a normal baubo, and also an oblong instrument of dark wood, like a flattened baubo, but with two large holes in it. Her skin was the purest alabaster, and the most fearsome yet enticing feature of the Lady was her thick, rich hair, piled atop her imperious head in a bun or beehive shape. Her hair was completely white.

It was not the grey-flecked whiteness of old age, but the radiance of ice, or diamonds, or snow. It shone with a starry lustre that radiated a goddess's power and purity. If Miss Letchford's manner was aloof, then her magnificent snowy mane gave her every justification. Previously, Sophia had glimpsed her at assembly wearing a little cap, and the blurred vision of her hair gave her to imagine old age – which was why Chaste's tales of dalliance with the males of Leaden Rodings seemed so odd. But Miss Letchford was young, and superb in her youth, scarcely older than Miss Duckett.

Yet, thought Sophia, what a contrast the two Ladies presented, like two poles: the one raven-haired, warm and sweet, the other ice-pure and regal, but no less beguiling. Despite her most English of names, there was indeed something foreign about Miss Letchford. Not just her hair, but a directness of manner, even passion: a singular disdain for those who took refuge in coyness.

'Today we shall learn about water, I think,' said Miss Letchford, as though to no one in particular. 'First, though, the new maid Sophia Derrière will approach my desk, and bend over to touch her toes, with her skirts up and her bare exposed. A spanking shall teach her submission.'

Sophia shivered in astonishment, as a ripple of excitement spread through the class. They had been waiting for this spectacle of shame. Shaking with rage, Sophia rose, her face reddened, but did not leave her desk.

'Miss,' she gasped. 'I have done nothing to deserve punishment.'

'You dare question me?' asked Miss Letchford, in a voice of amusement that was almost approving. 'My classes always begin with a spanking, to concentrate their minds.'

'I have not been improper,' insisted Sophia.

'All maids are improper,' drawled the Mistress. 'What were you thinking of?'

'I was not thinking of anything,' retorted Sophia.

'Well, that is an offence in itself. A Lady is supposed to think at all times.'

The class tittered, and Miss Letchford said easily that they were to keep quiet, or she would cane them all, and then they would learn nothing about water.

'Come up here, Derrière, and take your spanking,' she said, touching her dark wooden implement. 'It shall be the paddle, which hurts only a bit – just fifty to tickle you and teach you humility. All new maids take spanking as soon as they join my class. Or are you a cowardy-custard?'

'My derrière is already red, miss,' said Sophia in a sudden rush of quiet defiance. 'And you may see.'

With that, she turned and lifted her skirts, then lowered knickers to show Miss Letchford and the class her fesses still crimson from Miss Duckett's rod.

'I took number six from Preceptress Duckett, a few days ago now,' she said, 'so I am not scared. But I *was* thinking, Miss Letchford, and honesty impels me to tell you, although honesty also impels me to refuse your unjust spanking. The rules permit me to do so.'

'I shall decide what is just,' hissed Miss Letchford. 'I am not one of those do-gooder Ladies who thinks that a spanking teaches a maid virtue. I do not teach virtue, my pretty maid, I teach facts. I don't give a fig for virtue! I like to see a maid's naked bum squirm, and shiver and go deepest crimson under my cane or my hand or my baubo. To see her choking back the sobs and squeals as she takes punishment. An unjust whip-

110

ping is the very sweetest! You maids here are positively the worst class it has ever been my misfortune to encounter, and I promise that all of your bums will glow again and again from my lash before the year is out, you included, Miss Derrière. Your squirming bums, and *my* pleasure – that is virtue, Ladies. You know *my* rules – every lesson begins with a spanking, for humility, and if there is a new maid, why, it must be her bum that dances. So, tell, Sophia – *what* were you thinking? According to the sacred rules, I may ask you *that*.'

'I was admiring your wonderful hair, miss,' said Sophia – obviously in truth, for who could fail to do so?

Miss Letchford touched her piled mane, and her nostrils flared proudly. Her lips curled in a sneer, and she said that flattery would not spare Sophia her spanking. The two Ladies stared at each other in an electric silence.

'Not that hair, miss,' said Sophia quietly. 'I was wondering what your mink-hair looks like. You see, as I have been scrubber in your classroom, I found lots of little white hairs amid the chalk-dust, that could only have been from a mink – from scratching, perhaps.'

At this, the class erupted in laughter and Miss Letchford's alabaster face paled even more, in chilling rage. She took her flail of canes from her belt and rapped her desk, restoring order. She looked at Sophia long and hard, then a thin smile creased her shell-pink lips.

'You may sit, maid,' she said, to Sophia's astonishment. 'Your honesty has earned you a pardon.'

She stared at Sophia, a pink tongue-tip passing slowly across her parted white teeth. Sophia knew that it had not.

Miss Letchford rose, and walked to Sophia's desk, where she lifted her cane and tickled Sophia under her chin. 'You see before you, Ladies,' she said with heavy irony, 'a maid who knows the rules – who knows her own mind – who will not be spanked by her monstrous,

111

wilful Mistress. Well! What are we to do? Miss Derrière here obviously thinks herself better than the rest of you, and better than me, too. But a beating there must be — by my rule. Only with the crack of whip on flesh can your several minds be invigorated for their lessons. Tell me, Miss Derrière, do you think me monstrous? The truth, now.'

Sophia hesitated. 'Yes, miss,' she said, 'I must confess that I do. A whipping without just cause is . . . unruly.'

'A proper lawyer, a clever fish!' cried Miss Letchford. 'Well, Miss Rulebook, you will admit that being monstrous is a gross impropriety, will you not? Don't look so perplexed, maid. By the rules, it is obviously *I* who should be chastised. Don't you agree?' She bent and put her face close to Sophia's.

'I . . . meant no such thing, miss,' Sophia blurted.

'But you said it, and therefore *you* shall chastise *me*.'

In an electric silence, Miss Letchford unfastened her cane-rods and flung them contemptuously on Sophia's desk. Then she returned to the front of the class and took her waist-high stool from behind her own desk, placing it by the blackboard for all to witness. She lifted her skirts, bending over to reveal the tight white silk of her panties, which were cut quite high above her waist; to Sophia's surprise, her black boots were shown to come almost to her Lady's place, and she wore them without hose. Their leather fabric was so thin and lustrous that it served as stockings. There was a sliver of pure alabaster thigh visible between panties and boot-tops, which widened as Miss Letchford pulled her panties up very tight against her fesses, which swelled ripe and beckoning for Sophia's cane.

'I shall keep my knickers on, as it is a Mistress's privilege, even a monstrous one's,' said Miss Letchford sarcastically. 'Come on, maid! You must not keep us from our lesson, so I shall begin my teaching as you cane my bum. Mind you pay attention to my words.'

Sophia sensed that the class of maids expected her to obey and, trembling, she approached the tall woman bent over the stool and clutching its legs in the position of humiliation. The canes were much heavier than those her own fesses had tasted, and she reassured herself that it would be a matter of three or four strokes only, before she could return to her desk and be swallowed up in her embarrassment.

'I have never done such a thing before, miss,' she said.

'Then you shall learn something. Don't be shy, my haughty maid. You deem me monstrous, so I must be punished.'

'You mock me, miss! I never said –' began Sophia.

'Don't tell me what you said or didn't! Now, I shall require a stroke at intervals of, let us say, two minutes, and you shall keep stroking me until I order you to stop. But you will find that won't be soon. A Mistress teaches best by example.'

Sophia had no choice but to go through with this tormenting mockery. How she wished, as she fought back her sobs of shame, that she had taken Miss Letchford's spanking, and had not given way to improper foolhardiness. The Mistress had no right to put her to such grief, and the cunning Lady knew only too well the strange anguish that twisted the maid's heart at having to inflict, rather than receive, punishment! Suddenly, bitterly, she lifted the canes and whipped them squarely across Miss Letchford's spread silken fesses. Miss Letchford neither moved nor cried out, apart from a very slight shivering of her buttocks, which only Sophia could have noticed from close up.

'Water,' Miss Letchford began, without making the slightest acknowledgment of her punishment, 'is the mother of all life, and we must respect her, if not exactly worship her as the ancients did. The human body consists mostly of water, and the intricate system of rivers, sea and rain is a constant cycle which nourishes all life. We speak of the earth, but rightly, we should call our world the ocean, since most of her is water.'

Sophia lifted her canes and delivered a second stroke, which made Miss Letchford's buttocks clench slightly. Despite herself, Sophia was pleased to see a reddening under the translucent thin knicker-silk.

'The gods of the ancients were wisely chosen,' continued Miss Letchford, 'for they represented the cycle of life: the moon, causing the ocean tides; the sun, which evaporates the seawater to make clouds, whose rain falls on the land to make rivers flowing back to the sea. The whole procedure of water performing the kind duty of nourishing life. Our Essex ancestors even worshipped the rain goddess.'

Sophia laid a third stroke, as hard as she could, across Miss Letchford's croup, which gratified her now by trembling noticeably. Then, in an unconscious nervous mannerism, Miss Letchford reached below her to scratch her fount, rubbing heartily at her panties on her beautifully swelling mound.

'Essex is well supplied with rivers, and I expect you maids to know their names all: such as Crouch, mighty Thames of course, Lea, Blackwater, and our own dear Roding.'

Sophia's sorrow shame had dissipated, to be replaced by a fierce bright anger. This woman had sought to humiliate her and now she, in her submissive position, should be the one to suffer! Miss Letchford would play games with Sophia Derrière – she would discover that it was no game. Sophia took the heavy canes with both hands, and lifted her arms high to deliver her hard fourth stroke on the quivering bottom of the submitting Lady, who, if not yet supplicant, could be made so. Sophia would make her squeal for mercy. There was rippled admiration from the class; Miss Letchford's hand darted again to scratch her Lady's place. Her buttocks were twitching noticeably, and a crimson flush showed clearly through the knickers.

'Hmm!' she exclaimed brightly, and acknowledging her chastisement for the first time. 'That was rather a tight one, Sophia, you almost have my bum squirming. Do I surmise that you used both hands? It is quite lawful, you know, although I wouldn't *tell* you so.'

She sneered, and Sophia took a deep breath. 'How long do you intend this shameful chastisement to continue, miss?' she blurted. 'Until you have named all the rivers of England?'

'If I decide so,' said Miss Letchford complacently. 'Why, are you tired? Scared of taking punishment, but even more frightened of imposing it?'

'My brief history at Rodings has proved to all that my derrière is no stranger, and no enemy, to chastisement, Miss Letchford,' answered Sophia sternly. 'But in forcing me to make you my maid, you have mocked me. I have delivered four strokes, and that is mockery enough. Your chastisement may continue, but on my terms. I shall decide when it is to end. If you do not agree, then I shall resume my seat and listen with every attention to your fluvial wisdom. Well, Miss Letchford, are you monstrous enough to deliver your nates to the mercy of both my cane and my judgement?'

There was an awed hush. Miss Letchford scratched her fount quite furiously, and sighed with a strange distress that Sophia had scarcely expected. Her buttocks began to tremble and twitch quite openly now, as though the smarting from the cane was only just beginning to affect her.

'You are a curious maid indeed. Yes, I accept your condition. You will see what it takes to be a real Mistress, a real Governess as you no doubt aspire to be. I have flogged males, Sophia! I have been Governess at the Academy, and can assure you I know from males how to take a punishment well, laughing off the cane's kiss to my bare as though it were no more than a gnat's sting. Proceed, Miss Derrière, and see how I take my caning like a man.'

115

'Very well, miss,' said Sophia grimly. 'I can promise I shall make you squeal.'

Sophia recommenced her two-handed caning of the Mistress's spread buttocks. Each stroke now provoked a flurry of wriggles and squirming, almost as though Miss Letchford were taunting her punisher with this parody of torment. All the while her teacher's voice rang clearly with details of the moon and her tides, of hurricanes and typhoons and floods. Sophia felt a strange annoyance that despite her exertions, she was actually gaining profit from the class! As if to compensate, she made her exertions all the harder, and was rewarded with a delicious wriggling of Miss Letchford's reddened fesses, and the hint of a sob as she enunciated Lakes Titicaca, Baikal, and Okeechobee.

The caning of Miss Letchford by the maid Sophia Derrière continued apace, at the rate of one stroke every ninety seconds, not the prescribed two minutes, and at each stroke Sophia was ready to decree the punishment at an end, on the slightest hint of a squeal from Miss Letchford's anguished throat. But no squeal came; instead, she continued her lesson in a voice that, after an initial unsteadiness, had recovered all her regal authority and indifference to the fierce lacing of her buttocks. However, she kept up a constant nervous scratching of her Lady's place. Sophia recalled her own punishments: that a plateau was reached, after which the body accepted and adapted to pain. Miss Letchford obviously knew her plateau.

Miss Letchford's buttocks were vivid crimson beneath their flimsy knicker-silk by the time the lesson was at its end. Sophia was bathed in sweat and quite flushed, while her victim's face was as pure and serene as ice. Her knickers, Sophia saw, were quite shredded and no doubt improper, or else fit only for Submission Day; Miss Letchford smoothed them over her flogged buttocks as though nothing had happened, and did not even wince

116

at her fingers' touch of her reddened flesh. She must have taken at least thirty cane-strokes without seriously flinching. As the class filed out, she ordered Sophia to remain.

'I believe you were the last skiv to clean my room, Miss Derrière?' she gasped, through tight lips, as though suppressing some inner passion. Sophia nervously agreed. 'Well, you have left quite a mess! Clean it up now.'

'But that's impossible.' Sophia was silent as Miss Letchford pointed to a gleaming pile of white hairs, right beneath her punishment stool! Sophia knelt and tidied a good handful of hairs, and, cupping her palm, she offered them to Miss Letchford.

'No, miss. You dispose of them – or keep them as evidence of your untidy *impropriety*, should I choose to remind your buttocks of their owner's error. And another impropriety, apart from damaging House property by ripping my knickers . . . you have – Oh! – broken your promise, you have – oh! oh! – not . . . made . . . me . . . squeal!'

As she gasped these words, Miss Letchford was rocking in agitation on her sharp boot-heels.

'Thank you, miss,' said Sophia humbly, and hurried from the room, clutching her suddenly precious bundle. She looked back, and saw Miss Letchford's hand once more between her thighs, scratching herself nervously, as she lustfully eyed Sophia's person. Her other hand rubbed her fesses, as though in a caress of congratulation.

It was then that a piercing squeal of pain erupted deep in her throat, and her cheeks glistened with tears. But her eyes smiled.

'Oh! Oh! Oh!' she cried, quite uncontrollably, as her fingers feverishly rubbed the swelling of her fount. 'That *hurt* so, Miss Derrière!'

Sophia was sure Miss Letchford's unmistakable

117

movements were more than mere scratching. Inflamed by her lashes, the Mistress was openly diddling! She did not know whether she had made an enemy or a friend. Perhaps both . . .

7

Whipped at the Mainmast

At lunchtime, where Sophia was still a kitchen drudge, Miss Duckett interrupted her duties and, with a rather sulky expression handed her an envelope, behind a large steaming stewpot where the transaction went unobserved. It contained the key to the library. Sophia thanked her with a nod that was perfunctory and even regal, and was pleased with heself for her haughtiness. Miss Duckett turned on her heel and left without a word.

The evidence of Sophia's number six punishment gradually faded from her blushed buttocks, although she rather wistfully inspected her bottom every day in the glass, hoping it would not. At morning ablutions, she became aware of a curious pecking order among the maids who had recently undergone chastisement.

Those with the most vivid imprint of their canings assumed airs of superiority over their sisters, for as long as the imprint lasted. Sophia had basked in a glow of admiration following her session with Miss Duckett, as after her taking Miss Brace's baubo at her very first assembly, but the admiration faded along with the crimson of her nates. Unfortunately – in a sense – she was a conscientious worker, performed her skiv tasks thoroughly, and was careful to obey the rules, so that the two light spankings she took from Miss Tunney and Miss Sassi, for the offence of having her cardigan

119

improperly buttoned, were admittedly her own making, as though she courted the punishment.

The approaching prospect of administering chastisement to Miss Duckett's own bare was, she now saw, a cruel and even exploiting punishment: for all she knew, the Pres – and even Mistresses – had their own parades of chastised beauty, whose purposes she would serve. She was not sure how to deal with her rescuer; should she insist or plead to take caning as good as she got, for her own self-esteem?

The thought of Miss Letchford herself baring her nates for the inspection of her comrades – the crimson Sophia's cane had raised, contrasted with the delicious snowy white of her mink – made Sophia shiver. She kept Miss Letchford's mink-hairs in a little muslin bag in her drawer, uncertain as to why. Was it a sort of talisman, a possession of magical power over the stern Mistress? Or had Miss Letchford made her take her mink-hairs expressly for the purpose of holding Sophia in *her* possession?

Miss Sassi had delivered a baubo-spanking of only forty-one strokes – Miss Sassi said she liked to chastise with prime numbers – which scarcely hurt at all, and had done so with her usual wry chatter about lurid tales of derring-do in the far west. Miss Sassi seemed to have a thing with being tied to railway lines, which the Americans seemed particularly fond of. Miss Sassi said that the Americans had such long railway tracks, and such big powerful trains.

'Just imagine – Miss Katie Delilah, heroine of Mr James Z. Barsac's *Warlord of the Rio Bravo*, tied to the tracks with her long blonde hair draped over the desert sand, and her legs outstretched, an ankle fastened most immodestly to each rail, so that the circling vultures can see her knicker-silk as the El Paso Express thunders down on her. What an awful fate; imagine being cloven in two, between the legs, by that giant shining steaming locomotive! There are not yet many railway lines in

Finland,' she added wistfully, as though this ruled out any journey to her ancestral homeland. Sophia noted that her spanking arm shook a little after this evocation, but that her spanks became considerably fiercer.

When not dwelling on matters ferrovial, Miss Sassi liked to speak of hair, and in particular mink-hair. 'Your hair is so lovely, Sophia,' she said dreamily. 'It grows fast, and soon it will be time for another perm. Have you noticed I have been giving perms to many of the maids recently, and that they are well pleased?'

Sophia said she had.

'When are you going to ask me to shave you, I wonder? Down there, I mean? She is so moist and lush and shiny and I wager her scent is divine . . . Oh!' Miss Sassi was silent, as though she had exceeded the bounds of propriety.

'In truth, I don't know,' lied Sophia, 'I should have to give the matter some thought. I believe it itches awfully as the hairs grow again.'

Sophia secretly longed to have her fount shaven! But she was wise enough to bring Miss Sassi under her control by making her do the pleading. Miss Sassi observed coquettishly that there was a simple remedy – the maid should be shaved every single day.

'Although that would take far too much time, so I would have to restrict the privilege to a very few *suitable* maids. Mmm! your bottom is reddening nicely,' she said, as though to change the subject.

'Ouch!' cried Sophia without meaning to, 'it is quite tight, for a baubo spanking, miss,' as a particularly hard angular slap caught her right in the furrow at her lower fesses, near her anal bud.

After a little pause, Miss Sassi said that perhaps she should oblige maids to be shaved there, in return for being given a nice perm, if that were not too beastly.

'Some maids might find it nice, miss,' gasped Sophia, as the baubo landed again on her quivering bare bum.

121

'Would *you*?' said Miss Sassi drily.

'If it gave you pleasure, miss,' said Sophia.

'It would not be for my pleasure, but for your own good,' Miss Sassi replied.

'In that case, it would be improper for any maid to refuse moral improvement,' gasped Sophia, wriggling quite a lot now as the slaps from the baubo made her bare bottom quite warm and glowing. She added that she was curious, with Miss Sassi's permission, to see her collection of mink-hairs – she did not mention that with Miss Letchford's hairs she now had a collection of her own, as she sensed Miss Sassi would see it jealously as a kind of competition. Miss Sassi replied that it was not a good time, and she had not much hair in stock just at the moment.

The beating was nearing its end, though, and no further words were spoken on the subject. When she had taken the forty-first and final stroke, Sophia obediently knelt to kiss the baubo that had chastised her, and received Miss Sassi's ritual admonishment not to repeat her offence. Forty-one! Sophia's buttocks were left quite raw even from the simple spanking, and Miss Sassi's love of prime numbers reminded her that the sacred rules about number of strokes seemed honoured more in a Mistress's 'personal custom' than in strict observance.

In parting, Miss Sassi solemly expressed her desire that she should be spared the need to whip Sophia's bare buttocks with the cane itself. Both women's eyes met, and both knew that the words were insincere. As she left, Sophia found herself wondering what Miss Sassi meant about her stock of hair: surely, she either had a collection or she had not?

Sophia's fesses tingled pleasantly for only a short time after that and her other willed spanking, and as the day of her next meeting with Miss Duckett approached, she felt an unreasoning anger towards her rescuer, for having introduced her to the wicked thrill of a well-enflamed derrière. Miss Duckett would now refuse her the same hard bum-tickling, but make her deliver it to her own body. Though aware her resentment was improper, she resolved to make Miss Duckett suffer more than she had bargained for, then reflected ruefully that she would thus be giving her raven-haired Mistress just what she wanted.

In the library, Sophia found herself in paradise. After one or two challenges from Miss Flye and Miss Wyvern, the Mistresses for languages and sewing, it became known that Sophia was entitled to be there, as custom: custom, like advantage, seemed an important word at Rodings. She timed her visits for when she could be assured of solitude, and soon came to regard the musty leather-bound books she unearthed from the stacks as her own treasures. Many of them were too bulky to remove; the first she dipped into was only a small part of the rich lore of the County of Essex. Much of it described artful chastisements for various rural misdemeanours, and the country pastimes which at times seemed indistinguishable from those same misdemeanours. Sophia began to think that the Rodings Riders would not be something new, but the noble continuation of Essex's curious and exotic traditions.

One book, a huge volume in ribbed leather, apparently three centuries old, was primly entitled *Ye Boke of Essex Chastysementes*, and consisted of handwritten entries detailing the punishments of the miscreants and felons of the county, not least upon the naval cadets, or seafarers who had the misfortune to offend on their visits to the shore. Many of the older entries were in Latin, but most were in crabbed English whose spelling varied with each hand and each decade. Sophia thrilled wickedly at the corrections inflicted on the bodies of wrong-doers through the ages, and concluded that Essex must be either the most virtuous or the most wicked county in England. It was a kind of Domesday Book except that, instead of listing lands and properties, it listed offences and punishments.

Many of the punishments were quite mundane and even charming in their rustic simplicity, others, especially offences of sorcery, witchcraft, or against established religion – which seemed to mean anything at all – were awful. She had some idea what the pillory, stocks, and ducking-stool had meant in the countryside of long ago, where sheep-stealing, drunkenness, fornication, scolding, and unseemly behaviour with farm animals were recorded, but was astounded at the punishments which the young seafaring men, officers and crew alike, seemed content to undergo for the most trifling offences. The school at Shoeburyness appeared, to her warm curiosity, quite early in the narrative, having apparently been founded by King Henry I, or perhaps II. Was this, then, the fierce training, upon which the might of the Royal Navy, hence the Empire itself, had been founded? Apparently it was.

She could not tear her eyes from the descriptions of the punishments of the young sailors who served, or were about to serve, their King. The details were more than informative, and offered instruction, warning, and – Sophia admitted – a strange stimulation. Punishment with lash or cane was commonly described as 'taking crimson', and before the details of the actual chastisement, there were loving descriptions of the gradual, shaming stripping of the offender, the pulling down of undergarments – in some cases, not their removal, but the knickers being held tightly by the miscreant himself against his nates, as increased humiliation – and the knots or straps with which he was bound by waist, ankles or wrists; even gagged with a metal ball for the harsher floggings at the mainmast, with a cat-o'-nine-tails.

There was beating the tattoo, in which a victim was

124

suspended naked on a flogging-lattice with tiptoes on deck, and arms and legs splayed. The cat o'nine tails was applied with thirty or more strokes to buttocks, thighs and shoulders, in a criss-cross pattern which was artful and pleasing to the onlookers, despite the agony it caused to the naked victim. One such who bore his ordeal bravely was said to be well tattooed, and Sophia was surprised that many cadets actually chose this visible and cruel punishment against a straight buttock-caning, which, though just as painful, would be more discreet when unclad in 'fluvium.

One particularly common punishment among the young cadets was called the drumskin, and dated from the seventeenth century; the victim was obliged to hold the cheeks of his bare buttocks tightly apart and kneel, revealing his furrow and bum-hole. Since his hands obscured the main fleshy part of his fesses, the cane-strokes were delivered on the innermost furrow and down the backs of the thighs, perilously close to the bum-hole itself, and the dangling baubo with its precious life-sac.

Sophia imagined that no matter how hard or painful the caning, the miscreant dared not even shudder, for fear of one stroke slipping and causing unthinkable distress. Some of the accounts of this punishment hinted ominously that after its completion, the victim was obliged to remain in the drumskin position, with bum-hole open, for 'admonishment'. Sophia shivered to think what that admonishment might consist of, in an academy full of well-bauboed young men with cream to spurt. Yet her shivers were mingled with a growing wetness and excitement in her belly and Lady's place, which she could not, nor wished to, stop.

As Sophia read of the more orderly yet still stern punishment of kissing the gunner's daughter, where the miscreant was flogged naked and strapped to a ship's cannon, she imagined the scene. A bright winter's morning with the drums beating as the young man, shivering with cold and apprehension, was ceremonially led to the gun, kissed it, was stripped then tied to the metal, facing out to sea. The seagulls cawed and swooped over the grey northern waters as he stared towards Holland, perhaps, and felt the first lash of the cane searing his naked buttocks; he bit his lip at the fearful pain that lanced his young body, mindful that he must be brave and not cry out, to shame himself before his comrades, for to cry out would visit punishment on them all.

A naked young man flogged not just for oneself, but for others! It seemed to Sophia the noblest and most beautiful thing imaginable, and she swallowed, giddy with longing to be that young man, all those years ago.

An alternative was a flogging from the yardarm, the high crossbeam of the ship's mast. This meant that the mariner's naked body was suspended by very long ropes from the bar, his feet tethered to the deck but floating in mid-air about four feet above it. Thus suspended, he took his whipping on back and buttocks from a cat with specially lengthened thongs, whose strokes Sophia thought must have been fearful, delivered at such long range and with such impetus. She saw the young man, swaying naked in the wind, lost between sky and sea, like a gull, with only his pain for company, and thought that more beautiful still.

After a while, she noted curiously that the entries for offences were longer than those for the punishments awarded, and it became apparent that many of the entries listed offences as yet unpunished, or punishments decreed but for some reason unadministered. The *Boke of Chastysementes* was in large part a book of stored resentments for which it was hoped punishment would be imposed in the future. Was this to do with the *Long Book*? Sophia looked for the section dealing with the Roding Valley, and found none; or rather, she found a gap in the binding and pagination, where it seemed that a whole section of pages had been removed.

Disappointed, she nevertheless followed the entries for Shoeburyness and the Naval Academy, growing more and more agitated, and feeling the warm moisture in her Lady's place flowing quite uncontrollably. She was fascinated that the same names of chastised cadets kept appearing over the centuries, obviously in different inks, but often with reference to ancestors who had attended as cadets. It seemed astonishing that men would serve and endure the most awesome discipline, and then send their sons and grandsons knowing they would have to endure the same. She began to wonder if she would ever understand males, and had an inkling that only on presenting herself at Shoeburyness as governess of these strange creatures could she hope to understand what, if anything, went on in their minds.

The entries seemed to stop in the year 1763, after which the book announced 'End of The First Volume', in quite modern handwriting. The book had been continuously kept for three centuries! Which must mean that a second book existed, and was currently kept up to date ... furthermore, that it contained the *entire* story of Rodings in a separate volume.

The last story concerned a young midshipman who kissed the gunner's daughter, outside the College, and was then piped aboard ship, in a parody of a captain's welcome, to be flogged at the yardarm. His heinous offence was 'grave insubordination and conduct reductive of His Majesty's Discipline'. As Sophia read of his bravery, naked and helpless under the lonely lash, her flowing quim became quite insistent. Her nubbin tingled, her belly fluttered in her agitated warmth, and she felt her knicker-silk quite sopping with her oils. Almost but not quite unconsciously, her fingers crept beneath her skirts to the wet knickers, and began to rub the swollen lips of her Lady's place.

She found her throbbing damsel through the cloth, standing clearly, and her touch sent shivers of electric joy up her spine. She moaned aloud as she read the precise description of each stroke of the cat, the extent of the young man's shuddering, and the loving description of his naked limbs trembling like flower-stems. Her hand went inside her knickers, and pressed her naked fount; harder and harder, she rubbed her naked tingling damsel, feeling spasms of ecstacy as the oily liquid engulfed her fingers.

Then she felt three, no, four, of her fingers, penetrate her very slit, right to the sacred barrier of her maidenly purity. Trembling and sighing with her pleasure, she read the disapproving comment that punishment at yardarm was given with the miscreant facing only the sea, his face seen only by the Captain, and for good reason: this young man, throughout his punishment, had presented a baubo, or virile member, in a state of immodest and tumescent excitement, even as the lash stroked his naked body.

She had been unsure why the thought of a male's bare body whipped excited her so; at this revelation, she felt her belly heave, and mewled softly to herself, holding her cries of joy deep inside as her body flooded with the warm ecstacy of her spend. She saw in her mind's eye, not the young man from so long ago, with his proud baubo stiff before him, but the waving breasts and hair of her Mistress, Miss Duckett.

A cosy fire smouldered in the grate of Miss Duckett's study. There was no sound but the breath of the cold night wind outside the drapes. Sophia inspected her Mistress and rescuer with a petulant *moue* curling her lips.

'It seems wrong, somehow, miss,' she said in as surly a voice as she could muster. 'I have been obedient in my duties, and everywhere in Rodings we maids are taught humility and submission. We speak when we are spoken to, we do not go into forbidden rooms or corridors. My maid's place is to obey and submit, miss, not take improper advantage.'

'Then,' said Miss Duckett, stroking her cane, 'you shall obey and submit to me, by taking your ordained chastisement. That is, you shall lace me, Maid Sophia, very hard.'

There was a rustle as her black silk peignoir fell to the floor, and she unpinned her hair to let the raven tresses fall over her bare white breasts, gleaming cherry-tipped in the firelight.

'See, I am naked for my chastisement,' she whispered. 'You shall please attend to me, maid. That is my order as Preceptress. It is a proper chastisement. The number of strokes taken shall be entered in the punishment book.' She smiled coyly. 'It shall not say that it is I who take the strokes.'

'And if I refuse?'

'Why!' cried Miss Duckett, taken aback. 'Then . . . Then you must take the strokes on your own bare.'

'Suppose that is what I desire, miss?' said Sophia. 'To feel *my* bum dance as you redden her?'

'Damn you, I *know* that is what you want,' said Miss Duckett with a sad smile. 'Please, Sophia . . . I beg you. I shall kneel and beseech you, if you desire.'

Sophia reached forward with trembling fingers and touched the ripe firm fruits of Miss Raven's bare nipples, that shivered in their turn, and stood proudly before her maid like her own wilful servants. Then her hand smoothed Miss Duckett's belly, feeling gooseflesh, despite the warm room, and little downy hairs which shivered at her touch. Sophia swallowed hard. She allowed her fingers to rest on the very first strands of Miss Duckett's lustrous raven mink, feeling the hairs bristle. Her own fount moistened as she contemplated this woman's body placed in her power.

129

'There is no need to kneel, miss,' she said. 'I shall require more than that from you. I shall take my punishment – shall suffer! – in hurting you, miss, my precious rescuer. But you, too, must suffer. For your presumption, your impropriety ... Oh, it would be so much sweeter to love this body than to hurt her.'

'Perhaps, by hurting me, you will truly love me. No one shall hear or see us at our rites,' said Miss Duckett. 'You may do whatever you want with me. Please!'

'Hm!' said Sophia, suddenly businesslike. 'You will obey my orders, miss. Unquestioningly. I have certain ... ideas.'

Smiling, Miss Duckett nodded her grateful assent.

'Then your chastisement shall begin.'

First, Sophia ordered Miss Duckett to open her wardrobe – she was to dress again. Puzzled, Miss Duckett did so, and showed Sophia a pleasing array of robes and underthings. as Sophia inspected these, she ordered Miss Duckett to wind her hair up very tightly and bind it flat against her skull, like a boy's. 'We shall see about your phrenology, miss,' she said, half-joking. 'I intend to make a proper young man of you.'

After much rummaging, Sophia found a selecton of clothing which she approved. Soon, the short-haired Miss Duckett was attired in a white blouse, and a fetching light blue zoave jacket which came to a narrow hem just below her belly-button, and with balloon sleeves above the elbow, a fine female embellishment on its stern military origin. Sophia said it would do for a male's jacket; the trousers were to be a pair of thick ankle-length drawers in blue lawn cotton, tight-fitting and worn without further knickers. Miss Duckett put these on, saying they were only underthings, for beneath a ball gown, but Sophia decided they would have to do for trousers, being the right shade of naval blue.

'They match the jacket quite well, though not exactly, but then you are a male, and can't be expected to know such things. I don't think we'll have you shod, a barefoot chastisement is always prettier. Now – attention!'

Trembling, Miss Duckett faced Sophia and stood to attention, while Sophia inspected the cabinet of disciplinary tools. She found what she sought: a cat o'nine tails, quite fearsome in its quiet majesty; a whippy set of birch-rods, and a four-foot splayed willow-cane. These she showed to the Preceptress.

'Duckett!' she barked. 'You are a pathetic slave. You have no right to wear a cadet's jacket! Pull it over your head, if you please, I do not wish to see your face.'

Miss Duckett obeyed; next, Sophia ordered her to open her blouse down to the last button and, when this was done, she brutally pulled the blouse from Miss Duckett's shoulders, all the way to her waist, so that her arms were pinioned behind her back and her trunk bare. She led the trembling woman to the bed, and quickly moved the levers so that it cranked upright to stand as a punishment frame.

Miss Duckett was pressed against it, feet outstretched, and it was the work of a moment for Sophia to bind her tightly to the frame by waist and ankles. Muffled moans of protest, curiosity or delight, came from Miss Duckett's hooded face. Next, the pants were ripped firmly from the bare globes of her buttocks, and pulled down to just above the knees, rendering Miss Duckett truly immobile. Sophia was rewarded with a vista of bare flesh: the shoulders, back, buttocks and thighs naked and framed by the tousled clothing, like a sculpture devoid of human feature, its curves and hillocks pure geometric beauty.

She set to work on the croup with the willow cane, first of all, flogging her Preceptress's clenching arse-globes with casual strokes whose very ease was a warning to her victim that severity was unnecessary, since this flogging would be a long and arduous one.

'Do not waste your breath asking me how many you are to take, slave,' she said, 'for it shall be as many as

131

please *me*, not you. That is, after all, what you desire, my boy.'

Miss Duckett was silent, her only reaction a sinuous swaying of the body as her quivering buttocks delicately reddened under the caress of Sophia's cane. At the fifth or sixth stroke, Sophia began to lace harder, taking care now to cover the whole expanse of helpless bare skin, so that her crimson caress formed the prettiest of patterns on her Mistress's bare bum.

When the derrière was reddened to her satisfaction, she asked Miss Duckett curtly if she had had enough, and at once answered herself that of course she had not. 'Not by a long stroke, Master,' she whispered. 'How pretty a male's bum is when squirming! And there is so much of you to squirm – the fesses are just a beginning.'

With that, Sophia put aside her cane and, glancing up to the painting, at the twinkling arse-bud of the grinning centaur, she took the cat, and swished it reflectively through the air, without striking Miss Duckett's body.

'This should hurt,' she said, and laid a tentative stroke low down across the backs of her thighs. Now Miss Duckett had trouble in suppressing a squeal of surprise and anguish.

'That stung, did it?' Sophia said with a cruel chuckle. 'I have heard that boys don't like it there ... so that's where you'll get it, Master Duckett, my lad.'

The flogging proceeded in silence broken only by the sobs that clutched Miss Duckett's throat. Sophia found the cat so heavy that it seemed to direct the flogging itself: once the stroke was launched from the shoulder, it had a life of its own, and Sophia's role seemed merely to steer the thongs towards the shivering taut thigh-muscles, now reddened most awfully by the heavy braided leather. She felt her own body tremble, with the excitement that came from the idea of flogging a male; she could not see the face of her victim, and the hooding thrilled her, as did the pinioning of the hands twisted

132

behind her male's back. Miss Duckett's superbly female form assumed in her imagination the attributes of a beautiful young male, as though two different flowers could spring from the same bud.

She imagined the soft baubo of the male hardening, growing stiff and proud under her lacing, the fruit for her alone, and spurting the cream that was hers alone to taste, just from the caress of her whip. Her fount was moist, and the flow growing hotter and more copious with each whipstroke; she put aside the cat and, without warning, resumed the caning of the buttocks, to further sobs of choked dismay; then the cat, then the cane again, always making her captive dance in pain and despairing uncertainty.

Yet it was not enough, and when Miss Duckett's writhings had grown truly pitiable, Sophia told her she would now have to take the hardest part of the punishment. 'You are a midshipman, sir, and you shall take your flogging like a midshipman!'

Sophia had only the vaguest idea what a midshipman was, but her warning had a dramatic effect. Miss Duckett now emitted open squeals of protest as Sophia ripped the blouse away to free her arms, then balled the silk to make a gag which she pressed roughly into Miss Duckett's gasping mouth, silencing her moans. She took Miss Duckett's arms and stretched them high until they grasped the edges of the painting on the wall above, and ordered her to hold this position, since she was to be whipped at the mainmast.

She took up the cat, and now began to stroke Miss Duckett's shoulders, stepping a few paces back and rushing towards her for each stroke, and thrilling to the whistle of the thongs as they cracked against the Preceptress's naked back. She worked down from the shoulders until the whole of the upper back was crimson with lashes, and not once did Miss Duckett cry out; her sobs were stifled almost inaudibly in her throat. But her

133

body writhed, jumping as the heavy thongs of the cat rocked her. Sophia was pleased that not just the back, but fesses and legs too danced in a sinuous rhythm whose graceful beauty had her fount quite gushing with Lady's moisture. She knew whipping would not be enough. She had seen things in Miss Duckett's cabinet – unspeakable things, yet wickedly beautiful. Did she dare?

'You are taking your punishment like a man,' said Sophia in genuine admiration.

She thought she had given at least thirty to the back, but the birch lay untried. The flogging had now lasted an hour or so, Sophia reckoned, and she decided to award Miss Duckett the choicest morsel of pain: a birching on bare buttocks. She informed Miss Duckett of her decision, and heard a deep, low moan of despair. But the woman's despair was marked by resignation; she knew that she was receiving just what she demanded. Sophia saw that the inside of her reddened thighs were glistening with moisture, and thought briefly that Miss Duckett had made pond in her terror.

Sophia put her fingers firmly on the lips of the fount, letting the tips and nails penetrate the slit to a depth of an inch; she found them swollen and hot, and bathed in oily wetness that was no soiling. Miss Duckett was as excited as her chastiser! On impulse, Sophia put her fingers to Miss Duckett's breasts, and rudely tweaked and pulled at her nipples, which stood stiff and tensed like gnarled hard nuts. Sophia played with her breasts quite harshly, rubbing and squeezing the nipples, and rubbing Miss Duckett's own love-oil all over her naked teats until she groaned in pleasure rather than pain. Then Sophia replenished her hand-cup of Miss Duckett's fount liquor and smeared her own lips and tongue with the delicate hot fluid.

Gasping with desire, Sophia no longer resisted her impulse. She went to the cabinet and withdrew a wicked

134

cylinder, mounted on a firm belt of leather; it was a thick yellow baubo, curving slightly upwards, with grinning red lips painted on the helmet. This goddess's purpose was clear. Sophia lifted and pegged her skirts, then removed her panties, soaking with her liquor, and with trembling fingers strapped the totem around her waist. Quickly she tore the gag from Miss Duckett's mouth and, before she could gasp her words of exclamation, replaced it with the drenched wad of her own panties. Then she took the birch and lifted it high above Miss Duckett's inflamed bare nates.

'This is no fluffy little toy birch, boy,' she murmured. 'This is a heavy instrument of a good dozen lithe saplings, as you know very well. And your punishment for keeping such an implement shall be to taste her kiss to full endurance.'

The birch crackled drily as it hissed through the air and lashed the woman's glowing bum-skin. Now Miss Duckett could not restrain her moans as her bum danced madly in pain.

'Can't take it, boy?' sneered Sophia. 'You have only to say the word for your chastisement to cease, and you can don your girly's clothes again like a snivelling wretch.'

In her mind's eye, Sophia pictured herself as Governess at Shoeburyness, delivering the same words, and the same chastisement, to the hard, supple young buttocks of a true male, his baubo stiffening before him in his terror at his avenging Mistress's flogging tool . . .

The birch lashed the cringing slave a dozen times, before Sophia could stand her excitement no longer. She took the inflamed bum-cheeks and spread them to reveal the tender wrinkled bud of the anus. She put her finger in, which made Miss Duckett writhe quite uncontrollably, and gauged the dimensions, before approaching the body of her Preceptress and tickling the bud with the smiling tip of her baubo.

'This is what naughty boys get,' whispered Sophia, as

she pushed the instrument thrillingly inside the cavity of the woman's anus.

Miss Duckett squealed and her buttocks squirmed as though to reject the invader, but Sophia realised that she was clenching her fesses so as to make the baubo's ingress easier. She pushed hard, thinking it should never go all the way in, and then suddenly Miss Duckett moaned in deep, ecstatic relief as her nether channel seemed to sigh and yield utterly, and the baubo slid smooth as silk right to the very depth of her fundament. Sophia gasped; the baubo was equipped with a little tickling acorn that, as soon as the main shaft had sunk to the full, began to tickle her own throbbing stiff damsel.

Miss Duckett's bottom began to buck, as though begging Sophia to thrust the baubo into her anus in a fierce rhythm, to which Sophia quickly adapted as though it were the most natural thing; especially as each stroke of her hips caused the acorn to tickle her damsel to her shivering delight. She thrilled at the humiliation she delivered to her Preceptress, as though the thrusting into her most secret and tender part were the ultimate in penetration of her spirit. She thought of a male's fleshy baubo doing the same thing; doing it to his comrades, perhaps – as males apparently did – but more excitingly, doing it to her, Sophia Derrière. Clutching and spreading the buttocks drumskin-tight, she stroked deeply and her fount gushed with love-liquor so copious that she felt the hot stream trickle down her stockings and soaking them, almost as though she had made pond herself.

Miss Duckett's moans were now hoarse and rhythmic as she panted through her oily gag; Sophia reached forward and touched the swollen fount-lips, rapidly finding the nubbin, which was as stiff as her own, and whose touch made Miss Ducket squeal aloud. She began to flick the nubbin quite mercilessly as she stroked inside the quivering tight anus, wishing she had a real flesh baubo so that she could feel the rubbery warm pressure of Miss Duckett's silky hole. She felt the flesh of Miss Duckett's bum warm and tender as her own bare belly thrust against it, and with her other hand she began to spank furiously, to maintain the pleasing crimson her whipping had raised.

It did not take long before this new spanking, coupled with her insistent damsel-caress, raised Miss Duckett's voice to fever pitch, the cries coming hoarse and high; Sophia knew and marvelled that with this strange, thrilling thrusting in the bum-hole she would make the woman spend. Her own belly fluttered and tingled with electric joy as the baubo teased and caressed her nubbin at her every thrust.

'Yes,' she panted, 'you are taking it like a seaman, Duckett!' and at this Miss Duckett's body became quite uncontrollable, her love-oil flowing in gusts down her soft whipped thigh-skin as she yelped in her spasm of spending. She was utterly in Sophia's power, and Sophia felt herself goddess not maid.

Her mind whirled in fantasy. She was Boudicca, whipping and being whipped, she was Suetonius, his massive baubo spurting hot cream into the writhing anus of Miss Duckett, his raven consort; she was the *Bucentaur*, a massive ship like a baubo cleaving the hot sea of the female's love liquor; she was the goddess Baubo herself, then ... the very anal passage of the goddess, her soft walls filled with the huge, never-ending spurt of the cream from the centaur's own organ as his searing whip lashed her soft derrière.

Sophia could not restrain her own spend, nor her harsh yelps of ecstacy as her joy flooded her.

Their joy subsided, the two females – dressed as women once more – decorously faced each other. Sophia thought of Miss Letchford, of Miss Duckett, and of herself. Miss Letchford seemed a forbidding mountain, almost an enemy, her buttocks icy hills of disdain to be tamed by fierce crimson; Miss Duckett a sensuous lush blossom, to be nurtured by chastisement that was tender but no less fierce; herself, Sophia Derrière – what was *she*? Miss Duckett said, 'I hope you have learned your lesson, maid.'

'Yes, Miss,' said Sophia with bowed head.

'You are very wilful. I don't know if one chastisement alone is enough to discipline you, and no doubt you will have offended liberally before next week is out. So you may come at the same time again. And the week after that, and –' she wiped her brow, flushed and taking a deep breath '– and every week. If Baubo and her Master approve.'

She looked up at the painting and the centaur's gleaming anal bud, then nodded. It seemed that they did. Sophia wondered if Miss Duckett had told the truth in saying that no one else should see or hear their rites . . .

138

8

Shredded Silk

Derrière ... bottom, croup, fesses, the sacred portion
... Sophia lay on a night scented with the new air of an
early spring, and rubbed the bare skin of her own firm
young arse-globes. She felt naughty, thinking of that
word arse; more suitable perhaps to a male than a
female derrière, it had nonetheless a pleasing robustness,
a firm ... *Essex* quality. What a lot of words there were
to describe such beautiful and sacred orbs! Her fingers
stroked her furrow, touching the wrinkled little bud that
always tickled her belly with such a naughty, pleasant
shudder.

Beside her, she could hear Bella Frinton moaning
softly, and knew that she was pleasuring herself too.
Somehow there was a satisfaction in their being apart,
as though each alone in her separate pleasure was the
accomplice of the other. Her fingers toyed with her
nubbin, sending little spasms of joy through her body,
particularly in her spine, and with a special tingling at
the base, just at the top of her fesses and furrow. Truly,
that seemed to be the most magical part of her Lady's
body: somehow the queen of the other secret places, the
nipples that stiffened so sweetly, the damsel of course,
and the oily recesses of fount and deep slit. Sophia ran
her trembling hands all over her skin, naked, with her
nightie cushioning her neck. She felt that her body was
a temple, the nodes of pleasure, the worshipped icons,

and the curved hills of her buttocks, the altar on which others must some day worship as she worshipped.

Her skin was still smarting a little from the last, rather perfunctory, beating she had received from Miss Sassi. This time, she knew that she had courted punishment deliberately, and the spanking had proceeded as before. But she had artfully arranged to cut some of her mink-hairs and replace them in their bush, then ostentatiously scratched her fount, to make sure that Miss Sassi saw the hairs fall to her floor. Sophia knew that Miss Sassi would collect and treasure them, and this gave her a feeling of having the Purser in her domain, just as her keeping of Miss Letchford's hairs somehow had her in the tall white-haired Mistress's domain.

She took the pouch containing Miss Letchford's mink-hairs and began to rub herself with it, the soft fabric sliding deliciously over her quivering damsel. As her belly fluttered and her heart quickened, she found herself imagining Miss Sassi and Miss Letchford, their croups writhing into crimson as Sophia caned them both bare. And then, somehow, the two women were wrestling together, their bodies glistening and slippery with sweat, their prize being a thorough penetration with the giant baubo Sophia wore at her waist. Miss Letchford won but, between her legs, suddenly, Sophia saw she had her own fleshy baubo! And as she bent and spread her buttocks to take her prize from Sophia, Miss Sassi bent forward, receiving Miss Letchford's prong in her own anus. They performed their tribadic dance on a bed of wet silk panties, mingled with silky rose petals thrown by a throng of watching maids: Chaste, Felicity, Ransome, Bella . . .

At these images, Sophia brought herself closer and closer to a spend, her fingers moving with a smoothness born of her frequent artful practice. Then she took her forefinger into her mouth and bit on her sharp nail until the tip was smooth. She trembled; placed her finger at

140

the bud which was the entrance to her nether hole, and pushed a little. Her finger went inside about an inch, and she clenched her teeth. It hurt! Only a little, though, and it as a maddening, insistent hurt that was almost pleasure, and would not let go, but demanded more, a further and deeper penetration.

Her mouth was dry: she scarely noticed that her diddling finger was now stroking her stiff damsel with quite remorseless desire. She pushed again, trying to relax her bum-hole, and found that if she delivered herself to thoughts of pure pleasure, floating helplessly on the oily spend-juice that gushed from her slit, and which she imagined as warm ocean of joy, then her hole would admit the probing finger.

It did; Sophia gasped aloud as her index sank to the hilt inside her quivering bum-hole, whose elastic walls seemed to suck and caress the invading finger like a much-loved enemy. Her pleasure was maddening, irresistible, as though her anus chided her tweaking finger for her lack of girth, for not being longer and harder and smoother, like a baubo, or the spurting flesh of a male . . .

Sophia thrust annd diddled harder and harder, not resisting but enjoying the smooth gush of her joy as she convulsed in a spend that left her quite breathless for long moments afterwards. She felt a glow of satisfaction, that she had established a further domain over a part of her own body; her thoughts turned to the forthcoming meeting of the Rodings Riders, and she resolved that it should be her task to establish domain over other maids' parts too. Moments later, her reverie was disturbed by a heavy familiar pressure as a body slid under the covers beside her.

'Why, you woke me up!' hissed Bella. 'I was listening. I expect the whole dorm was listening. You were making enough noise, puffing like a grampus! Whatever were you up to?'

As she said this, her hand nimbly raised Sophia's nightie afresh and slid down her bare belly, after a friendly tweak of the nipples, to snugly cup her fount-lips and stiff damsel, which she began to rub gently.

'Still stiff,' she said admiringly. 'Mmmm ... You don't mind? I had to listen to you – feel me, I'm all wet!'

Sophia put her arm around her friend and said that she did not mind, then told her what she had been doing. Bella took hold of Sophia's moist index finger and slid it into her own furrow, on to the anus bud, which she wiggled a little so as to part the wrinkle.

'Would you do it to me?' she whispered, flicking Sophia's nubbin quite hard now. 'Go on.'

Sophia felt neither inclined nor able to refuse, and firmly pushed her finger into Bella's anus, causing her a happy little squeal of excitement. Bella twisted her body, parting her thighs so that they were both comfortable, and drawing her knee up to place her foot on Sophia's thigh as both maids diddled each other. Sophia indicated that it would be too awkward for Bella to do her in the bum at the same time, and that a fesse-stroking would be acceptable; in truth, her bum-hole was still quite tender after her own finger's ministrations. As each maid worked at her gentle task, she found herself obliged to interrupt herself momentarily to push up her nightie which slid down with the gentle frottage of their writhing bodies and quims.

'Isn't clothing a bother?' said Bella. 'It would be so nice to scamper round naked, like lambs, and diddle each other whenever we wished.'

'But it is a pleasant bother,' answered Sophia gravely. 'Where would Ladies be without the lovely feel of silk against our skin, the smell of leather and freshly laun-dered linen, the sweet rustling of skirts and the swish of stockings as our thighs move? As for underthings, Bella, don't you have a thrilling feeling just from their very tightness, of knowing yourself bound and made prisoner by such beautiful garments?'

142

'Making commode is such a fuss, though,' said Bella merrily. 'All the straps and knickers and everything ... and the same for a spanking.'

Sophia thought for a moment, feeling her friend's body sweetly squirm as she approached a spend. 'How I wish I could spank your bare bum right this moment,' she whispered. 'You are a naughty minx, making me so wet in my Lady's place. But your punishment shall be to spend and gush your wet over my fingers, without crying out. As for your idea, why, it should not be difficult for a clever maid to alter her intimate clothing to make pleasurable operations both seemly and convenient. What if our knickers were flapped, a little slip we could lift to reveal our lips and furrow, when we needed to make commode?'

'Or to diddle!' cried Bella enthusiastically.

'Or, indeed, to diddle. There could be knickers with no front at all, frontless panties – that would be rather daring. And corselets or bustiers with open places at the breasts, so that we could slip our hands in and ... feel each other's teats. But I think such dress would be improper.'

'Not on a Submission Day!' Bella exclaimed. 'On a Submission Day, maids can wear what they like. Torn stockings, soiled knickers, anything that betokens humiliation. But there must always be stockings. Oh, Sophia, don't stop rubbing me – I must tell you – don't you get the loveliest feeling when you rub your thighs together, and feel the silk of your stockings so smooth and ladylike? Sometimes, in class, if I'm bored, I do that under the desk – yes, rub my thighs together, ever so secretly, and make mysef all wet. And cross my legs ... not ladylike, but no one can see me. Oh, I'm so wet now for you. Don't stop your diddling! Make me spend, Sophia, with your clever fingers.'

Smoothly, Sophia brought Bella to her gushing wet spend, and gave her own body to the other maid's eager fingers, bathing in the warmth of her own little shudder, milder and more friendly than the spend she had caused herself, yet enriched by the thought of the sheer, smooth stocking-silk that Bella had described. She thought of herself, a little nubbin, trapped and caressed beteeen the giant firm thighs lustrous with silk, and rubbing her. Miss Letchford's, Miss Duckett's? Her wetness flowed as she thought of milky hard stockinged thighs, squeezing her.

Bella's spend, though, was not friendly, but ecstatic in its frenzied writhing – the more so because of Sophia's ordained silence. Sophia marvelled at the power of her finger's slightest twist or pressure inside Bella's clutching soft bum-hole. She asked her gasping maid when the next Submission Day would be, and received the answer that it was after Sowing Day.

'Hadn't you noticed? It is nearly springtime, and then we must sow the fields of Rodings. It is supposed to be very historic with all sorts of rituals, but hard work for us. Sowing week! Well, we maids must work. I'm so looking forward to the meeting of the Riders, Sophia. These games you speak of, that you have learnt from the books – perhaps we shall learn some ways to make our sowing tasks easier.'

'Yes,' Sophia joked. 'We could be horses and oxen for each other, just think!'

'Well, we have to be that anyway,' said Bella glumly.

Sophia's questions were stifled by the arrival of a Preceptress at the far end of the dorm; a patrol threatened, and Bella slipped back to her own bed without a word. When the Preceptress had passed, Sophia found that her pretence at sleep rapidly became reality, and with a drowsy contented murmur to Bella, she slipped into soft dreams.

'I do wish you'd tell us what sort of games you have planned, Sophia,' said Ransome, as she opened the creaking old door of the barn.

'You are going to find out, aren't you?' answered Sophia. 'They are Essex games I found in the old books. Things that Queen Boudicca used to play with her warriors. She said that to tame a male, you had to play games with him, and eventually you could ride him like a horse.'

Sophia was pleased at the maids' unspoken admission of her natural leadership, stemming from the authority of her book-learning and her avowedly superior derrière.

'Have you ever ridden a horse?' said Bella. Sophia admitted she had not.

'I have,' said Chaste Marsh. 'It is like riding a man, although not as smelly. Pooh! It stinks a bit in here.'

'It is the old cowshed,' said Ransome, 'just at the edge of bounds. None of the Pres shall find us, and if we spot one coming, then Felicity shall whistle and we shall all escape over the fence.'

'Then we shall be breaking bounds,' said Sophia, 'which will be two crimes.'

'But they shan't find us, or know who we are,' replied Chaste.

'She will know *somebody* was here,' insisted Bella.

'I shan't blab!' cried Felicity.

'But we will be honour-bound to own up,' said Chaste Marsh, 'although that is a mug's game, if you ask me.'

'No one shall find us, and that is that!' Sophia cried. 'Now, we shall begin with some little girlish games, to get us in the mood. Then we shall try riding each other, and . . . well, you'll see. If you play properly, then you shall all be full Rodings Riders. Eh, Ransome?'

She ordered the dozen maids, giggling nervously, to remove their jackets and skirts, then peg up their petticoats. When some of the maids said this would be cumbersome, Sophia decreed they might take off their petticoats too, and play in stockings, blouse and knickers.

145

'We may get a but dusty,' she said, 'but it doesn't matter, since it will show we have been good drudges.'

She inspected 'her' maids, as she suddenly viewed them: a spectacle of entrancing eager beauty, a dozen firm young derrières swelling ripe beneath the thin tight silk of the knickers.

'Aren't you going to disrobe, Sophia?' asked Chaste rather mischievously. 'Or will you just watch?'

'No, no,' said Sophia, blushing, and began to take off her things, well aware of the earnest eyes which gazed upon her baring. Almost, but not quite, unconsciously, she undressed in a slow and provocative way, not gaily disrobing like the other maids, but taking her time with straps and buttons, teasing them until she finally revealed her own fesses and made a great show of pulling up her knickers well into her slit and furrow, so that the silk shone like a second skin. The excitement of her little show made her feel a little damp between her thighs, and she wondered if the wet patch would show on her knickers, then decided that she did not mind at all.

They played Blind Man's Buff, and Ring-a-ring o' Roses, falling down with shrieks of laughter, then Hide and Seek – which was not really a success, since the shed offered few places to hide, and those few covered their fugitive with smelly straw. Then there was a tumultuous session of leapfrog; their mood became gay, and then Sophia decided they should play Musical Chairs.

Since they had no chairs, she decreed that half the maids should kneel and serve as chairs for the others, while Chaste Marsh hummed a tune. 'Musical Maids', she called it. When the tune stopped, those maids who were seated should leave their seats, and one of the seats would rise and join their number. When the tune started again, they should scramble to occupy the fewer remaining seats, and so on until the last seated maid was the winner. This was merry sport, although fisticuffs threatened to break out on occasion, and Sophia devised a refinement – that, while the maids were sat upon, they should buck and kick in order to dislodge their incumbent, like wild horses.

Susan Westham was the winner, successfully taming her steed, Clarissa Slim. This led naturally to a picka-back race, although there was some confusion whether the riders were supposed to aid their carriers in winning, or hinder them, and the riders did not stint in delivering vigorous slaps to their carriers' buttocks. All were merry and flushed, and Sophia announced that they were now ready to be proper Rodings Riders, that is, teams of Mistress and horse.

She had noted the barn was well equipped with saddlery and other country appurtenances and, when lots were drawn to assign roles, it was a delight to adorn the steeds with bit, bridle and harness, and to marvel at their submissive grace as they padded obediently around the floor of the barn, whinnying and snorting charmingly, for all the world like real horses, while their riders, all brandishing short heavy crops, looked on in admiring impatience.

The display was a thing of rare beauty: to see the maids, who a moment before had been gambolling and shrieking in flushed, happy sport, now cool and dignified in their new role as horses, the equine submission seeming all the more beautiful because of the muscled power that trembled beneath the flanks. The leather fetters tightly strapping the maids' bodies seemed to emphasise their feminine grace straining beneath the bonds. A spectacle, however, was not enough; some thought a proper race was in order, but that would necessitate the risk of going outside. Sophia decreed a game of polo, the barn's floor being a large enough terrain to accommodate two small teams.

A swift consultation with Chaste Marsh informed Sophia rather vaguely of the substance of polo; it seemed to involve chukkas and wallahs and other things which Chaste had learnt from one of her Hackney acquaintances, a subaltern in the Indian Army 'with a lovely rider's bum'. However Sophia soon made up her own rules, thinking games far too important to be left to mere males.

Ransome and Susan Westham, having won at the other games, were designated team captains. Each end of the barn was designated a goal area, and the aim of the two teams was to propel the ball into their opponents' goal. Riders sat impatiently on their steeds, flicking their tethered horses on the buttocks with their crops; the steeds were enjoying themselves hugely, pawing the ground and dribbling, snorting and braying like real thoroughbreds. Their knees and elbows were thickly padded for comfort, but – what to use as a ball? Furthermore, Chaste said that the ball should be whacked with mallets, of which there were none.

'It is quite simple,' said Sophia. 'There is an odd number of horses and riders, so a maid shall be the ball! We don't need mallets, the whip shall be enough.'

At once, there was a chorus of volunteers; she chose Bella Frinton. Quickly and expertly, she trussed Bella and bridled her, then set her loose like a riderless horse, except that her forearms were bound together, as were her calves, both with extra padding, so that she was obliged to proceed in an awkward hopping motion. The rules were that the ball was to be directed by whip-cuts: a stroke to the left flank drove her to the right and, when stroked on the right flank, she must turn left. The flank was defined as shoulder, upper back, or outer thigh. A stroke square on the buttocks meant that she must proceed straight forward, while – Sophia hesitated, but decreed nonetheless – if any rider were agile enough to lean underneath her and deliver a stroke to the pendulous breasts, then Bella must stop in her tracks. Her eyes shone: no one was more impatient than Bella for the chukka to begin.

148

Chaste was to act as referee along with Sophia herself, and asked what sort of penalties there should be for infringement of the rules – that is, foul play. Sophia was slightly taken aback.

'We are Ladies, Chaste!' she exclaimed. 'I do not think there can be any question of foul play.'

'You have still much to learn about being a Lady, my maid,' said Chaste. 'I suggest that if a player offends – strikes another player with her whip, for example, or another player's horse – then she should receive a penalty point. We must not interrupt the game, of course, but at the end the points shall be added up, and . . . well . . .'

'You mean each penalty point shall be a whip-stroke to the croup,' murmured Sophia, feeling her heart leap in excitement. 'To be administered by myself.'

'There is also the question of reward for the winning team,' Chaste added. 'That is, whichever has scored the most goals before poor Bella gets tired.'

Bella huffed and whinnied behind her bridle, to indicate indignantly that she would never get tired. Sophia said that it seemed rather coarse and unladylike to reward victory, rather it might be better to punish failure. The winning team would accordingly be invited to spank the bare bottoms of the losers. This was agreed, with resentment and sly jubilation in equal proportions, and the game began.

'You know,' said Chaste thoughtfully as the game got off to a brisk and uproarious start, with whips cracking on flesh clothed and unclothed, 'men are always so concerned about playing things by the rules. They take games so seriously; in fact, they sometimes say that life is a game. With their uniforms and regulations! But a Lady finds it much simpler to make up her own rules.'

'Rules are necessary for good discipline,' said Sophia sternly. 'And the males look *so* nice in their sailors' or soldiers' uniforms! As though all that formality hints at the brute strength beneath. I am looking forward to being a Governess – at Shoeburyness, you know, and inspecting all those young men, with their uniforms so nice and crisp and smart; if there is *one* crease not perfect, why then . . . bare bum, and a good dozen with my Governess's cane! *In front of all the others . . .*'

This last comment, which had only just occurred to Sophia, made her quite weak with sudden desire. The thought of caning a naked male bottom: that was enough on its own to make her moist. But the idea that he should squirm in front of his comrades was somehow naughty and voluptuous.

'I have heard that the cadets at Shoeburyness play a game called buggerball,' Chaste remarked cheerfully. 'The aim, like most ball games, is to get the ball to the opponent's goal, but buggerball is distinctive in that it has no rules at all. One is not even obliged to play for the same side all the time, if a sufficient bribe is offered. In the old days, I believe murder was quite common.'

'Oh, stuff and nonsense!'

'It's true!' said Chaste, po-faced. 'You do not know the male. It was, of course, punished, but only after the game was finished, games taking precedence over just- ice. My ensign – he had a tattooed Indian radish, or *mooli*, on his baubo, that he got in Calcutta! – said that sometimes a game could take hours, days, or even weeks, and that there was as much play off the field as on – nobbling, wounding, and seductions of one kind or another. It was almost like real life! And sometimes, he said, you could not tell whether it was real life, or a game of buggerball! The *mooli* was a good luck charm signifying potency, by the way.'

'And did it work? The mooli, I mean.'

'Yes,' said Chaste.

'Well,' exclaimed Sophia, 'anyone playing buggerball when *I* am governess shall be soundly thrashed!'

'That,' said Chaste, sucking her thumb, 'is all of them.'

A loud squeal drew Sophia's attention back to the game. Bella had received a strong stroke right across her buttocks, which would have propelled her forward into the enemy's goal even had the rules not decreed it.

'Oh,' she said. 'One point to nil, I suppose.'

'It was a foul!' cried Susan Westham.

'Was not!' retorted Ransome.

'She lashed her right in the furrow! Of course she shot straight to goal! It ain't fair.'

'It is unladylike to say "ain't", Susan,' said Sophia gravely. 'As for a furrow stroke, well, it may be unorthodox, but it is certainly skilful, and not against the rules. Play on.'

After half an hour of vigorous and increasingly anarchic play, Sophia called half-time. She had by now awarded over a dozen penalty points for various offences, including striking across the face or breasts of an opponent rider. Now, it was time to reverse the positions. The steeds and riders changed places, and Sophia told Bella that she was to replace Felicity Straw as lookout, after her sterling service as ball. Bella made a face.

'But you must be awfully tired, Bella,' said Sophia. 'And I saw you take four or five quite hard strokes to your breasts! That must have smarted.'

'Yes, it did,' said Bella smugly, 'but I didn't mind. Don't tell me you didn't enjoy watching, Sophia. Your face is as red as my bum!'

Chaste Marsh grinned at Sophia's discomfiture, for Bella's words were true. Throughout the spectacle, Sophia had exalted in her position of power over the combatants, and the resulting moisture steadily seeped between her thighs as the maids rode each other and lashed buttocks and backs in superb equestrian dominance: it seemed that the riders were as keen and adept to lash the buttocks of their steeds as to stroke the ball. Felicity came in, while Bella, walking gingerly, replaced her outside; Sophia said they had plenty of time for the second half, then for whatever penalties were to be paid, and after that they should return to the House. But Felicity seemed unsure if she would make a good ball.

'We must have a ball, Sophia, eh?' said Chaste somewhat mockingly. 'I wonder who.'

'There are no volunteers,' said Sophia firmly, although she had not asked for any, 'so I suppose I must do the job myself. Chaste, you will please referee, helped by Felicity.'

'Must, Sophia?' said Chaste. 'Must, or want?'

Sophia blushed fiery red. Chaste saw into her heart. She swallowed, and ordered herself to be bound and, on impulse, as bit and halter were readied for her mouth, she said that, for a bit of jolly sport, she would be tied hand and foot to be whipped around the field like a *real* ball.

Gasping with a pleasure she had never before tasted, she drew her thighs up to her breasts and clasped her ankles, permitting Chaste and the others to lash her securely with ropes and thongs into the tightest of bundles. She balanced, teetering on her croup, and could not move except to roll on the dusty floor. She practised a few manoeuvres and discovered herself quite adept at directing her body like an egg towards the goal, even at directing her motion. Gagged, she could not speak, but nodded to Chaste that proceedings should recommence.

The first stroke lashed her almost at once full across her croup, and she had to force herself not to cry out – not so much in pain as in shock. Frantically, she rolled in the direction indicated, only to be halted by a stroke to her left thigh; she rolled to the right, another stroke caught her on the right, and she retraced her path. There was neither mercy nor ceremony in the way her helpless body was beaten: by her simple binding, she had ceased to exist as a maid, and was a mere object, to be used and abused for the entertainment of others. That thought excited her curiously and powerfully as the whips lashed her.

Then, a fearful stroke took her straight across the tops of her breasts where they peeped between her trussed knees, and, her eyes brimming with tears, she came to a halt. The respite was brief: further strokes rained on her defenceless bound body, driving her willy-nilly across the field. From time to time there was a cheer, as a goal had apparently been scored, and then Chaste unceremoniously rolled her back to midfield to begin the next chukka. Sophia's tears were now tears of joy. She felt her flesh glowing and reddening with the searing smarts of the riders' whips, and did not care. She wanted it never to stop: she was a slave, and loved her helplessness.

More than that: at each furious lash, her belly fluttered and her spine tingled, and she could feel her little damsel stiffening sweetly as her fount became wetter and wetter, so much that under her hail of blows she found herself worrying if the wet patch showed on her tight knickers. From the ribald whoops of her tormentors, she guessed it did, and was rather proud of herself. The moistening became a flow, and to her delighted shock – yes, oh sweetness, it was *coming*! – she felt herself approaching a spend! It seemed absurd – she was alone and reduced to a plaything rolling on the dirty floor, her clothing no doubt improperly scuffed and dirtied, and yet her belly trembled with lustful pleasure! The knowledge that she was going to spend brought her spend nearer and made her more lustful, until the cracks of the whip to her tortured fesses and thighs were drowned briefly by her high peals of yelping pleasure as her spend engulfed her.

'I'm not sure if that should count as a goal,' she heard Chaste say, 'nor who has scored it. But the match is over now, and the score is a draw, fourteen all!'

Gasping, Sophia was unbound, and she smoothed her soiled clothing, then wiped her brow. Chaste handed her a crop.

'Since it is a draw, there are no losers to be spanked,' she murmured, 'but there are thirty-three penalty points to be paid, and that is your job, I think.'

She showed Sophia her notebook, in which the offenders and tally of offences were carefully listed. Every single maid was to receive chastisement, the steeds being noted for biting, head-butting and spitting.

'They are a lawless lot,' Chaste continued, 'and one or two strokes, even on the bare, is not great chastisement. I suggest that you modify the rules, Sophia, not to increase the number of decreed strokes, but their intensity.'

So saying, she took each of the riders' crops and bound them with a wire handle, until Sophia had a flail of at least a dozen thongs, which her hand was only just large enough to grasp. The maids looked on with fearful yet lustful expectation, their faces flushed from their game; Sophia wondered how many of her equestrians had been brought to their own spends by the thrill of combat, and the insistent pressure of a bucking steed between their thighs, or a merciless whip to their fesses.

The maids were made to stand in line, hands behind their backs and holding up knickers tightly sheathed. All were pegged, and Sophia suddenly thought it would be exciting to see if with one or two strokes she could shred those tight knickers with her heavy flail. She announced her decision – that punishment was to be taken on the knickers, and was greeted with wails of dismay.

'It's not proper! Punishment must be on the bare!'

'Come, come!' said Sophia gaily. 'Just one or two strokes shan't damage your precious silks . . . not much, and anyway, you may keep them for Submission Day.'

But the protests continued, until Sophia raised her

arm for silence. 'Maids! You are now fully-fledged Rodings Riders. Just think of the pleasure when we can play polo with real males . . . naked ones, and lashed by proper hard whips! But, for the moment, we need a badge of honour, our sign of being Rodings Riders. I had thought of a brooch, a bit or spur or something horsey, but that would not be secret.'

Ransome spoke, with some defiance. 'You act as though you, the new maid, are already in charge of the Riders, Sophia,' she blurted.

Sophia laughed. 'Jealous, Ransome? Do you want to put the matter to the vote? Or shall we be tickled for it? I am ready.'

Sophia sensed that the maids were all for her, but to her discomfiture there seemed understandable interest in a tickling match. She decided to take a risk. 'New maid I may be, but my name, Sophia Derrière, makes me known to all. My sacred portion is supreme, the finest and sweetest of any maid's, my virgin purity is unquestioned, and if anyone wishes to challenge me, then we shall devise a suitable contest. Ransome, my sweet, I wish to love you and be nice to you, and could never ask you to divulge the secret of your own name.'

She paused to look at Ransome's fiery eyes, but her head, at last, deferentially nodded in obeisance, and Sophia was pleased that her authority was now unquestioned. The Rodings Riders applauded, and Chaste whispered that Sophia had guessed unerringly: Ransome had been the slave of a wicked Master, and the Board of Rodings had indeed paid a ransom for her liberty. Ransome was no longer virgin.

'So now,' cried Sophia, 'beating shall be on silk, and I decree that our badge shall be . . . the torn knickers of the true Rider! Let the first maid bend over!'

It was, by her own insistence, Ransome herself; the maid bent and drew her knickers to their fullest extent, so that her bottom shone like two hard gleaming moons under the translucent silk. Sophia lashed her once, twice, each time to the gasps of approval of her maids; the skin reddened in a sweet blossom of pain beneath the silk, the many rods suffusing the blush like the petals of a huge anemone on Ransome's clenched bottom.

Sophia forgot her list of ordained penalties – to no objections – and continued to flog until the knickers were well shredded into fluttering little ribbons. Sweating hard, she wiped her forehead and called for the next – it was Jane Broad, whose derrière, flat and vast as the Essex marshes, lived up to her name – repeating the process until the badge of honour had been conferred on buttocks and knickers alike. And all the time she felt a swelling pleasure once more in her own fount. She longed to touch her throbbing nubbin, her longing made more acute by her certain knowledge that behind her, the phalanx of waiting victims were diddling themselves at the sweet spectacle of another's writhing pain.

'This shall be our secret badge,' panted Sophia as she flogged, 'and it binds us, for it contains the delicious risk of punishment if our impropriety is discovered.'

At last, every maid had been flogged and witnessed the flogging of her comrades, and the air buzzed with happy, rueful squeals of discomfort as bottoms and shredded knickers were touched, compared, and admired. Then Chaste nodded to Sophia and herself bent over, advising her she must not be forgotten. Chaste hummed as she took an even sterner punishment than the others, and Sophia saw that as Chaste's ripe bottom squirmed, the other maids were now openly diddling, fingers reaching through furrow and slit, to touch each other's nubbins; unconsciously her fingers crept between her own thighs.

At each stroke to Chaste's prettily writhing buttocks, Sophia felt a spasm of tingling joy shock her, so that when the punishment was finally over, Chaste stood happily rubbing her raw globes through the gaping web to which Sophia's flail had reduced her knickers. Then, Sophia obeyed with secret delight when Chaste said, as she had hoped, that she must earn her own badge. She bent over, and said that her flogging was to stop only when she gave word. As she felt the first stroke of the flail on her thinly silked buttocks, she jumped in surprise: the instrument truly was heavy, and she would show them all that her status as Chief Rider should be unquestioned.

At the second stroke, she knew that she was already at her plateau of spend; her bottom glowed and smarted awfully, Chaste's hard strokes adding to the discomfort of her hearty whipping as polo-ball. Her fount flowed hot and oily with her liquor; the third stroke brought her to a cry of spasming happiness, as her fingers delved openly between her soaking slit-lips, rubbing the stiff damsel as she shuddered in the joy of her spend. Chaste paused in the flogging, but Sophia told her to continue, and she took stroke after stroke, her body jerking and squirming in a dance of humiliation and submission and happiness.

'To lead,' she murmured to herself through gritted teeth, 'one must first learn to submit.' Each stroke of the awsome flail seemed like a lover's caress, warming her in the afterglow of her spend, until Chaste panted that the punishment really must end – Sophia's knickers were shredded to nothing at all!

Sophia stood and gingerly rubbed her crimson glowing bottom, which she twisted to inspect with a thrill of approval. She had the reddest and surely the most smarting derrière of all the maids! Ransome said wonderingly that she had no knickers left at all, and Sophia saw it was true: her glowing bottom was caressed by nothing more than a few wan strands of silk, like the wisps of a kiss-curl.

'That's it, then,' she said triumphantly. 'We all have our badges as Rodings Riders. You maids shall commit

157

the impropriety of wearing shredded knickers, while I, as Chief Rider – as your *Mistress* – shall improperly wear *no knickers at all*.'

Suddenly she remembered that Bella Frinton was still outside keeping watch, and must receive her own badge. She was about to tell Chaste to fetch her, when there was a squeal, and the door burst open. Before them stood Miss Sassi, holding Bella by the hair, and beside her the glowering, triumphant figure of Miss Letchford.

'I didn't see them coming,' squealed Bella. 'Honest! I kept watch – but they came up from the village, over the fence, from outside bounds.'

'Quiet, slut!' barked Miss Letchford, and delivered a stern blow to Bella's knickered buttocks with the leather pouch she carried. It was large, almost a sack, and resounded against the maid's flesh with the heavy chink of coins. Sophia thought of Miss Letchford's previous excursion to High Roding, when her lesson was taken by Miss Flye, and wondered what business she and Miss Sassi could have there.

'I don't know what is going on here,' said Miss Letchford, 'but it looks improper. A full report shall have to be made to Miss Brace, perhaps to the Board, after each of you has made a separate statement. Who is the ringleader?'

Her eye fixed on Sophia, but before Sophia could own up, there was a chorus of, 'I am the ringleader! I am! I am!'

'Your loyalty does you credit,' sneered Miss Letchford, 'but I can guess.'

'I alone am to blame for this scene of impropriety, miss,' said Sophia. 'And I shall take flogging for all.'

'Well, punishment there shall certainly be, when the true facts have been ascertained, and no doubt hearty flogging will grace your maids' bottoms. But flogging is not the only punishment, especially not for a ringleader, whatever ring it is you are leading, Miss Sophia

158

Derrière. I think haircuts are in order to start with, and you may all report to Miss Sassi tomorrow – a *complete* haircut, I mean.'

Miss Sassi grinned fondly, no doubt thinking – as Sophia was – of the young maids' founts gradually shorn of their curls, bared under her razors and scissors.

'But as spring is early,' Miss Letchford continued, 'sowing shall commence within the next few days, and the just punishment of flogging is sweeter when allied to hard labour and useful purpose. It shall amuse me to think of your founts itching unbearably as your sprouts grow back under your heavy leather breechclouts. In the case of ringleaders, it is fitting too that punishment should be exemplary. Sophia Derrière, I think we must make an example of you – you'll agree, I'm sure.'

'You wish to whip me publicly, like Queen Boudicca, miss?' said Sophia with some defiance. 'I gladly accept.'

'Oh, it is an agreeable thought, and I shall no doubt act upon it,' said Miss Letchford pleasantly. 'But sowing seed means attracting birds, miss – you city maids being ignorant of country ways – and Miss Wyvern insists birds be kept away from our fields. For that, we require a scarecrow . . .'

As the maids filed sheepishly, yet with strange exultation, back to the forbidding silhouette of the darkening House, Sophia said to Miss Letchford that she was sure she could explain things satisfactorily. Miss Letchford placed her hand on Sophia's bottom for an instant, in a gesture that was almost one of affection.

'Don't trouble yourself, sweet maid,' she said, her eyes and lips bright. 'Miss Sassi and I heard every single thing.'

9

Ploughmaid

Sophia was to be fount-shaved: that much was certain.
With a certain excited foreboding, she lined up early on
the appointed morning with the other Rodings Riders
at Matron's surgery, where Miss Sassi was to perform
the multiple operation. Miss Lord gloated in attend-
ance, ready to minister with salves and ointments. The
other maids looked anxiously at Sophia, their leader,
and cheerfully she assured them that this would be
another badge for their select group; that if it pleased
her, she would decree they must keep their founts
shaven permanently. She knew deep down that it would
please her, that the idea of having a naked fount, a 'bare
slice of cake' as Miss Lord rather indecorously put it,
excited her enormously.

'And just think,' she whispered, 'when we have males
to tame and ride, why, they shall have to be shaven too,
and I believe that is the most frightful shame for them!'

Chaste Marsh, of course, was no stranger to the
operation, opining that there were lots of crabs to be
caught on Hackney Marshes. Miss Letchford overheard
her remark, and ordered Miss Sassi to pay especial
attention to Chaste's crevices, then told Miss Lord that
she was to apply her harshest disinfecting agent all over
Chaste's Lady's place, to make sure of cleanliness.
Chaste made a rueful face but said nothing, and seemed
the most cheerful of them all when Miss Letchford

ordered the operation to begin, saying that they must all watch and be watched as they were shaved, and this ignominy was part of their punishment.

It seemed that Sophia was to go last, perhaps because Miss Letchford wanted her to feel apprehensive. She felt so, as she watched the other maids parting their thighs and going under the razor; yet Miss Sassi was so expert, and the shaving so clean, that Sophia became quite excited, particularly as the swish of razor on strop reminded her of a lovely leather whipping crop. She was excited, too, by Miss Sassi's deft and indeed shameless fingers; such was her dedication that she quite openly inserted her thumb or index into a maid's slit, where necessary, or took one or other pink gash-lips firmly in her fingers, to pull it away from the fount and seek out any mischievous stray hairs. When the fount was shaven, the maid turned in the armchair and presented her spread fesses, upon which Miss Sassi repeated the process, delving into furrow and even into the arse-bud itself, until both fount and furrow were smooth as ice.

After a while, the mood of the Rodings Riders lightened, and mischievous glances were exchanged as they rubbed their founts and sighed at their new discomfort, yet in sighing exhibited a rather daring pride. This came to Miss Letchford's attention, and displeased her, yet it was too late to change things; Sophia smiled as she mounted the chair, lifted her skirts and revealed her naked fount, then obediently spread her stockinged thighs. She saw that Miss Sassi had three separate bags for the mink-hairs she collected, according to colour.

'What!' cried Miss Letchford furiously on seeing Sophia's bare thighs and bum. 'No panties, maid?'

Sophia replied sweetly that since a bare fount would be required for the punishment shaving, she was knickerless, to save time.

Miss Letchford's anger turned to a leer. 'Well!' she said thoughtfully. 'Impropriety on impropriety,

161

punishment upon punishment. We can't have your page in the book overflowing, maid, so I'll ticket you for this – a number three. You may elect to take it here and now. It means the cane, as you well know, and since you have had the foresight to be disgracefully knickerless, you shan't have the trouble of lowering panties.'

She stroked the shiny smoothness of the yellow cane at her waist, then began to unfasten it, very slowly, and rubbed its splayed tip with fingers that she put to her lip, as though savouring the odour of the maid's buttocks with which it would soon be impregnated.

'You'll all itch and smart when you're yoked for sowing,' she said, 'but Miss Derrière here shall smart threefold, for I am going to lace that bum of hers as she has never been laced! I may give you thirteen for a number three, and thirteen it shall be, very tight, and you shall regret your girlish playfulness.'

'Why, Miss Letchford,' said Sophia coolly, 'I gladly accept your ticketing, and I assure you my bum won't flinch. She has taken worse, and from stronger arms.' Sophia gulped and rather regretted saying this, as she was aware she exaggerated.

But it was too late, for Miss Letchford advanced and lifted her cane high. 'Then you won't mind taking your lacing as Miss Sassi shaves you,' she hissed. 'It will save time, which seems to concern you so much, and you say you will not flinch.'

Sophia was positioned kneeling atop the chair-arms, with her thighs spread almost painfully apart, and her buttocks stretched and fully presented. She thought that her furrow would be quite defenceless – a cruel or thoughtless stroke from Miss Letchford's long cane could easily flick and slap her right across the anal bud, and even reach her quim. But there was nothing for it but to submit. She rested her arms on Miss Sassi's shoulders as the Purser reached down her belly and continued to lather her Lady's place.

'Isn't this fun, Sophia?' she exclaimed brightly. 'You are such a *brave* maid: just like Texas Jake when he was flogged by the preacher's wife in Amarillo State Penitentiary, for spitting in chapel! There is a time and place for such things, just as there is a time and place for wearing knickers.'

Sophia felt the scissors trimming her unruly luxuriant mink, then the first caress of the razor, as Miss Sassi applied short, sharp strokes to thin down her luxuriant bush to a stubble. Miss Sassi cooed with delight, and said she would keep Sophia's hairs specially. The strokes became longer and smoother, gracefully slicing against Sophia's trembling fount, and interspersed with tickling brush-strokes. She forced herself not to stir, even as her tender places were tickled, for she knew that when the cane fell on her naked buttocks, one sharp move could mean anguish.

'I shall try to be as brave as Texas Jake, miss,' she said hesitantly, 'or as Queen Boudicca of Essex!'

This brought a murmur of approval from her maids. At once she heard the whistle of the rod; she clenched her teeth, and her jaw tightened as her bare buttocks flamed with the first lash of Miss Letchford's cane, squarely across the centre, and only inches from Miss Sassi's placidly slicing razor. Miss Sassi appeared not to notice at all, except to say she imagined it hurt quite a bit, as though commenting on the weather.

Tears welled in Sophia's eyes, and her gorge rose in her pain. Yes. Oh, yes, how it hurt! She could not help but flinch a little, vainly clenching and unclenching her bum-muscle but without moving the outside flesh. A second stroke landed, and in quick succession a third, and now Sophia was trembling. A low, anguished moan clutched her throat. The silence in the room was electric as the Ladies observed Sophia's torment. Miss Sassi paused to wipe the tears from her cheeks and continued placidly at her shaving.

'When Miss Letchfrd has finished, we'll turn you round, maid, and then I can do your derrière,' she said. 'I expect she'll feel uncomfortable as I shave her – she'll be all red even before she has the razor! – but it can't be helped.'

A fourth stroke took Sophia unawares at the tops of her unprotected thighs, just above her stockings, and the pain that seared her seemed unimaginably cruel. How could she ever have thought that caning was just a game, a pretty conceit to play with sweet Miss Duckett?

'Oh, your poor thighs,' whispered Miss Sassi. 'How it must hurt. I should love to kiss them better – and your bum too.'

Now her hands were pulling apart the lips of Sophia's gash – she felt two hesitant fingertips penerate her, and realised that her slit was moist! – and as the flogging continued implacably, and Miss Sassi continued to shave, it was she, not Sophia, who trembled.

'Oh,' she gasped, 'I do hope you are going to finish soon, Miss Letchford.'

'On the contrary, Miss Sassi. There are seven strokes left, and I intend to skin her nice and slowly.'

Now there were longer intervals between the strokes; Sophia counted to nine, her buttocks smarted with white heat, and she wanted to beg Miss Letchford to give the remaining strokes quickly. But she would not lose her dignity, and she knew it would be useless. Besides, her attention was distracted; the pain of flogging no longer seemed to be an intrusion on her private self, but now, rather a distant warmth which she could somehow control.

What she was unable to control was the insistent pressure of Miss Sassi's hand on her intimate places. As her buttocks cried out for mercy, so did her wet fount cry for more of Miss Sassi's gentle touch. Her fount seemed to be utterly smooth, yet still the Purser lathered and shaved, spending longer and longer on the caress of the lather-brush.

'Such a brave man, Texas Jake,' stammered Miss Sassi. 'And flogged on his naked back, by a vengeful woman! Perhaps she was avenging his prowess with Ladies, since he had spurned her lustful advances. Vengeance is sweet . . .'

Sophia wondered if she would be spurred by vengeance to punish the naked bums of the sea-cadets, when she became Governess, but Miss Letchford cried harshly that just correction was sweeter still.

She cracked the cane firmly in the crevice of Sophia's furrow, the tip flicking her anal bud and making her screw her eyes in distress as the pain shot through her – a tickling pain that was somehow an act of the lash's adoration of her sacred portion. Her heart swelled with pride: her portion was taking it, and in taking the flogging was accepting the homage both of her chastiser and all those – priestesses! – who witnessed her sacrifice. Miss Sassi too worshipped at the altar of her gash, tweaking the stiffened damsel as though at prayer and, with this knowledge, Sophia felt a spend well within her. She wanted the flogging to continue, wanted to spend and glow with the adoration that her humiliation bestowed upon her squirming body.

The Rodings Riders knew that a sacred event was taking place; Miss Sassi's hand slipped for a moment, and the bone handle of her razor dwelt for a moment in the parting of her thighs, where Sophia could see a wet patch. Miss Sassi touched herself and groaned, and her belly fluttered with her harsh breath. Miss Sassi's fingers were feverish inside Sophia's trembling, swollen slit; another cane-stroke kissed Sophia's bare nates, and she shook too in a shuddering flow of joy which flooded the lather on her shaven slice and made her naked thighs a soapy river of glistening spend.

'Thirteen,' came Miss Letchford's voice, as though from afar. 'I hope you have learned your lesson, maid.'

'Yes, miss,' said Sophia, gasping, as Miss Sassi

carefully wiped the lather from her fount. She looked down in admiration at her own bare beauty; she had never realised the sculpted elegance and purity of a naked Lady's place.

'Well,' panted Miss Sassi, 'I think that is the finest shave I have ever made! You are lovely and smooth, maid – a pity that the hairs must grow again. If you wish to come every day for a shave, I shall accommodate you.'

'Not for a long while,' rapped Miss Letchford, 'for her punishment is to itch as the bristles grow, in the leather panties of a field-drudge! Yours, Miss Sassi ... that is another matter.'

'Whatever do you mean, Miss Letchford?' stammered Miss Sassi, going as white as her stern companion.

'You know, miss,' said the snow-white female. 'Why, Miss Lord and every maid in the room know. The wet on your Lady's place gives you well away. You have spent, Miss Sassi, have you not? The most indecorous of improprieties.'

Now Miss Sassi blushed a fiery and charming red.

'To take improper pleasure with a maid is a most serious offence for a Preceptress or Mistress,' drawled Miss Letchford. 'I cannot ignore it, not in public.'

'I thought you were my friend,' said Miss Sassi bitterly.

'And so I am, sweet Kutti. That is why I am not obliged to place your name in the book. We are of equal rank. I cannot order you to take punishment – only Miss Brace or the Board can. But I can *offer* you punishment – a purging.'

She swished her cane, leaving the Purser in no doubt as to her intentions. Miss Letchford's eyes glowed as red as coals in the snow-pockets of her wide eyes.

'Well ... it is all right, I suppose,' murmured Miss Sassi. 'I admit I did take pleasure from shaving Derrière, and – yes, I did spend. I could not help it, but I shall pay for my laxity. You will please cane me, miss, if – if you promise we can still be friends, and go to –'

Miss Letchford put her finger to Miss Sassi's lip, to silence her. Sophia wondered what she had been going to blurt out – was it the secret of their trips to the village? Without more ado, Miss Sassi pegged herself and lowered knickers, then bent over and touched her toes.

Thirteen strokes of the fierce yellow cane were delivered to Miss Sassi's bare, and the caning took place in total silence. Apart from the slightest of quivering, Miss Sassi gave no evidence of the torment that her blushed fesses must be enduring. When the punishment was over, she kissed Miss Letchford's cane and hugged her chastiser.

'You are right, Miss Letchford,' she murmured. 'You are always right. How I needed that! Now we can be closer friends than ever. And in token of my esteem, please take this.' She thrust the little bag of Sophia's mink-hairs towards Miss Letchford.

Miss Letchford took it, lifted her skirts, very coolly, and placed the muslin bag in her panties, at her fount. Then she smiled at Sophia. 'Well, maids,' she said, 'you have witnessed two chastisements, which must give you a taste for your own that is to come. I shall make my report to Miss Brace this afternoon, and no doubt she will summon you individually. In the meantime, Miss Wyvern awaits: it is time for your labours in the fields.'

'Look on the bright side,' said Chaste as they trudged to the ostler's stables. 'At least we are getting a rest from the classroom. All that book-learning! That isn't what being a Lady is really about.'

'I suppose ploughing fields *is*,' said Felicity Straw sarcastically.

'In a manner of speaking, just so,' answered Chaste with a sly smile. 'By the way, Sophia, do you think the Letch has a pash for you?'

They were in a good mood: at assembly, after their shaving, they had enjoyed looks of awe from the other maids, and certain Riders had made play of scratching their founts, yawning nonchalantly as they did so.

'Don't be silly!' retorted Sophia.

'I bet she has,' said Bella eagerly. 'Look at the way she kept your mink-hairs!'

'Oh, it is just in play,' said Sophia, not meaning it.

'Probably she is putting an old Essex spell on you,' said Chaste, matter-of-factly. 'Did you know that, in the old days, there were more witches in Essex than all the other shires of England together?'

'Even Queen Boudicca was a witch,' said Ransome. 'Julius Caesar said so. Or the Venerable Bede. Or somebody.'

'Stuff and nonsense,' replied Sophia. But as they entered the stables she thought of Miss Letchford's own mink-hairs she had picked from the floor . . .

There were as many maids again as the Riders. They nervously awaited accoutrement for their drudgery, under the eyes of the Preceptresses, including Miss Tunney and Miss Duckett, who eyed each other warily and with ill-disguised enmity. Chaste murmured that pashes were terrible things in the wrong hands. Sophia almost wished Miss Letchford were there – not at that very moment tattling scandal to Miss Brace – to give her an object for her own proud defiance.

Sophia had no time to think about pashes as Miss Wyvern made her entrance to take charge. Miss Wyvern was as striking as Miss Letchford, but where the one was ice-white, Miss Wyvern was distinguished by her very ordinariness. The maids and even the Preceptresses quailed at her entrance; Sophia could not understand why.

Miss Wyvern was of medium height, and possessed of a full derrière in keeping with the traditions of Rodings, but slightly individual in that her fesses did not swell

168

ripe and full like other maids' but thrust up hard and pert, like two fruit buns, or even a young maid's breasts. That Miss Wyvern was not as young as her appearance suggested was confirmed by her breasts themselves, which were very full and long, and hung under her tight starched blouse without benefit of corset or stay. Her mousey hair was plaited in two neat pigtails tied with blue ribbon to match her skirt, and it was this which made her seem almost absurdly younger than her Mistress's years.

She did not wear the decorous long skirt of maid or Mistress, but a short blue tunic with shoulder-straps and a starched pleated skirt which stood out like a ballerina's, allowing a full view of her snow-white frilly knickers, garter belt and stocking-tops.

Her white skin beside the tight knickers showed not a sign of mink-hair, and Sophia wondered if she too were shaven. Her white blouse was fastened with a neck-tie, dark blue like her skirt, and with the golden image of a long ship. Her heels were high even by Rodings standards, so that her gait was prim and precise, and the gold-rimmed eye-glasses perched on the end of her charmingly upturned nose conspired to give her the aspect of a very young and rather awkward junior schoolgirl. She carried no cane; Sophia could not understand how this quaint and almost lovable figure could seem to inspire such awe – until she heard her voice.

'Fieldmaids! Attention!' said Miss Wyvern softly.

Her voice was not raised above a polite conversational tone, yet it was deep and mellifluous, and its very mildness thrilled Sophia with such power and menace that she at once stood to ramrod attention with the other females.

Miss Wyvern slowly walked up and down the line and inspected them, saying quietly, almost regretfully, that they were a sorry crew, and it would take much fieldwork to put muscle and sinew on them, and turn them into fit Ladies.

'Happily, we have no shortage of fieldwork,' she said. 'Today, you shall work on Fallow Field, by the boundary fence. Your Preceptresses shall of course take a dim view of any attempts to hop over the stile to shirk.'

Sophia remembered that it was the very place where their Riders had met in their barn, near the stile over which Misses Sassi and Letchford must have 'hopped' on their way to Great Roding. Perhaps the place was a well-known thoroughfare for escapees.

The maids were divided: they would take turns at ploughing and sowing. It was then that Sophia looked closely at the fearsome array of agricultural implements which filled the ostlery, and made it resemble an arsenal: scythes, ploughshares, hoes and shovels, all razor-sharp and gleaming bright; harnesses, yokes and, above all, the heaviest leather whips Sophia could imagine, suitable to tame the fiercest bull. As if guessing her thoughts, Miss Wyvern said brightly that newcomers must be aware there were no animals at Rodings, as the Board did not believe in cruelty to dumb creatures. Therefore the maids, who were sentient – most of them – performed the necessary work, since their powers of thought enabled them to reap moral benefit and instruction from it.

'Cruelty to maids is all right, you see,' whispered Chaste sarcastically.

Her insolent words echoed more loudly than she perhaps intended. Miss Wyvern did not bat an eyelid, nor even look in Chaste's direction. Instead, she held out her hand, not looking at it, as though to receive a cloakroom ticket; Miss Tunney promptly hurried to fetch a harsh bullwhip, whose braided handle she placed in Miss Wyvern's palm. Miss Wyvern's fingers snapped shut around the whip handle.

'Assume the position, Chaste, please,' she murmured apologetically, looking up into space.

Chaste blanched and looked helplessly at Sophia

before taking a step forward, bending over, and lifting her skirt over her back. Miss Wyvern thoughtfully pulled down her knickers to the tops of her calves, and loosened her garter belt to lower her stockings and reveal a further expanse of creamy thigh-flesh. Then she nodded, and Misses Tunney and Duckett took Chaste in a tight hold by the shoulders.

Miss Wyvern seemed to exert herself not at all, but suddenly the bullwhip was swung high in the air, there was a whistle and a crack, and Chaste's body shook, as a deep red blossom sprang on her naked buttocks. Sophia understood why she needed to be pinioned by the Pres: the weight of the whip was enough to topple a body. Sophia shuddered as Miss Wyvern rested from her single effort, and continued to address the maids as though nothing untoward was occurring. She explained that the Rodings plough was a device whose invention, by the Board, stretched back to Foundation itself, although successive modifications had been made, notably by dear Mr Bucentaur. With this apparatus, the horse followed the plough, and the driving Preceptress followed her horses, three or four to each Pre.

The ploughmaid's torso was stretched on to a bare wooden board, or chassis, with two large wheels. Her legs were held and directed by her horse, as a gardener would push a barrow, the horse being another maid who was harnessed and reined, and whipped on by the Preceptress who held her reins. The ploughmaid held a ploughshare, a curled sharp wheel with which she turned the earth: a human intelligence directing each slice of the wheel was more artful and efficient than the blade alone. Sophia could not fault this logic, however brutal.

Suddenly, a second whip-stroke rang through the dusty èstable; poor Chaste's body trembled savagely as her buttocks squirmed and clenched in an agony that had her dancing on tiptoes. Sophia marvelled that the

171

slender Mistress possessed such strength, and found herself excited despite herself at the spectacle of Chaste's blossomed croup. The hint of moistness between her thighs, as she waited with longing for another stroke, made her ashamed.

The third stroke came and, after what seemed an age, a fourth. Chaste was trembling almost uncontrollably as she was helped back to her feet and led to her place in line. Her face was red and she seemed close to tears, her breath harsh under heaving breasts. Sophia longed to caress and cuddle her, but dared not. And she found herself thinking that Chaste *had* been insolent, *had* merited chastisement, though not perhaps such rigour. Field discipline was obviously harsher, and no doubt with reason.

Miss Wyvern held out her arm and let fall the whip, without looking; it was caught and replaced by Miss Duckett. Miss Wyvern did not look at her victim, nor comment on her punishment, but wished the maids a fruitful day's work, and said that she would be on hand to supervise discipline.

Sophia was to be a ploughmaid, with Felicity Straw to wheel her, and scatter the seeds into the furrows Sophia made. Miss Duckett helped her into her strange work costume, and was rather ashamed, but whispered to Sophia that all maids had to undergo this labour, and that it would make her a Lady – *more* of a Lady. Sophia did not see anything ladylike in her new costume, but kept silent. It was a bizarre garment, all of a piece, and designed to cling to the body of any maid, in order to keep off the mud and smuts of the field. It was made of very thick black rubber.

First, she was obliged to strip naked, and don a pair of heavy panties made of coarse thick leather, which Miss Duckett said that all the maids had to wear, by Miss Letchford's decree, as part of their punishment. Sophia grimaced as she put the panties on; already she felt uncomfortable, even though Miss Duckett assured her there would be little itching, as her newly-shaven fount had not yet begun to sprout mink-bristles.

Miss Duckett showed Sophia how to clamber into the rubber – the garment was folded, then unrolled over the naked body like a pair of stockings, and Sophia found the effect not unpleasing and oddly sensual. Miss Duckett grinned ruefully, seeing her pleasure, and said she was afraid it would get very hot and sweaty, but that could not be helped.

'Think of your poor horse, spurred on by my whip!' she added mischievously, and, remembering Chaste's torment under the strokes of the bullwhip, Sophia thought perhaps she had got the better bargain, even though it would later be her turn to be bridled.

Rubber, of course, could easily be washed clean; leather, not so easily, and her new panties smelled richly of the founts of previous wearers. Strangely, Sophia found the heavy aroma not disagreeable, and even exciting; she thought of the generations of maids whose fount-lips had sweated and perfumed – and even, she started, made commode! – in these very panties, and dreamed that perhaps Queen Boudicca herself might have graced them.

She lay on the narrow plank, which bit into her fount and furrow quite uncomfortably, and her waist and breasts were firmly strapped. Miss Duckett tied a sweat-band to her brow, and then she was given her plough blade, the curled wheel with which she was to cleave the earth. It fitted on to the front of her chassis, so that her arms and weight of her torso were only half-supported by it. Being a ploughmaid would be strenuous muscle-work, while being a horse seemed more humiliating: the horses wore bridle and reins, were gagged by bits and harnessed, and wore only the harsh, chafing leather panties, together with incongruous rubber boots named after the Iron Duke.

173

Otherwise they were naked, the buttocks and shoulders bared to the whip, and even the breasts naked to the air, held firm by twin circles of leather which formed part of the harness, and from which they peeped like cherries in a cake. Sophia guessed that the long tongue of the whip was quite capable of reaching around a maid's torso to stroke those helpless bare cherries. Felicity, harnessed, reined and gagged, lifted Sophia by the ankles and tilted her until her face was inches from the ground; Miss Duckett cracked her whip and they set off.

The work, under a growing hot sun, was more arduous than Sophia had dreamed. She was glad of her short hair, more so of her sweatband, which she could feel rapidly soaking. From ground level, the field seemed unutterably vast, and there was yet a pleasing symmetry in the dispersed ranks of yoked drudges who laboured under the whip, as though a growing part of field and sky. Sophia concentrated on churning the rich earth with her plough-wheel; behind her, she heard Miss Duckett's yells of encouragement or reprimand, and the crack of her lash on naked shoulders, followed by squeals or moans of discomfort. Her legs, firmly held by Felicity, shook from time to time as she heard Felicity cry out after a loud whipcrack, Miss Duckett apparently taking care to alternate her lacing between buttocks and shoulders. Sophia did not know which was worse, and her thought was interrupted by a sharp shock of horrid pain as the long whip snaked expertly across her own sheathed buttocks.

'No slacking, ploughmaid!' cried Miss Duckett. 'Don't think you get off lightly.'

Even through the thick rubber, Sophia's fesses smarted abominably; she consoled herself by imagining the vengeance she should wreak on Miss Duckett's own croup – naked, and bound, and unprotected! – on their next session of punishment under the centaur's arse-bud.

Throughout the ploughing, drudges passed with drinking water. After two hours, there was a break, when the drudges could rest; Susan Westham brought an urn of tea and some currant buns.

'Doesn't your fount itch awfully after shaving?' she said gleefully. 'Mine does – red hairs grow faster, you see.'

Sophia, groaning in every muscle, was not sure whether to admire or sympathise. The pause was short, though, and soon it was her turn to be yoked as horse. The thick rubber came off, revealing her naked body a veritable bath of sweat, and promptly donned by Felicity Straw, the advantage of rubber being that it clung to any maid's shape. Felicity mockingly turned up her nose at the smell, and Sophia said she should be glad they did not have to swap panties too.

'You should be glad!' cried Felicity. 'I've had to go lots of times, and once, even . . . well, I needn't say! But it's not so uncomfortable after a while – quite nice, in a funny way, and anyhow it is the least of a drudge's worries.'

And she rubbed her glowing red shoulders and bum as though to prove what needed no proof. Sophia saw that, all around, the maids were attending to their ablutions quite openly and with no regard for shame. Here in the fields, it seemed natural, and she remembered her experiences on the road from London. So she lowered her itchy leather panties, squatted and, in full view of Miss Duckett's lustful eye, relieved herself copiously on the freshly-turned earth.

Sophia was yoked and bridled, the metal bit snugly depressing her tongue, and the harness fixed tightly round her bare breasts. She was glad of the cool air on her skin, although she dreaded the whiplashes she knew would be her lot. Now she clasped Felicity's ankles, and her brief feeling of power was cut short with a searing lash of the bullwhip across her bare fesses, which made

175

her jump, though the bit stifled the cry that jumped in her throat. She had not known the whip would hurt that much, with just one stroke. What poor Chaste must have felt, taking a whole four in succession, from the cruel Miss Wyvern!

She had no time to think further, but started on a fresh furrow, directing Felicity with twists and jabs to her ankles; the steering was harder than it looked, and made no easier by the rain of blows with which Miss Duckett graced her naked flesh – far more, she thought, than the other drivers. But their force was moderated, Miss Duckett wisely or lustfully deciding that quantity was more important than intensity; she alternated strokes to buttock and shoulder, so that by the end of the first furrow, Sophia already felt herself well crimsoned.

She found herself looking forward to the water-carrier, and refreshed her sweating body with copious draughts, letting the cool liquid dribble down her breasts. There was a break for luncheon, a pot of watery stew, and more tea, and the roles were reversed once more; a further break for tea, and Sophia was the driving horse again. She could not say which role she preferred, for even as ploughmaid her soaked rubber coating received more than her just share of very strong lashes. Her only amusement was observing the fate of all the tea they had drunk, as little puddles appeared beside the maids' footfalls – including her own copious emissions. Miss Wyvern seemed to take a special interest in these evacuations, and Sophia's in particular.

The sun grew low, and finally the maids were told that their labours were at an end. Miss Letchford arrived and joined Miss Wyvern and, as the maids thankfully began their trudge back to the stable, Miss Letchford told them that they would all be interviewed by Miss Brace before fieldwork, on the morrow. She had asked for the most severe chastisement to be admin-

176

istered, and she was pleased to tell them that Miss Brace
had provisionally granted a number ten punishment: a
communal, public flogging. There was a chorus of
rueful, yet somehow defiant, moans, and Sophia felt a
glow of pride. But her own passage was stayed.

'Not you, Miss Derrière,' said Miss Letchford. 'You
are the ringleader of these miscreants – I have advised
you that further service is required from you than the
mere offering of your naked fesses. It is twilight, when
the birds like to swoop in search of the seeds you have
sown. I have promised you to Miss Wyvern as scarecrow.'

Numbly, Sophia followed the two Ladies to a coppice, where she saw a stack of baubos, life-size and
curiously curved, as though the goddess were inclining.
Although these breasted baubos were clearly female,
they had a smaller baubo raised at the fount, just where
a male's should be.

'That is your perch,' said Miss Wyvern in her silky,
menacing voice. 'Scarecrows must be comfortable.'

They came to the centre of the ploughed field; over-
head, Sophia saw flocks of birds. She was made to strip
naked in the chilly dusk air and, with pain in her eyes,
she lay down and allowed her wrists to be bound to the
very top of the baubo, her ankles to the base of the
shaft, and found the smaller baubo protruding obscenely right between her thighs: a perch indeed, but a very
uncomfortable one, pressing cruelly against her slit and
furrow. The base of the baubo permitted it to stand
securely; the two Mistresses raised Sophia until she
hung suspended, more sacrifice than scarecrow, a
straight arrow of quivering naked flesh, with her tiptoes
barely touching the ploughed earth. Both Mistresses
uncoiled their whips and stroked them.

Now she understood why the baubo inclined; it meant
that her naked body hung open to caress or assault from
any side, her front as unprotected as her back.

'How have I offended?' she stammered. 'I have worked well. Any punishment I deserved was awarded by Miss Duckett as I laboured.'

'You have soiled the earth,' said Miss Wyvern. 'You made commode, and more, on numerous occasions! I observed you.'

'But all the water and tea we drank –' began Sophia.

'Excuses!' cried Miss Letchford. 'An impropriety, itself deserving of punishment. You see, Sophia, it is getting cold and dark, and the birds must be aware of a living warm body in their midst to deter them. Therefore we must make your body glow, a beacon in the earth.'

Sophia felt tears of disappointment at this extra and unjust humiliation; her dismay increased only slightly when it became clear that both Mistresses were to flog her at once, Miss Letchford on her shoulders and buttocks – already crimson and smarting from her overseer's whip – and Miss Wyvern on her front! She gulped in horror at this enormity, but her gulp of astonishment turned to a choked sob as Miss Wyvern's first expert lash took her square and hard right across the unprotected nipples of her exposed breasts. It was like the kiss of a viper; shortly after, Miss Letchford's whip caught her full on the buttocks, and her body could not help dancing in the cool evening breeze.

It seemed that no inch of her skin was spared. Miss Wyvern took particular delight in stroking her breasts and belly, and even placed deft strokes at her shaven hillock, as well as giving a bountiful lacing to her tightly closed thigh-tops. Meanwhile, Miss Letchford used her ferocious, mannish strength to crimson further Sophia's squirming nates and thighs, almost down as far as the backs of her knees. Sophia shook and trembled at each stroke, the lashes following in rapid, seemingly unending succession. And yet there was a dreadful excitement in her very solitude and humiliation, alone on the earth with only her searing pain, the cawing birds and the lash of the whips as her company.

Her bottom glowed with fire that belonged to her alone, and her breasts smarted with caresses that were those of the whip, her fierce lover. She thrilled, suddenly, at her power as the receiver of everything and anything the whip could give; a maddened exultation at her utter humiliation seized her. She shuddered, losing all control of her maddened body, giving herself utterly to pain, her Mistress. Sophia felt the hot trickle as she gave way to her body's helpless and joyful insistence: the moisture and warmth of her own body puddled her flesh and the earth below her. The whipping stopped as the two Mistresses watched, gloating.

'She has soiled herself anew,' said Miss Letchford. 'Who would have thought she had so much in her! That enormous bum, I suppose.'

'We must rejoice at her sacred portion, for, in soiling the earth, she has nourished her, as is her Lady's duty,' said Miss Wyvern in a new, kindly voice. 'The earth has her sacrifice, Sophia, and your fruits, your nectar, have enriched her. And now we shall leave you to contemplate the importance of our earth, and our female role as bringer of richness, and protector of growth ... against the thieving birds, the *males!*'

'How long must I remain?' Sophia sobbed, her body glowing hot in the cool lonely air of twilight.

'Why, until I feel like releasing you,' said Miss Lechford airily. 'Or until you may again enjoy the company of females, for your next chastisement! You are learning what it is to be a Lady, Sophia.'

10

The Sacred Pole

At first, Sophia felt a fierce exultation in her trussed solitude. I am alone with the earth of Essex, she thought; I have always been here, part of it. Night fell; Sophia's beaten body still smarted, but its glow ebbed with the waning light, and as darkness came she began to shiver. She at first felt submissive elation at being thus offered to the force of earth, but this too waned, leaving her a naked maid, cold and alone, surrounded by the hostile squawking of birds. She fell into an exhausted and unhappy doze, and was awakened as gentle hands unbound her. Moonlight fell on the faces of Chaste, Felicity and Susan, and they cloaked her in a warm robe as they took her from the sacrificial baubo. A hot flask was pressed to her lips, and she drank.

'A right beast, that Letchford,' said Chaste. 'I *think* she would have taken you down before nightfall, but I couldn't be sure. Where a pash is concerned, you know, there can be all sorts of horridness towards a loved one.'

Sophia was not sure if she liked being in a pash.

'Well, there are pashes and pashes,' said Chaste philosophically. 'The Duck is all right, really. She is a bit soppy. The Wyvern, now she would have left you there all night, doubtless. She has all these funny ideas: it is a Lady's job to suffer and fertilise the earth and such like.'

'So I gathered,' said Sophia, rubbing her sore limbs.

'Pooh!' said Susan. 'You do stink! You are all mucky and sweaty and everything, and I bet your bum smarts like fury.'

Sophia admitted this was true.

'You can slip back into dorm,' said Chaste, 'for the Letch and Wyvern can't admit what they did, you see. Not exactly against the rules, but doubtful. Best wait a while – what you need is a bath. The River Roding is not far.'

'Won't that mean breaking bounds?' said Sophia timidly.

'Yes,' said Chaste, and led her on to the stile.

The River Roding was smaller than she had expected, a silvery stream with water waist-high and perhaps ten feet across. Here, they knelt, and Sophia's cloak was held as she slipped into the cool water. She felt enriched and ennobled as she bathed, her wet breasts glistening in the moonlight, which made little stars of the water-beads clustered around her nipples. Her maids stripped too, and joined her, then washed her tenderly, silently, and she felt like a goddess receiving their homage. Twigs and pieces of tree bark floated in the lazy stream; Sophia, on impulse, caught a large piece of birch-bark, like a sheet of card, and deftly fashioned it into a little boat.

'There! she said. 'Now, where does the Roding flow?'

'Into the Thames,' said Susan, 'and then into the sea.'

'By Shoeburyness?' asked Sophia coyly.

'Yes, eventually, I suppose.'

With a kiss and a flourish, Sophia sent her little vessel bobbing downstream. As she did so, she clasped the naked folds of her shaven fount, in benison.

'Then my boat shall carry me to Shoeburyness, one day,' she said gaily. 'It shall be my *Bucentaur*!'

Laughing, they decided on a swimming race, to the little bridge which crossed the water not far away.

Sophia won easily; she knew they let her win, but

181

accepted this deference as her right. They clung and embraced under the little bridge, giggling. Suddenly Chaste called for silence. She heard footfalls.

From their hiding place, they looked up: Miss Letchford and Miss Sassi were proceeding across the bridge, and towards the village. They were dressed in sober Rodings uniform, but carried cases, and suddenly disappeared behind some trees. When they emerged, they had only one case, and were dressed quite fantastically. Sophia was reminded of some of the gaudy Ladies on bleak Commercial Street.

Miss Letchford was arrayed all in black, her skirts and boots shining as though of some lustrous rubber or even patent leather. Her waist was corseted to a pinpoint under a clinging black jacket of the same fabric which thrust both breasts and shoulders into sharp conical points, like twin turrets. Miss Sassi was in white, her mane ribboned and plaited, and her lips and cheekbones painted bright red; her long skirt was of soft summery muslin, and she wore red shoes to match her lips. Miss Letchford carried both a cane and a coiled whip; Miss Sassi a bouquet of bluebells.

The maids waited unseen until this strange duo had passed, and then without question they rose to follow. They padded noiselessly on the rutted track, keeping the pair at a long distance in their sight, following the river until they came to the outskirts of the tiny village: some cottages with thatched roofs and bottle-glass windows, an ostlery, a few shops and taverns with gaudy inn-signs. It was one of these taverns, named The Essex Bargee, that the two Mistresses entered.

It seemed from the inn sign that at some unspecified time in the distant past, the Roding had been large enough to accommodate throngs of merry bargemen on their way to the Thames. Their descendants seemed to congregate there still, for the tavern contained a gaggle of fair, muscular youths who, if not bargees, looked as

182

though they might be. All were beardless and had cropped or completely shaven heads, with earrings and bright neckerchiefs. Sophia thought them curiously appealing and almost romantic in a gypsy fashion.

The Ladies did not stop in the tavern proper, but passed through the rear door, to the ale-garden, where they were promptly followed by all the customers. The landlord, a slightly more mature version of his customers, with gleaming shaven head and two earrings, bolted the door and followed them with a jug of wine and pewter goblets for the new guests. The ale garden was surrounded by tall trees and bushes; amongst these stood statues of Roman or Greek provenance, naked males and females, or various maritime gods and heroes at the prow of ships. Sophia thought this most cultured for a small village in Essex.

Concealing themselves in a hawthorn bush, the maids watched and, for once, Chaste seemed to offer no explanations. Misses Sassi and Letchford took place at a table, before a glowing brazier of logs, and were served wine, although the males favoured Essex ale.

The arrival of the two Ladies, the only ones in the place, caused much rejoicing among the beardless youths, and it was not long before their table was surrounded by admirers, some of whom were permitted, with a haughtily crooked finger, to sit or even squat on the grass. Miss Sassi clutched the heavy bag as Miss Letchford surveyed their admirers. It was evident that the males wanted to see what the bag contained; Miss Letchford, however, teased them, making them compete to quaff their ale the fastest, or bring her further wine-jugs, until the company was most merry. Miss Letchford crooked her finger for silence and Miss Sassi delved into her bag. From it she withdrew a shimmering, lustrous wig of dark curly hair, and waved it teasingly at the males.

'And which of you maids has earnt this fine wig?' she

183

drawled, at which voices were raised pleadingly, and hands waved shiny gold sovereigns.

Miss Letchford thoughtfully accepted the proffered coins and lifted her skirt to place them in a purse strapped to her naked thigh, for she wore no knickers. The males gasped at the fleeting, heavenly vision of her naked fount. Then she took the wig, and stroked it. Her gaze alit on two of the most strapping youths, whose musculature seemed to Sophia quite well-formed and almost bursting from their skimpy shirts. Miss Letchford ordered them to turn and present their bottoms, sheathed in coarse linen trousers.

She touched their fesses, and stroked the wig over them. Then she tapped each male on his buttocks and said something which was obviously a command, and made them blush. Nevertheless they obeyed. Each of the young males sheepishly removed his trousers, and stood with naked baubo before the two Mistresses. Sophia noted with some excitement that Essex bargees evidently did not wear knickers. The young men's baubos hung naked and menacing, curious pink shafts of flesh with large bulbous sacs beneath them, and to Sophia's surprise they were as shorn as the males' heads, naked like her own fount. The baubos trembled and seemed to speak to Miss Letchford as their crimson helmets swelled slightly and rose, like puppies begging.

Miss Letchford laughed. 'You are frisky,' she said. 'Well, you must fight for your prize! Off with those shirts, my maids.'

The males obeyed and stood completely naked before her, their bodies glistening in the firelight and their baubos now wondrously quivering and stiff. Miss Letchford reached out with the prized wig and tickled the ball-sacs of each male, making the baubos rise to their full stiffness, just like real baubos. Sophia's interest was more than mere curiosity; she felt her pulse quicken, and shifted uneasily in her robe, as her quim grew warm and moist. There was to be a wrestling between the two males, the prize being the sumptuous dark wig. Despite their coyness, the males did not seem surprised by this turn of events, and it was rather as if all were playing their parts in a familiar ritual.

Their bodies were oiled until they shone like pale gold, and then the two males set to their wrestling. Sophia had never seen such fury: kicking, punching, and scratching which left no part of the body unpunished, save for the baubos, which stood stiff despite the ferocity of the contest – or perhaps, Sophia thought, because of it. At any rate, it seemed that the male shafts and their precious ball-sacs were sacred even in the most heated combat. Sophia found it quite thrilling to watch the power of the oily naked bodies writhing and grappling, and thought that bodies so hard for combat must surely be just as hard for love.

At length one of the youths had the other pinioned to the grass and was sitting on his shoulders, twisting his arms in a way that permitted no escape. He was the winner, and rose triumphantly to receive his prize, cheered by his fellows. With great ceremony, Miss Letchford adorned him with the wig, in which he primped and preened for all the world like a real maid – the more so when he was presented with a pink silken petticoat, corselet, belt and stockings, and ordered to dress, which he did with evident relish. He then took a place on a bench beside the glowing brazier; Miss Sassi removed another wig from her bag, a red one this time – Sophia heard Susan gasp – and two more males were selected.

The process was repeated until eight of the young men sat demurely on their bench in lustrous female underthings of different pastel hues, fiddling with their hair, stockings and garters in nervous delight. The process of elimination continued: now, each pair of winners must strip again and fight each other, until only four were left. Then they fought, until there was a crowning finale and a single winner, a surprisingly slim and even girlish young man who had won by his prowess at the slippery wrestler's art. Sophia wondered what the prize could now be, since each contestant was permitted to keep his new attire.

Without more ado, Miss Letchford lifted her own skirts and pegged herself, revealing her croup and Lady's place bare. Miss Sassi delved once more in her sack, and retrieved a gleaming black device dangling with straps, and Sophia gasped: it was a wooden baubo of ferocious length and girth and, quite calmly, Miss Letchford strapped it around her waist. Then she gave a resounding slap to her bare croup, and motioned to the winning wrestler that he should bare himself likewise. The winner's petticoat and stockings were blue; decorously, he accepted the pins, and pegged himself so that his manly portion was as naked as Miss Letchford's.

His baubo stood straining and stiff, an engine of wondrous size. Sophia was awed at the muscled girth of this shaft, and quite unable to understand how such a soft pink thing could swell to such monstrous loveliness. The winner turned his back on Miss Letchford, then bent over and touched his toes, his thighs well spread as though for a beating. She tickled his ball-sac and stroked his manhood, as though making sure of its stiffness, then whispered to Miss Sassi.

The Purser defty pegged her own muslin skirts, knelt on the grass before the young man, and lowered her panties to her knees, presenting him with the sweet smooth moons of her ripe derrière. The young man straddled her with powerful thighs; Sophia gasped as Miss Sassi reached behind her and spread the pink, swollen lips of her precious Lady's place, the glistening petals of her gash! The swollen bulb of the male's baubo touched her lips, which seemed to suck him hungrily

186

inside, for with a single thrust the male had been swallowed by the slit of the female, and all that was visible of his manhood were his tight pink balls.

He lay trembling in this position, as Miss Letchford firmly parted the cheeks of his own bottom and revealed his anus bud. She applied oil to the giant baubo between her thighs, until it glistened menacing and huge, then tickled the male's anus with its tip. He shivered apprehensively, but did not move or speak until Miss Letchford, with a stern and vigorous thrust of her hips, drove the wooden engine deep inside the young man's bumhole! It was then that he let out a moan of distress, or perhaps of joy and, as though to comfort himself, began to buck furiously in the gash of Miss Sassi, while Miss Letchford dictated his thrusts with powerful ones of her own to his plugged anus. Their fesses gleamed in the baleful moon's eye, and Sophia imagined centaurs with whips emerging from the trees.

The male's thrusting grew more and more vigorous, his moans more agitated, and Miss Sassi's buttocks bucked too. The trio formed a monstrous tableau, like fauns at worship, until both Miss Sassi and the male cried loud in their spends. At once, Miss Letchford withdrew her glistening baubo from the clutches of his bum-hole and, taking her cane, began to beat his naked buttocks very severely, with neither pause nor ceremony.

'You would, would you?' she hissed fiercely. 'Well, you'll take *this*, my fine girl!'

She flogged the naked male, still fixed in his spread position, and was quite merciless, not pausing formally between strokes, but lashing the rapidly reddening skin with every appearance of real fury. At each stroke, the locks of his shiny wig bobbed most prettily in the moonlight, and his moans harmoniously echoed the lapping of the nearby river. Miss Sassi scrambled away, then turned round and knelt beneath his balls, clasping

187

the orbs quite firmly and directing the now-limp baubo into her own mouth. She began to suck and lick on the organ with noises so enthusiastic that Miss Sassi might have been engrossed in one of her favourite American adventure stories.

Sophia was very excited by this lustful spectacle – she could not think of it but as a ceremony of pure desire – and allowed her quim full freedom to moisten and drip with her lovely hot oil, as her damsel tingled and began to stiffen. The male's baubo was hardening again under Miss Sassi's vigorous tonguing, and with the beautiful squirming of his naked bum lashed by Miss Letchford's magnificent female fury.

The charm of the tableau suffused the watching maids, and Sophia reacted with a soft coo of pleasure as she felt firm hands around her waist and on her bubbies, rubbing her Lady's place and her already stiffened nubbin. She responded, the probing made all the more delicious by her not knowing whose tender flesh she penetrated – was it Chaste's, or Felicity's, or Susan's? Her nostrils filled with the glorious scents of spring and excited female perfume. She felt herself on heat, like an animal, and it was as though the draughts of wine and ale in the garden communicated themselves to her own spirit.

Now all the males, and the innkeeper too, were bending to bare their bums for the vengeful rod of Miss Letchford. Those attired as females lifted their petti-coats and with squeals and twittering made passable imitations of females in mock-terror, while the bargees dropped their coarse trousers and groaned in protest that their Mistress must not be too hard on them. A dozen hands caressed the soft body of Miss Sassi as she brought the flogged male to a spend, allowing the creamy fluid to dribble over her lips and chin, and licking it with every evidence of satisfaction.

Then, as Miss Letchford lifted both whip and cane,

Miss Sassi passed at a crawl beneath the straining baubos of the others, licking and kissing the hard balls under the engorged members. Their groans redoubled, as Miss Letchford belaboured their nates with her flails, and Miss Sassi cunningly tantalised their baubos with her kisses, but without dwelling long enough to make them spurt. Sometimes she reached up with her fingers and rubbed a particularly stiff, gleaming helmet, quite harshly, so as its owner begged her to 'finish me, Mistress!'. But she would not.

'You all want to spend, my Trojan bargees?' she cried. 'All in my wet northern cunny, eh? Well, you must catch me, and only the fleetest bargepole shall have me! Bend over, now, show me your girlies' bums!'

Laughing, she took her posy of bluebells and stuck one flower by the stem deep into each proffered anus. 'Now you are the fairest Essex maids of spring!' she cried.

The lights in the inn went out, and the figure of a buxom female appeared silhouetted in the doorway. 'Closing time, my dear,' called the innkeeper's wife.

'It is bargepole night, my sweet!' cried the landlord. 'Come join us, won't you?'

'What, again?' said the Lady, not entirely displeased, and went inside to fetch something; she returned with a garland of berries and a flute, with which she adorned the head of her half-naked spouse, giving his ball-sac a playful but quite firm tweak with her hand, then smacking his stiff member with straight fingers.

'Be my Pan, then, sir,' she said. 'What lore these Mistresses do teach us!'

In the darkness, lit only by moon and brazier, she stripped herself stark naked, and took her man's shirt from him, so that he was nude also, and then in a sudden movement leapt on to his lap, scissoring her bare thighs and ankles around his loins, so that his baubo sank fully inside her quim. Like the others, he was shaven. Sophia was agog; her own slit was flowing most copiously, and her fingers at Chaste's – or was it Susan's? – swollen damsel flicked quite feverishly. Miss Letchford flogged the landlord's buttocks with enthusiasm, and he groaned that if she went on, he should spend in his dear maenad's gash.

'Not yet!' cried Miss Letchford. 'To the river! Bring the bargepole! We must offer, my men and maids.'

From the coppice of trees, an extraordinary instrument was fetched, a sapling or narrow tree trunk, with prongs at the end like a trident, except that there were seven of them, spread like an enormously wide garden rake.

'Poseidon's wand!' cried Miss Letchford. 'The position, maids! Boast, you boasters!' At a flick of her fingers, seven of the males – or maids! – jostled into a scrummage, and seven pairs of bare nates were presented, all well crimsoned from their Mistress's whip, and all prettily adorned with a poking bluebell.

This was not enough. She continued the treatment, with one arm caning the innkeeper's buttocks, while his wife bounced on his supporting baubo; and, with the whip in the other, lashed anew at the gleaming moons that the maids presented, until Sophia thought they glowed from flogging, not like moons, but suns.

The cries of the tormented maids were beautiful, mingling as they did the sweetest pain and the sweetest adoration. She felt her own belly tremble and her quim flow with moist warmth, and knew that she could spend, when she decided to release her floodgates. But she felt those tickling fingers on her stiff nips and damsel and fount-lips, with a whole hand – whose? – right inside her wet gash, and wanted to tease herself by delaying her climactic pleasure. She asked Chaste what 'boast' could possibly mean, and Chaste said it was a matelot's term, and very rude.

'It means "Bend over and spread them",' said Susan Westham, with smug erudition. 'How I wish we could!'

'Who knows?' gasped Sophia, as tremors of joy pulsed from her stiff throbbing clit. 'It is moonlight, and spring in Essex, and anything may happen. Let us follow them.'

The others accepted her lead and, in truth, she was pleased that they were on territory as yet unfamiliar to the cognisant Chaste. The party of celebrants was preparing to move; Sophia saw Miss Letchford carefully position her seven-pronged wand, each shaft gleaming dark under the moon, and suddenly the tips were deep in the young males' furrows – she thrust hard – seven shafts disappeared inside the bending males' anal buds, filling them completely! Sophia imagined it must tickle to have a bluebell pressed right inside one's bum-hole. Miss Letchford cracked her whip.

The winner of the contest, resplendent in his – or her – wig and petticoats, nimbly but shyly climbed onto the prong of Miss Letchford's waist-baubo, lifted petticoats and, with knees clasped and feet resting on Miss Letchford's powerful thighs, sank once more onto the prong of her huge shaft. The engine plunged full into the male's anus and once more he groaned. With his hands reaching behind to clutch her spiky breasts for his balance, Miss Letchford began to carry him forward, each step a firm thrust of the baubo deep inside his anus. Sophia imagined it must hurt awfully – yet be awfully nice too.

'To the river, my bargemen!' she cried. 'Poseidon shall follow Pan.'

She handed her cane to Miss Sassi, who took charge of the landlord and his lustfully writhing spouse, whom he carried on his baubo as the merry cortège began its progress throgh the coppice in the direction of the Roding. Sophia beckoned to the others to follow, which they did, grudgingly disentangling from their mutual embraces. She guessed that all were near a spend, and thought that this lightness and delirium of spirit would excuse any seasonal lewdness.

191

Sophia and her maids followed at a distance, hearing them begin a strange chant, to the plaintive whistling of the innkeeper's flute. Miss Letchford whipped on her groaning pack, their buttocks writhing both at the smart of the lash and the pressure of the baubos that filled their holes, and Sophia saw that she carried the weight of the bewigged maid quite easily, with her legs wide apart and her thighs rippling. The maid's baubo was trembling, stiffening again; Miss Letchford had artfully positioned her whipping hand so that the shaft of the whip was clutched against the shaft of the manhood, and each flick of the whip had the effect of rubbing the organ closely and hard, until after only a few steps towards their fluvial destination, it stood ramrod stiff once more.

'How I wish Mr Bucentaur were here,' trilled Miss Sassi.

'He shall come!' cried Miss Letchford. 'He shall grace us with his presence – one of these nights. It is for him that we make our offerings to the river. He shall sail to us . . .'

They emerged once more beside the Roding, gleaming still and mellow in the moonlight. From the trees, Sophia and her maids watched as the strange ceremony was complete; now they could thankfully recommence their embraces and touching, and Sophia knew each maid was flowing wet, lost in her own private dreams of lustful pleasure.

A flick from Miss Letchford's wand, and the males straightened, still with the prongs inside their bum-holes, their cheeks clenching the baubos to them. All stood with organs proud and erect, facing the lapping waters; all had bums that glowed like starlight, in homage to their Mistress's whip. The innkeeper gently deposed his spouse and stood beside them, his own manhood stiff. Miss Sassi reached into her bag, and withdrew an armful of hair. She passed along the line to affix a little tufty wig in the shape of a female mink, delicately to the hillock of each shaven male, above his baubo, squeezing each ball-sac and kissing the tip of each straining helmet to betoken her work satisfactory.

Their whipping recommenced, more gently now, and in a slow, almost hypnotic rhythm. Miss Letchford permitted her rider to dismount, and suddenly began to vigorously rub his organ, squeezing the purple helmet so hard Sophia was sure it must hurt. But the maid rolled her eyes, and seemed to be in heaven, until, inspecting the tip closely and judging the moment correct, Miss Letchford ordered her winner to join the ranks of offrants.

Apart from the crack of whip on bare, there was silence. Caressing each other, the maids watched with baited breath, until Miss Letchford hissed, 'Now! Make your offering, maids of Essex, men of Troy!' And as one, the rank of organs trembled and bucked in the cold air, and spurted sweet jets of creamy white fountains over the waters of the Roding, to fall in droplets and anoint the stream. Sophia thought it the most beautiful sight. Her spend came, making her bite her lip so as not to cry; she shuddered as her thighs were sopped with her love liquor, and she thought of a giant black baubo, thrusting into her pulsing slit and cleaving her utterly, and knew it must belong not to Miss Letchford, but to Mr Bucentaur.

The offrants turned to face Miss Letchford, their baubos limp once more and glistening with the cream they had spurted in tribute to the river. Miss Letchford's face was flushed and her eyes narrow. Her nostrils flared as she addressed them and told them they were both maids and men of Essex, had offered themselves to the waters, and must now show their manhood with an offering to the land. Sophia could scarcely believe her eyes: Miss Letchford lay on her back on the soft grass and lifted her skirts, spreading her thighs and lifting

193

them in the night air. Her Lady's place was bare, and she held her huge pink lips swollen and open, the pink portion glistening like a flower of savage, rapacious beauty against her snow-white fount skin.

'My pleasure, now,' she hissed. 'Each and every one of you slaves! What is a male? A beast that talks and obeys, and ruts to order. A slave of the earth. Take me! Rut me!'

Miss Sassi began to embrace the first of the flaccid males, first taking the soft flesh in her mouth, sucking on it. Then, when it had filled her mouth, she released it and set to a stern tickling and rubbing, which seemed to Sophia most painful, until to her pleased surprise the baubo stiffened once more under this regime of vigorous squeezing, and presently rose to its full hardness.

'You see?' gasped Chaste, four of her fingers deep inside Sophia's slit. 'That is what males do when they diddle. They rub their baubo, as we rub our damsels. They do it to themselves and to each other, but I imagine they prefer it when a Lady does it. We have softer hands, you see.'

Now, the erect male knelt over the prone figure of Miss Letchford and put the tip of his organ against her fount-lips. She clasped his reddened buttocks and suddenly thrust him fiercely inside her slit, so that only his balls were visible, red against her white thighs. Then, with both hands, she began a furious spanking of his bare bottom, so that he was moved to buck and squirm fiercely, seemingly as though to escape the force of her raining blows, but really thrusting in search of the beauty that Sophia knew lay within a Lady's belly. So this was what men and Ladies did, she thought, her quim soaking and longing to be touched.

During this time, Miss Sassi was sucking and rubbing the second offrant to arousal and, when the first had finally spurted inside Miss Letchford's gash, with lovely helpless sighing and moaning, the second was ready to take his place. This was done so that Miss Letchford's gaping red slit was empty for scarcely a second before he was bucking on top of her, and Miss Sassi was sucking the organ of a third. So it went on until all the males of the company had pleasured the writhing Mistress. The riverside glade resounded to the slap of palm on bare. Sophia wondered how much cream the male could contain. It seemed an awful lot, which was nice for Ladies, she supposed.

The hidden maids were arranged in a circle, and each maid had a hand fully inside the soaking slit of her neighbour in this 'ring-a-roses', while free hands caressed naked bubbies and squeezed and pulled stiff tingling nipples with the gayest joy and abandon. Their moans grew louder and, in their heat, they were oblivious to discovery. Sophia was panting with the warm glow of spend, and it came as no surprise to her when the branches rustled and Miss Sassi stood before them, a picture of innocence all in her white girly dress, except for the glisten of spurt on her lips and chin.

'Gosh!' said Miss Sassi. 'Naughty maids!'

Sheepishly, they stepped forward, Sophia was their head, defiantly smoothing her hair from her brow. 'Yes, miss,' she panted to Miss Letchford, 'I am the ringleader once more. However I dare say you cannot punish us for witnessing *this* . . .'

'Sophia, my angel!' cried Miss Letchford, her thighs glistening with the cream of the worshipping males. 'However could you say that? Punish you? You have been kind enough to grace us with your presence. I welcome you to our joyous celebration!'

Sophia felt herself engulfed by the blurred rapidity of events. It was like a dream: Chaste, Felicity, and Susan were all on the ground beside their Mistress, and joined by Miss Sassi. All were naked, now, except for Miss Letchford, who kept her strange steel corsetry with the conical pointed breasts, sharp as daggers. Their thighs were spread, their moans of pleasure unabated as the males took them in turn, swiving sometimes two at once, in slit and bum-hole together. The baubos of the males seemed inexhaustibly stiff now, as though, drained of cream, they stayed erect and splendid for the women's pleasure.

The innkeeper's wife joined in, her husband beaming as the muscled lads swived his spouse, and she tenderly kissing him as he rammed his massive baubo into the anus or gash of one or other of Sophia's friends. Miss Letchford pleased herself by kneeling behind a swiving male and, with expert dexterity, pushed the conical tip of her breastplate deep into his anus as he pleasured his maid, causing him to cry out in pain, surprise, and delight as her vigorous breast-swiving mirrored his own.

Sophia was robed still, but her hand crept to her fount and, at the spectacle of rutting worshippers, she diddled herself shamelessly, bringing herself to gushing spend after spend. She longed to join them, to part her thighs and feel a hot male shaft cleave her flesh, and Chaste and the others beckoned her to do so, their cries of joy ringing in sweet melody over the lapping wavelets of the Roding. But something held her back. The time was not this one. Special flesh awaited her body's precious opening. And a more pressing urge – her Lady's need – lanced through her body. She must be touched by touching others' flesh: by whipping.

She seized Miss Letchford's whip and cast her robe from her. Naked, like a vengeful goddess, she strode among the writhing company, applying careful strokes to buttocks, breasts and even founts. She was afire with her glorious nakedness, and the nakedness of her squirming victims. No croup was spared; already red, they glowed now like fire from her tireless flogging arm, and the squeals of pain were music to her. She diddled herself openly now, the sight of writhing buttocks flailed by her lash sweeter than any baubo inside her, the feel of a neck or waist pinioned by her foot as she whipped its owner's bare nates was sweeter than honey. She spent, shuddering in ecstacy, and felt herself all-powerful.

At last the gathering grew quiet and still; birds chirped, and the rays of dawn were peeping over the tree-tops. All rose and formed an orderly and silent line to make their way back to the inn. Their smiles were the smiles of those who had done their sacred and pleasant duty.

Miss Letchford put her arm around Sophia's waist, and kissed her. She sighed and smiled, then motioned that they must not speak a word of these events. Sophia nodded agreement: how could she betray such sacred rites?

'Still virgin, Sophia?' Miss Letchford said, without mockery. 'I admire you for waiting, the stripping of your petal will be all the sweeter. Oh, doesn't the day smell so wonderful! The sweet Essex air, the spring flowers, and – Oh, Sophia, when a Lady has her fill of cream, of the male essence – when the deep waters of her womb are touched by the breath of the spirit – she is in heaven! Some day soon you shall know for yourself. Meanwhile, it is back to school for all of us. You have your meeting with Miss Brace.'

Playfully, she touched her own, then Sophia's lips. 'Quite a flogging in store for you, my maid . . . on your naked bum! *That* will bring us down to *earth*.'

11

Moonlight Raven

'Well, Sophia, you have been very candid, and I commend you,' said Miss Brace, absent-mindedly stroking the glass case of one of her antique baubos. 'I have spoken with your friends, and they were brave in your defence, but it is evident you are the ringleader. And after so short a time in House! Your name already features well in the Punishment Book – your sacred portion must be handsomely crimsoned by now. My first lacing of it evidently did not deter you from further malpractice.'

She spoke with a slight curl of amusement to her lips, and her eye was merry, as though she did not entirely disapprove. Sophia shifted uncomfortably in her chair, sitting bolt upright and submissive, with her hands around her knees. 'I take full responsibility, Mistress,' she said humbly. 'I am indeed the ringleader, and beg you to visit all chastisement on my fesses alone.'

Miss Brace smiled, and her fingers strayed lovingly to her rack of shiny canes. 'It is not as simple as that,' she said. 'where there is a ringleader, there must be a ring which chooses to be led. And a Lady is responsible for her choices. Did you not choose to board my carriage, in Commercial Street? Have you not chosen to remain a Rodings maid? There is a railway ticket and a shilling for you at any time.'

'Never!' murmured Sophia defiantly.

'Then you must know that these ... "Rodings Riders" constitute a grave offence. The structure of Rodings is a delicate pyramid of power, with the Board – and Mr Bucentaur – at its apex. Any disturbance to the foundations of the pyramid, any rival group, with its own leaders, can disturb the House's very foundations.'

Sophia said that she agreed, but that the Rodings Riders were only a bit of fun.

'There is no such thing as a *bit* of fun,' retorted Miss Brace. 'You are apparently practising to ride the male of the species – a bit of fun, indeed! – and when you do catch one of these beasts, you shall fnd that they are considerably more trouble to a Lady than a bit of fun. You might be tempted to go further afield for your riding – to break bounds in search of willing males – and breaking bounds is a desperate crime.'

Sophia bit her lip; she longed to tell Miss Brace of the events by the river, that she had seen males and females together. Then she wondered if Miss Brace was well aware, and playing a game with her. She sighed. 'I'll take my punishment, Mistress,' she said, 'however harsh. All I can do is beg you to go easy on my – on the other maids.'

'Easier than on you, Sophia, I can assure you, but it will be tight nonetheless. In public – a number ten or eleven, I think. Submission Day is approaching, and I think your misdemeanours were well timed, for the spectacle of a sturdy public flogging will be a fine incentive to the maids' humiliation. And look on the bright side – your submission will surely earn you a place in the disciplinary annals of our House. Just think; in years, or centuries, to come, maids will read of the stirring spectacle as Sophia Derrière is flogged to the limits of endurance, her bare bum twitching in the bright Essex sunshine.'

Miss Brace paused and wiped her brow. She was

flushed; Sophia saw that her words, and the vision of chastisement they conjured, were causing her agitation. 'Tell me, maid,' she said earnestly, 'have you come to understand our ways? The ways of discipline, and the perfection of sound chastisement on the bare?'

'I think so, Mistress,' said Sophia carefully. 'When I am flogged on the bare, there is pain, of course, but also a wonderful joy in my humiliation and the knowledge I am gaining – that a maid's place is to submit, just as a Lady's is to dominate.'

Miss Brace went to her bookcase and took down a large leather tome, which she placed on the table beside Sophia. 'And is there excitement in taking punishment, other than that of enlightenment, Sophia?' she asked, somewhat coyly. 'I mean a bodily excitement, a rush of blood and a pulsing of your private places as you feel your bare nates wriggle at the kiss of the whip?'

Sophia nodded shyly. 'Oh, Mistress – please don't think ill of me – but I love to be tied, and made to squirm under the rod, my buttocks exposed to the eyes of all! I admit to taking pleasure, and admit that sometimes my Lady's place is . . . excited by my thrashing. Cruelty can be very gorgeous.'

Miss Brace opened the book. 'That, Sophia, is the history of human art, hence human civilisation. Suffering is human life, Sophia, and none suffers as much as womankind – that is why Rodings teaches the art of discipline, for only by accepting and coming to relish our inevitable pain may we transcend it. King Alcibiades of Lydia, for example, was fearful of being poisoned, so accustomed himself to swallowing a grain of arsenic each day. It happened that he became used to this dose, and in fact craved it, so that when an enemy did try to poison him, he was made happy! We take the necessary and just pain of punishment, a thing of horror, and, with artful rules and ceremonies, we make it a thing of beauty. To take flogging – joyfully! –

is to rule over the flogging, and its administrator. It is all in the mind, and that is why humiliation is such pleasure to a true Lady. Do you not think that deep in Queen Boudicca's heart there was triumph and joy as her squirming nakedness submitted to the Roman lash?'

The pages showed elegant woodcut drawings of maids in various stages of undress and restraint, submitting to chastisements of the most subtle and awful ingenuity. Each print was neatly labelled with name, date, and offence, with a description of the miscreant's composure under her punishment. The bound folios were in different parchments, and each seemed to have been placed into the book at varying stages of antiquity. Miss Brace had opened the volume seemingly at random: Sophia longed to peruse it herself, eager to find how far back the entries extended.

The first tableau she opened showed a maid, or rather the naked derrière of a maid, who was strapped firmly over a flogging-frame, with her bottom bared to the vigorous birch of a Mistress whose sternness was apparent in coiffure, frown, and dexterity of the rod's application. The artist was most clever in depicting, by line and shade and pure suggestion, the squirmings of the afflicted maid, the swish of the birch, and the flutterings of her lowered petticoats, as well as the strong crimson blush beginning to suffuse her bared nates. The detail was loving and painstaking; there was even a tuft of mink-hair sprouting beteen the folds of the maid's furrow. The caption read: *Eliza Softheart, affixed to the chastisement ponie, to receive 3 doz. with Miss Farthingale's birch, for the offence of making favourable observations on the manhood of the Hollandish matelots, with which Nation it pleaseth our Gracious Majesty King Charles II to be at Warre, Anno 1667.*

The chastisement pony was a curious curved table, whose head was supported by a little stepladder, with wrist-cuffs, and anklets at the base of the convex frame, into which Miss Softheart's extremities were firmly strapped. Her head was supported on a chin-rest, her long hair covering her features which, judging by the piteous state of her flogged bare bum, no doubt expressed a certain discomfort. Sophia licked her lips. Miss Brace ordered her to clasp her hands behind her back: she must not touch the fragile book.

The next plate, much older, showed a maid out of doors. She was fully naked, and seen from the rear, suspended upside down by her chained ankles from the branch of a tree which overhung a small pond. Her legs were spread very wide, and her arms pinioned behind her back by a chain which looped tightly between her fesses, against her furrow and crevice; her long hair was unpinned and floated on the surface of the pool like a lily-pad, while a fully-clothed Mistress ministered to her crimsoned croup and shoulders with a flail of birch-rods. Although her face was not visible, it seemed she wore an iron gag or bridle. Some ravens perched on the branch beside her straining ankles, inspecting her squirmings with mild interest; in the distance were two all-too-human scarecrows. Sophia shivered as she read: *Samantha Allkiss, gagged as a scolde and chastysed with birch rods four and fortie strokes for the horryd sayinge that Pan was a Lesser God. The Yeare 1552 of Oure Reckonynge.*

The next tableau also appeared to belong to the sixteenth century, but was somewhat more light-hearted. It showed a bevy of Mistresses in fine ruffs, bodices and starched skirts, all served with sweetmeats by a maid who was similarly attired, except that the wide pleated skirt was entirely backless. Sophia thought this extremely bold but nevertheless quite enchanting, as the maid was bare-bummed and stockingless in her perilously high-heeled shoes, whose toes curled quite bizarrely. Each Mistress carried a *fasces*, and one of them was in the act of applying the rods with great force to the maid's naked fesses, even as she performed her servant's duties, and evidently admonishing her not to let any morsel slip from her tray. The caption drily commented that Prudence Epping was being counselled in ladylike manners and deportment.

With each new display of chastisement in all its wonderful and myriad modes, Sophia became more excited, her excitement tempered by foreboding, and yet stimulated by it too. She knew that punishment awaited her Rodings Riders, with the choicest reserved for her, as their ringleader, and sensed that Miss Brace was teasing her with this display, or testing her mettle. She gasped as she recognised some of the punishments from the *Essex Boke* she had seen in the library: the Rodings book which she now perused was restricted to the maids of the House, yet complementary to the more general volume.

Here, too, punishment was sometimes referred to as taking crimson and she recoiled in shocked delight as she recognised young maids, naked or bound with only wisps of clothing for their modesty, suffering beating the tattoo or the drumskin, just like the males at Shoeburyness. For this latter, which seemed to be popular throughout the centuries, the anguish of the various maids was the same, despite their subtle differences in hair or demeanour, as they held their tightened bumskin to receive the stroke of a subtle cane directly on their furrow and cruelly tickling the exposed wrinkle of their anal buds.

Beating the tattoo was quite awful; the humiliation of the naked maid spread-eagled on the latticework flogging-frame, with her tiptoes helplessly dangling, in order to receive an artful criss-cross of strokes across shoulders, thighs and fesses, made Sophia sigh and shudder in sympathy. Sometimes the maids were hooded or gagged, or fastened with intricate black straps that cruelly tightened breasts or waist into wicked contortions of submission. Yet beside the flogged maid stood groups of her comrades, wearing the rather curious and daring backless dress; they smiled as though in encouragement, and proudly showed off the crimson which criss-crossed their own naked backs, or even lifting skirts to show knickerless blushed croups!

She reflected that across the centuries, the beauty and pain of the female buttocks spoke a truly universal language. And yet it was a language that she – that her derrière! – longed to speak, a sisterhood of humiliation to which she proudly felt she had been admitted; as she sighed over the pictures of flogged maids, she imagined herself thus bound and punished, and felt herself tingle and moisten. Those maids, Rodings maids, had bowed and knelt and abased themselves for their just training, for the fulfilment of the lash on their bared sacred portions, and Sophia knew it was her destiny also.

The collection seemed to end in the eighteenth century, roughly at 1763, the date that Sophia remembered was the termination of the *Essex Boke*. The earliest tableaux, crude woodcuts apparently from the fourteenth or fifteenth centuries, showed that devices of stern confinement, such as stocks or pillories, were favoured at that time. There were ducking stools, and even a bizarre punishment from the reign of King Henry VII involving a windmill on the flat Essex marshes: a number of maids were strapped naked each to a blade of the windmill, which slowly turned, and as each maid's body passed at ground level, her bare croup and shoulders met a flurry of birch-strokes from the assembled Mistresses. There was also a tradition of birching on pick-a-back, the offender holding onto a comrade's shoulders, or even being tied to her, her skirts up in disarray while the Mistress fustigated her bare nates with the familiar birch-twigs.

There was not just the birch: Rodings, over the ages, had devised an intricacy of restraints which was match-

204

ed by the artfulness of the flogging tools themselves. There were whips, of course, and baubos and canes; Sophia saw maids' buttocks blushing as fiercely as hot coals, under the tender attention of bundled steel rods, or thin knotted chains; some of the flails were fashioned of seashells or woven nettles and ivy, even strung pebbles or, apparently, cured and hardened strands of knobbled seaweed. Miss Brace noticed Sophia's curiosity with a smile of approval.

'You will be pleased to know, Sophia, that some of these antique implements are still extant. In fact, I have a collection, upon which you may gaze.'

She unlocked a large cabinet, and showed Sophia delicate rows of just such flogging devices and restraints as she had seen in the book: Sophia thrilled to think that they were in all probability the very same ones, their cruel beauty speaking to her from the distant past. She still held her hands behind her back, though she longed to caress the thongs that had caressed so many naked bottoms before. As if guessing her thoughts, Miss Brace said she might not touch, but that certain of the implements might grace her with their own touch before long.

'Your bare bottom, that is, maid,' she said softly. 'We must think about the suitable punishments for you and your co-conspirators. It is Submission Day – I mean to make it the finest Rodings has ever seen, and Mr Bucentaur shall be as pleased as punch! Your suggestions shall of course be welcome, Sophia and, although you may pale at suggesting punishments for your own bare, you know that it is a Lady's duty to concur in her own discipline. Think of your derrière as you, yet something apart, and greater than you – an admirably yet unruly work of art of which you are the guardian, and which must be bared to be varnished by the lash, so that her beauty may shine more sweetly.'

Miss Brace pulled a bell-rope, and smiled at Sophia as she touched one after the other of the sinister, beautiful instruments of correction; after a short while, Miss Duckett knocked, and entered, greeting Sophia as though her presence were a matter of course.

'I thought it appropriate to discuss your punishment with your rescuer, Miss Duckett,' said Miss Brace. 'My, Sophia Derrière, you have come such a long way from your sadness in Commercial Street, unrescued, unchastised and unladylike!'

The two women proceeded to discuss details of the Rodings Riders, their confessions and demeanour, haughty or otherwise, and the appropriate chastisement. Sophia agreed that it would be fitting for her maids to appear *very* sluttish, with torn corselets and stockings, blouses smutted and skirts unpressed, and that she would communicate this to them; she was secretly delighted at Miss Brace's tacit acknowledgement of her authority in the matter.

'As to knickers,' added Miss Duckett benignly, 'none must be worn on Submission Day, Sophia, not even shredded ones. That way, an errant, or even a quite innocent maid, is ready to receive a stroke of playful chastisement whenever a Preceptress pleases, or feels vengeful for an instant. The beauty of unkempt apparel is that maids are automatically in error, and merit punishment by their very being. Such lashes are of course unbooked and unticketed, even if playfulness extends to many, many lashes . . . You are wearing your knickers now, of course?'

Her last remark was phrased as a casual aside, but it was plain she had been leading up to it all the time. Sophia reddened, and asked Miss Brace if she was permitted to remain silent.

'Certainly not! Are you wearing knickers, maid?' retorted Miss Brace.

'No, Mistress,' said Sophia.

Miss Brace smiled grimly. 'Yes . . . Your stalwart adherence to your principles as ringleader of the so-called Rodings Riders . . . It does you credit. However, when we have discussed your punishment in the near future, we shall have to proceed to your punishment here and now. Unless you agree to go and fetch your knickers immediately, and return suitably attired.'

Sophia took a deep breath. 'I . . . I cannot agree to that, Mistress. It would be failing my maids, my comrades – breaking my word to them. It would be like . . . sneaking!'

Miss Brace nodded and smiled thinly, then brightened and continued her discussion of the collective punishment. It was mooted and agreed that various punishments should be imposed on the maids, as a delightful exhibition and reminder of Rodings' honourable traditions. There would be beating the tattoo, the drumskin, the stocks, the pony . . . Miss Duckett suggested the ducking stool, but Miss Brace called it a little too quaint. Sophia murmured that it would not be quaint if the miscreant were ducked, strapped to the stool, and then flogged on her bare shoulders and even buttocks, if a suitable position could be achieved, whilst under the water. A heavy steel rod would no doubt have to be used, to overcome the slowing effect of the water. She spoke half in jest, and was both pleased and apprehensive when Miss Brace's thin smile told her the suggestion was taken seriously.

Miss Brace sighed. 'Well then, Sophia – as for you, I think you can guess.'

Sophia swallowed nervously. 'I must kiss the gunner's daughter?' she murmured.

'Nothing else will do, will it?'

'No, Mistress,' said Sophia.

She wondered how her friends would take the news of their planned chastisements, when they demanded it from her, as she knew they would. She decided against asking Miss Brace for permission, fearing it would not be accorded.

'Good!' said Miss Brace briskly. 'I think Mr Bucentaur will be pleased, and I am sure he shall honour this Submission Day with a visit. But in the meantime, Sophia, before it is time for tea, I am afraid we must attend to your punishment for coming knickerless to my presence. As leader of the Rodings Riders –' Sophia thrilled that she used the proper name, without a dismissive *so-called*! '– you are obviously familiar with the equestrian arts. So I think it will be pleasant sport to take you on horseback. Miss Duckett, as the maid's rescuer, you shall oblige – take her on pick-a-back, if you please. Sophia, mount your rescuer, lift your skirts up high, so that I have a good panorama of your delicious bare. And hold on tight. I am going to cane your naked bottom eighteen times, and if you cry out once, it shall be eighteen more . . .'

Miss Brace's cane, her heaviest and whippiest, made a fearful whistling as Sophia clung to the perfumed body of Miss Duckett, her special friend, smelling her sweat of fear and excitement which mingled with Sophia's own. Her body jerked as the cane stung her with horrid hot force, sending her quim rubbing frantically as she squirmed against the thin silk on Miss Duckett's back. Miss Duckett's strong arms gripped her firmly below the thighs.

At every stroke of the cane, she bucked violently, her shaven quim silky smooth against her carrier's straining back, which rubbed her fount and shivering damsel, with no hairs to cause impeding friction. As the lashes continued to sear her croup, Sophia's eyes swam with tears, and she choked back her sobs of anguish; at the same time she felt Miss Duckett's silk become sodden with the liquor that began to seep, then flow, then gush uncontrollably from the swollen lips of her fount as her nubbin tingled at the pressure of her friend's body. She did not cry out, though she longed to; her squirming bare nates and maddened shudder at each smarting cane-kiss were her cry. But when Miss Brace finally panted, 'Eighteen,' Sophia did moan, for her fount gushed hot and long in a sweet, trembling spend.

'Well, if it must be, it must,' said Chaste ruefully.

'It's rotten, that's what it is!' cried Ransome.

'We have to be chastised one way or another,' said Felicity. 'Otherwise it would be improper.'

'I don't care if they chastise me or not!' cried Bella Frinton. 'My bum will take it. I'll wiggle her at you, all crimson and smarting, to show I don't give a fig!'

'It does seem unfair for us to be singled out,' said Susan Westham, 'especially after the Letch and her chums –'

Sophia put a warning finger to her lips. 'It shall be,' she said. 'And it is harsh, but fair. It is the way of Rodings. Look!' She lifted her skirt and showed her bare, glowing from her caning by Miss Brace not ten minutes before. 'I took that without complaint. I was horsed on Miss Duckett's back. I took it because I was knickerless, and true to the Riders! And if we maids can ride, then we must show we can be ridden.'

Glumly, the maids nodded agreement. They pressed Sophia for details of their individual punishments, ignoring her pleas that they did not really want to know. They did want to know, and their glumness became apprehension as they heard their planned punishments, which would take place outside the House.

All maids would first pass a gauntlet of Preceptresses, who would rip their garments from them until they were nude. They would then be bound with varying degrees of severity, with leather or chains, or even gagged with iron balls. Then they would all bend over in line and receive thirteen strokes of the cane on the bare. This was to warm them up for their formal punishment, and there would be a ten-minute pause after this first caning, during which they must squat motionless on all fours, with their chins on the grass. Then they would all rise, and re-form their line before all the House, to witness each other's punishment: in ascending order of severity.

Bella Frinton quavered, her previous bravado gone, when she learned she was to be beaten in tattoo, along with Susan and Felicity. Chaste was to be flogged on drumskin *and* in tattoo; she made a face on being told, but said nothing. Gulping, Sophia described as best she could recall the degrees of restraint – leather, ropes, or rubber – which each maid would have to endure, the number of strokes, and the implements to be used: flail, whip of shells, cat o'nine tails, simple cane, and even bare-bottom spanking with the hand, as a kind of sardonic *envoi*.

'There is one thing,' she added to her dismayed friends, 'but I don't recall if it is to be used. I think it *might* be, as a sanction for wilfulness or defiance. Miss Brace said she would discuss the matter with Miss Wyvern and Miss Letchford. At least it is not the windmill.'

To try and lighten the mood, she described the windmill, adding that she had not seen any of these structures in the Essex of today.

'They will probably build one specially,' said Felicity gloomily. 'Mr Bucentaur is fond of surprises. But what is this other dreadful thing? You *must* tell!'

Sophia had no choice but to describe the ducking-stool, the flogging of a bound maid immersed naked in the pond. The maids shuddered.

'I bet the Letch will insist on that,' said Chaste with a whistle. 'What a fiendish device! Who could have thought of *that*? Such cruelty ... Why, any Lady who countenanced such a thing should ... should be made to kiss the gunner's daughter!'

Sophia took a deep breath. 'It was I who thought of it,' she whispered. 'And that is the end of my story – my punishment. I *am* to kiss the gunner's daughter.'

* * *

That night, Sophia lay awake, curiously calm, her hands cupping her breasts and fount not in stimulation but in friendship, reassuring herself that after her ordeal, her body should still be hers, be whole, and that her spirit would pass through her chastisement gloriously enriched. Gradually she became aware that Bella Frinton was sobbing. The House was asleep; cautiously, she lifted Bella's bedthings and crept between the sheets, putting her arms around her friend in a soft embrace.

'What is it?' she whispered. 'Are you thinking of your punishment? Be brave, sweet. Submission Day is not yet and, in the meantime, we are all spared further punishment.'

'That's just it,' moaned Bella. 'It is the waiting — oh, I wish it were over! I know the other maids feel the same ... It is wicked, but there was talk of defiance, even of escape. Of taking our shilling.'

'But that would be unthinkable, Bella,' said Sophia, slipping her hands under Bella's nightie to caress her bare belly. 'Your friends are at Rodings — your friends *are* Rodings. Think of all the lovely kisses and spanks you'd miss. And don't you remember the scenes by the river? It was wonderful, but fearful too. Think of all the forces there are hidden in the Essex countryside that seems so friendly, the male forces, threatening to destroy our woman's purity. Isn't the House a bulwark against those forces, the life power of the male?'

Bella murmured that there was perhaps something to be said for the life power of the male, judging by their excitement and pleasure at the river.

'It's like King Alcibiades of Lydia!' blurted Sophia. 'He accustomed himself to taking small doses of poison, so that when a real poisoner threatened him, his body was able to cope with it. So must the power of the male be tamed, by tasting it and controlling it. That is why the sacred baubo, with which males are bodily graced, is by us fashioned into the shape of a female. We

211

females may have no baubos of our own, Bella, and no balls to spurt cream, but we can use the males to spurt cream for us. But who needs to talk of males, when we have ourselves, and our damsels who never tire of our caresses?'

Her fingers slipped to Bella's nubbin, and she found the folds of Bella's shaven quim dry and subdued. Sophia resolved to recall to Bella the womanly joy of which she must not deprive herself, and began to rub tenderly. She was rewarded with a slight moistening of Bella's fount-lips, and a tremble in her damsel, as her loins began to shift at Sophia's stroking. Wordlessly, her own hand crept between Sophia's own thighs.

'Spanks are one thing,' she said, 'but the drumskin! The tattoo!'

'Why, males get it all the time, at Shoeburyness,' said Sophia. 'I think. And anyway, what about me? I am to kiss the gunner's daughter.'

'You are our leader,' said Bella, wriggling cosily and with well-moistening quim. 'Your sacred portion is strong.'

'Even a leader can shiver,' said Sophia, and redoubled the force of her caresses so that her shivering would seem to her as well as Bella to be the product of lustful desire rather than fearful apprehension. And as the two maids brought each other to a cooing, gasping spend, the bedclothes writhing like a caged beast, Sophia reflected that her estacy contained elements of both.

In the days leading to Submission Day, Sophia found herself rather wistful; she missed the spanking attentions of Miss Duckett, who seemed to have grown inexplicably distant: perhaps because she was jealous of Sophia for meriting a nobler chastisement than she could give, or take herself. Sophia imagined herself, strapped naked to the gun barrel, and found that her diddling grew more intense as her apprehension grew and the day approached. She rubbed her swollen nubbin, bathing her fingers in liquor that seemed to flow without end, and caressed the globes of her croup imagining the kiss of a cane that was utterly powerful and utterly merciless.

It would be a noble punishment, and she vowed she would submit more than any maid of Rodings had ever submitted. The thought of her complete helplessness and the pain of the lash searing her bared nates as the whole House looked on in awe, made her spends an ecstacy of liquid golden honey. It was in particular the idea that her humiliation should be in public, like Boudicca all those centuries ago. The watchful eye of the centaur's anus in Miss Duckett's room seemed paltry by comparison ... and Mr Bucentaur would be – *must* be – there to witness her utter humiliation!

Her uniform of submission was prepared: she would be knickerless, of course, but had cleverly shredded blouses and stockings, a corset soiled and ripped, and her only concession to cleanliness was in conscientiously visiting Miss Sassi for a sadly perfunctory shaving of her fount. The delights of her first shaving were not repeated, though the operation continued to give her pleasure; Miss Sassi had a long queue of maids for her attentions. The episode by the river was not mentioned, although Sophia once jokingly asked about the fashion in wigs, Miss Sassi responding with an equal pretence at humour that the price of wigs was very favourable at the moment, especially for hair of quality.

'Virgin hair is the most prized,' she said succinctly, 'as it has a perfume all its own. The Chinese in particular are very fond of it. There!' She stroked Sophia's shaven fount to make sure it was silky smooth.

'Now you are fit for your showing tomorrow. I won't have time to shave you – a busy day for all of us! You poor, brave girl ... how I feel for you! How I –' her voice lowered to a whisper '– how I envy you.' And her lips brushed Sophia's in a chaste kiss.

213

After her shaving, Sophia went to one of the less frequented 'fluvia to try on her costume of ripped and soiled garments, and it was there that she was surprised by Miss Letchford.

'Oh,' she said, embarrassed at her semi-nakedness. 'I didn't think ... You, Mistress, in a maids' 'fluvium!'

Miss Letchford grinned. 'Nature abides no waiting, maid,' she said. 'What are you about? Come, fetch a sponge and towel and attend me.'

Uneasily, Sophia positioned herself beside Miss Letchford as the Mistress casually squatted over the gurgling channel, and lifted her skirts and petticoats to reveal her naked fount. Miss Letchford emitted a hearty, 'Aaah!' of satisfaction as the noise of her evacuations echoed in the chamber. Her face inches from Sophia's laddered stockings, she wrinkled her nose and took a deep breath.

'My,' she sighed, 'you stink so, and your stockings are so improper. You are a veritable slut, Sophia.'

'I have left them soiled, and ripped them, Mistress, specially for Submission Day, and my ... chastisement,' said Sophia humbly. 'My chastisement shall be my washing.'

'Your stockings are splendid,' said Miss Letchford, and put her fingers through a particularly dramatic gash. Sophia felt her thigh tickled and the silken fabric pulled, making the rip even larger.

'So splendid,' she added, her face quite flushed. 'You were rescued from Commercial Street, weren't you? Yes, a ... a *tart*, a proper little madam, a whore.'

'Mistress! I was not a whore.' cried Sophia.

'But with stockings like these, you should be,' cooed the white Mistress. 'A filthy, painted whore, like Chaste Marsh, lying on dirty straw and stinking of ordure and cheap toilet water, taking men by the dozen between her bulging cheeks, into her filthy bum-hole and her reeking red gash.'

214

Sophia protested that Chaste was a good maid –
now, at least – but Miss Letchford seemed not to notice.
With one hand she pawed and picked at Sophia's ripped
stockings, and rubbed her nose at the torn thigh-band,
breathing deeply of the perfume of Sophia's unclean
quim – which Sophia had to admit was quite rank –
while her other fingers quite openly played up and down
between her own thighs. As she sighed with the pleasure
of her evacuations and the heady perfume of Sophia's
soiled garments, Miss Letchford was diddling herself to
a spend.

'Oh! Yes! Yes . . .' she blurted, in a cry that was
almost a howl. 'Oh, Sophia, you filthy slut! How I look
forward to seeing your bum redden as you kiss the
gunner's daughter. Yes! Oh, my sweet slut . . . Now, a
sponge and towel, please.'

Miss Letchford stood and bent over to present her
bare fesses to Sophia, who dutifully wiped and sponged
her. When Miss Letchford was dressed again, she be-
amed at Sophia and put a finger to her own lips and to
Sophia's.

'Not a word,' she said. 'You still possess my mink
hairs, do you not?'

Sophia blushed and nodded yes.

'Then you own a part of me, and I am in your
possession, so I may do what I want with you. Don't
ask – you'll understand. I'm yours, Miss Derrière, and
that means I intend to own you, by hook or by crook.
And not a word about the village and the river. It was
all for your benefit . . .'

Sophia's mood the evening before Submission Day was
serene, and after diddling herself twice with full fingers
in her gash, she fell into a contented sleep. She was
shaken awake amid sounds of agitation. Rubbing her
eyes, she looked up at Miss Duckett. It was dark night,
and the moon shone.

'My chastisement, so soon?' she murmured, then looked round, following Miss Duckett's pointing finger. Bella's bed was empty.

'Where have they gone?' cried Miss Duckett.

'They?'

'Bella – Chaste – Felicity – Ransome, oh, the lot of them! They have fled their submission and their just chastisement! I shall be a mockery! You *are* a ringleader, curse you!'

Sophia sat up and clasped Miss Duckett's shoulders. 'Calm yourself, miss,' she said. 'I swear I know nothing of this. Does anyone else?'

Miss Duckett, almost sobbing, shook her head. 'No. I have told no one. When Miss Brace finds out . . . Oh!'

Sophia hugged her. 'My sweet, Miss Brace shall not find out,' she said. 'I am, as you say, a ringleader, and I shall find them and bring them back. They will listen to me, if no one else. Give me until daybreak. I promise. Would I lie to you?'

Miss Duckett smiled ruefully through her tears. 'Only if you are a true Lady,' she said, 'and I am afraid you are.'

The night air was cool on Sophia's face as she ran across the moonlit fields towards the stile. Her anger, tempered with sympathy for the errant maids, was rapidly turning to uncertainty as she realised she had only the vaguest idea of where they had gone. She ran among the menacing figures of scarecrows which seemed to track her with their sightless gaze; although she forebore to look closely, she was sure, and thankful, that none of the figures was the strapped figure of a maid. All she could think of was to head for the village, and the river, where the maids might have sought shelter from the cold at the Bargee's Rest; if indeed shelter were all they sought . . . Her thoughts were interrupted by a startling, 'Pssst!' of a human voice.

216

She stopped in terror and looked wildly round. There was no one in sight save a dark scarecrow. Peering closely, she saw a slight tremble of breath. The scarecrow was human! It was a maid, tethered and bound in a most imaginative and certainly uncomfortable contortion. She was not suspended as Sophia had been for a scarecrow; rather, she was lying on her belly, her body perched atop the pole on a small crossbeam, to which she was strapped. Her arms and legs were bent behind her in a sinuous curve so that her wrists and ankles met above the small of her back, and were fastened together with cuffs, attached to the grotesquely huge iron shoes and gloves in which her extremities were encased. Sophia was reminded of the horrid Spanish instrument of torture called the Seville Boot. Her torso was forced into a horribly tight corselet of black shiny material which Sophia guessed to be rubber, and from which her bare breasts and buttocks bulged most severely and uncomfortably.

To balance her body on the beam, taut chains stretched from heavy rings that pierced her big strawberry nipples and lush fount-lips, all the way to the base of the pole. Her head was covered in a black rubber hood, with holes for nose, mouth and ears only, so that she was sightless. Her head was held up and back by two more chains which attached her grey iron earrings to the cuffs at her ankles. For her further anchorage, the end of the crossbeam was curved and raised, and Sophia saw that it became a thick baubo, whose tip was deeply embedded in the maid's gash, while standing from her bum-hole was a thick plumage of black feathers, crammed fully into her anus. She was fully bound and pinioned, and utterly helpless. Sophia's hand flew to her mouth in dismay. Her own scarecrowing had been one thing; this was intolerable! She must find a way to release her.

'I know what you seek, Sophia,' came the creature's

lilting voice. 'This raven on her perch knows all. *Your* birds have gone to the water. To seek a bird, find a boat, to seek a boat, find the boatman.'

So she had been right! They had made for the Bargee's Rest, to find a boat, and ... what? Escape down the river to the Thames? It made no sense. Surely Chaste and Bella and the others could have simply chosen to take the Rodings shilling, to go outside forever. Unless they suspected it to be a trick, that there *was* no shilling ...

'I shall release you first, poor maid,' said Sophia.

'No!' cried the scarecrow. 'Only a Mistress with a sharp whip may release this raven for her crimes, with lovely, lovely chastisement to ruffle my naughty feathers! Go and find your birds, and let them trap you. Ha!'

The tethered maid flexed her ripe pressed buttocks and ruffled her splendid bum-plumage, then let out a cackle that sounded just like the squawk of a raven. Yet as Sophia sped onwards towards the stile, she knew there was no mistaking the silky voice of the raven. It was Miss Wyvern.

12

Eels

Sophia ran to the stile, crossed it, and was out of bounds. Was that a crime, or a mission for the good of Rodings? And what of the events by the river? Even attended by Misses Sassi and Letchford, had she been improper? Everything seemed so confused. The countryside slumbered under the moonlight and as she retraced a familiar path, her worries eased with the familiarity of tree and coppice. There the river – there the outline of the darkened village – there, the inn with the faintly glimmering light. She went around the back and crept through the bushes by the ale garden, then waited, catching her breath.

At this time in the small hours of the morning, the inn was understandably silent. She thought of the jovial innkeeper and his wife, snug asleep in their bed, and shivered, wishing she could join them, wishing she could go back to . . . to what? To the chill misery of Commercial Street, to the callous blows of Mr Lee, her cruel Master? No – she belonged to Rodings now, and must serve the House, as the House, in its timeless wisdom, would serve her. She became aware of a soft noise within the ale-house, like the clanking of a spoon, as though someone were at dinner. She crept across the yard and heard a low croon, somewhere between singing and humming. She scented food, and suddenly felt cold and hungry as she peered through the window.

By the light of a single candle, a figure was stirring a cooking-pot at the glowing fireplace, upon which a grill of golden pies was set. Sophia was quite astonished, for the crone – she assumed it to be a crone – was fully covered in a robe of dark purple, emblazoned with golden stars. Sophia expected the costume to be completed by a witch's hat, and hat there was, but not the conic one of legend. The crone wore a wide circular bonnet, plump and raised, like a gaudy cushion studded with moons and spangles. Beside her footstool lay a black cane, but it was not a cane, really, as it had a handle in the shape of a golden star, and a golden tip too, and Sophia knew it must be a magic wand.

The witch's face was hidden, all but for her eyes, by a kerchief that shrouded her nose and lips, like one of the desperados Sophia remembered from Miss Sassi's illustrated adventure books. But this kerchief, like the rest of the costume, was dark purple and starred with golden flecks. The pot steamed, and the pies grew crisp over the coals, while the crone stirred, crooning to herself and leafing the crackling pages of an antique leather book. Sophia thought herself indeed in a fairy tale, and was scarcely surprised when the witch called to her.

'Come to me, and warm yourself, Sophia Derrière, and bring your sacred portion with you.'

The witch's voice was a beautiful contralto, deeper than Miss Wyvern's but with the same imperious tone that sang of obedience. Sophia obeyed and, wide-eyed but strangely unafraid, opened the door to the alehouse. She thought the command odd, not because the witch knew her name – witches would, wouldn't they? – but because she could hardly forget her sacred portion, as it was attached to her, and indeed had given her her name in the first place. Sophia *was* her sacred portion – her fesses were her spirit. She would enlighten the witch on this point. Moreover, she was hungry.

'You are curious about my book,' said the witch, without turning her head. Sophia sighed at the beauty of that deep voice, like a cool kiss that hung in the musty air.

'I – I'm awfully hungry,' blurted Sophia.

The witch turned and looked at her, with wide smiling eyes that were dark jewels in a face whose skin was ebony. So, thought Sophia, with a tiny gulp, this is what witches look like. They have black skin, like – like the African prince of my dreams. Of course there is no African prince for me; my darkness is fated to be an Essex witch – a hag! Yet she could not believe there was anything but sumptuous beauty beneath the starry folds of the robe: the voice, and the eyes, could not lie.

'The raven sent you,' said the witch, matter-of-factly. 'She is a good raven.'

'It was Miss Wyvern!' cried Sophia.

'Yes, that too,' said the witch. Come and sup, and you may sit on my knee, maid.'

Sophia did so, feeling firm and muscular thighs beneath the witch's robe, where she had expected spindly frail limbs of a crone. This witch was no crone, but perhaps as young as Sophia herself. She could smell the tangy freshness of the witch's body, an odour that was not girlish, but enchanting and mysterious. It spoke of knowledge and power.

The witch dipped her ladle into the cauldron and drew out a brimming cupful of oily green liquor, which she proceeded to pour over the dish of pies. She placed one of these on a pewter saucer, which she handed to Sophia along with a fork. Then she withdrew from the cauldron a ladleful of glutinous rubbery things which she served on another saucer. Sophia balanced the plates on her lap, and nervously began to eat. She found the food delicious, and her questions were stayed until she had finished every morsel. As the witch was serving her second helpings, she asked what it was.

221

'Pie and liquor!' cried the witch gleefully, as though at some triumph. 'That is what we eat in Essex. And eels!'

'Eels,' said Sophia, somewhat taken aback.

'Jellied. Heat them until they are nice and hot, melting a little, but still jellied . . . an old Essex art. An Essex pie, anointed with the eel's liquor. The eel is a sacred creature – like a male's seed, or his very organ, darting in the warm female sea. Every eel here in England is born across the world in the Sargasso Sea, a monstrous pond of weeds, and swims back across the ocean to spawn. You think me a witch?'

Her imitation of a crone failed to disguise the silky beauty of her voice. 'Because I am dark of hue, and eat jellied eels? Are not all females witches? I am just a simple traveller, waiting for a boat to take me to the sea.'

'At this hour of the night?' asked Sophia, incredulous.

'Boats come at any hour of the night,' replied the witch.

'Look at my book, maid, to pass the time.'

'I must look for my friends,' protested Sophia. 'I have no time.'

'Your friends are gone, because they have gone,' said the witch helpfully. 'Therefore, if they want you to find them, you shall, and you can find them as well here, by the warm fire with plenty of pies and liquor, as outside in the cold. If you are a good maid, I shall permit you to kiss me.'

Sophia felt a pleasant drowsiness, and the witch's words seemed eminently sensible. Here by the fireside she was comfortably far from the cruel world of beatings and scarecrows! And something in her tingled at the thought of embracing this golden-voiced witch . . .

'There is a boat, for example,' said the witch, pointing to an illustration in her book.

The volume seemed like the one Miss Brace had

showed her, except that the persons depicted seemed to be young males instead of maids. This particular print was entitled *The Rudder* and showed a bevy of strapping young males in tight naval breeches standing in a small skiff, with canes in their hands. The object of their attentions was another male, but naked, who was strapped to the stern of the craft with his bared buttocks high in the air and obviously well flogged and crimson.

His shoulders and chin rested in the water, on a floating cushion, and the caption explained that this was the Shoeburyness method of training in the principles of navigation: the trussed young man was the craft's rudder, and had to steer by responding to cane strokes on his left or right buttock, depending on the desired direction. The picture's detail was fine; Sophia found herself scrutinising the trainee's well-crimsoned buttocks, and eyeing with some delight the very tight ball-sac which hung beneath his furrow – tight, no doubt, with cold or distress – and noticed that it looked curiously, and sweetly, like the folds of a maid's well-swollen fount.

That tableau seemed to date from the seventeenth century; the next was a little more modern, and some of the young males wore powdered periwigs. A young male was stripped to the waist and had his sailor's pantaloons lowered, so that his back and fesses were naked while they scourged him most cruelly at the mainmast of the little ship. The piquant part was that the young man was the mainmast. To his arms and legs were attached heavy sails, so that as well as the punishment of flogging, he had to endure their weight; as an afterthought, the ship's ensign flew from a crooked pole embedded quite clearly in his tender bum-hole.

Silently, the witch turned the pages, and Sophia found her excitement growing. Some of the tableaux seemed almost lewd, but their antiquity seemed to excuse that. She wondered if the male of the species were perhaps even more inventive in devising punishments – or lessons – than the female: unless, of course, these punishments had in fact been devised by a female unseen. Certain of them looked as though they had: males were confined most ingeniously in harnesses and chains for floggings in dank underground dungeons, their naked bodies stretched and splayed to the limits of discomfort, their heads hooded or gagged, and Sophia wondered what sort of improprieties the male cadets could have committed in the barbarous centuries past, to merit such correction.

She slyly wondered, too, if such chastisements still existed in the new Shoeburyness, under the benign rule of Governesses, and if she, as Governess, should have the power to impose them. And at this fancy, she felt her fount moisten. There was an added refinement to these scenes, whose details seemed constant, no matter what the century or costume – the costume of the flagellated one was eternal! – and it consisted of various fitments to the male baubo and ball-sac, which seemed to have the effect of increasing their size, sometimes to quite an alarming degree.

The naked representation of the male baubo no longer shocked Sophia; she was perturbed to see the shafts of the naked baubos girt with narrow metal corsets, which had the effect of squeezing the shaft into greater length, and making the domed helmet swell intriguingly large, as though they had become fruits, or balls. The balls themselves were often stretched away from the body of the baubo by a similar metal tube which squeezed their skin container, so that the delicate orbs hung very low, almost a mirror image of the stretched baubo above. Sophia found this awful, but very thrilling, especially as she noticed that in the pictures of later centuries, where the breeches were tight, frontal views of the males revealed swellings no less intriguing, as though they never took off these enhancing devices.

The witch noticed Sophia's eager gaze.

'That is part of a cadet's training,' she said softly. 'They do not wear the *garamanches* for punishment – at least, only at first training – but for beauty. To command at sea, a male must be long of baubo and his eggs must hang low.'

The witch became more animated, wetting her ebony finger with her tongue as she turned the pages. 'See, there is the flogging-horse of Hockley, the whale's back, the Burnham crane.' She pointed to a variety of intricate flogging-frames with their masked squirming victims securely strapped and lashed: a spectacle awful in its beauty.

'Males can be so cruel!' she whispered, her hand idly caressing Sophia's thigh. 'You have heard of the game known as buggerball? A ferocious sport and punishment in one. Like football, but with no rules at all. In the olden days, murder was common, and was of course a felony – at the Board's pleasure – but went unpunished until the end of play. Sometimes a game might take weeks, or months, and sometimes never end at all. See, here the game is pictured.'

Sophia noticed that her perch on the witch's thighs had grown somehow less comfortable, and she shifted uneasily.

She thought the game of buggerball had a horrid name, but was thrilling in its naked passion. The line drawings managed to convey the speed and turbulence of the play, the naked power in the fierce wrestling and combat of the male bodies. The males were contorted not in hatred, but in sheer ferocity, as though the opponent pummelled, lashed, twisted or pinioned were no person, but merely an animal to be tamed.

Possession or direction of the leather bladder seemed secondary to the imposition of punishment on the opposing team. The witch explained that in the absence of rules, there was also an absence of team loyalty, and no limit to the number of teams. Thus, players switched sides according to whim, bribery, affection, or the threat or execution of violence. Buggerball, in short, was a perfect training for life itself. Sophia found the players' steely dominance very moistening, and thought longingly of her own body as prey to the merciless, muscled clutches of one of the virile cadets who sported themselves over the centuries, for the greater glory of the Royal Navy.

The nakedness of the combatants added piquancy to the savage spectacle of male power, as though the spirit's powerful lusts were truly revealed by the baring of body. Sophia imagined warriors in ancient times, before the dawn of history, or even more recently: in Boudicca's time, the Ancient Britons going naked into battle, painted in fearsome blue woad, their baubos – surely erect! – more potent and frightening weapons even than their flashing swords.

'I wonder why maids do not play buggerball,' murmured Sophia. 'I am sure we would be gentler and more . . . tasteful.'

'Would we?' said the witch, turning the pages. 'We do not play this game, maid, because we cannot impose the ultimate submission. We have neither baubos, nor balls. See.'

Sophia gasped. This game was not merely sport, but something more. In the depictions of pitiless detail, she saw the truth of the witch's words.

'No!' she cried. 'Surely not that! It must hurt so!'

'No more than when you maids baubo each other,' said the witch, stroking Sophia's belly, and her fingers straying idly towards the breast. Sophia shifted again on her increasingly uncomfortable perch.

'You know that there are no rules in buggerball,' chuckled the witch, 'any more than in this harsh life. The rules of Rodings are a blissful exception. Males are not subtle enough to appreciate rules, which is why females must impose them on the creatures, often with-out their knowing. Buggerball was devised, or permit-ted, by a female Governess, of course, far back in time. She knew what males get to when they are confined with each other, like apes in a cage, and so she decided to make a game of it. Outside the game, it is forbidden, like most pleasures, in the interests of morality. That is why we females know how to take our pleasures by calling them punishment, or submission.'

The pictures of the males attending to each other spurred Sophia's fount to greater moisture, and she tingled in naughty, voluptuous delight. The males were so strong, so ruthless and . . . hard, there, in their virile places. Their bums so hard, so tautly knotted in the ecstacy of their discomfort, that naked flesh begging for the kiss of cane or whip! She longed to possess such flesh – to chastise young men – and more, to feel their hardness penetrate her own gushing slit, cleaving her to her very heart. She wanted to bare herself utterly to the male force she saw painted, to feel her breasts, her belly, her sacred portion caressed by a thousand baubos, whipped by a thousand rods. Her quim was flowing copiously in the flush of her imagined pleasure.

It was then Sophia felt a definite tremor in her host's supporting thighs. She looked down between her legs and, puzzled, saw the skirts of the witch shift and expand. She put her hand to touch, and felt a monstrous hot limb, throbbing and stiff between the witch's thighs.

'You . . . a witch?' she gasped. 'Wizard, I think! You have deceived me.'

'You insult me thus, maid,' said the witch, gently easing Sophia from her lap. 'It is part of a witch's art to make herself a warlock as she pleases. And by insulting me, you have insulted yourself, your own sacred por-tion, which is *your* art. She must be punished for it. I require you to take the position and bare yourself.'

'You . . . you have no authority!' cried Sophia.

227

'I have every authority,' replied the witch calmly, 'for I have balls.'

She rose, then swiftly raised her robe and pegged herself.

Beneath the robe she was naked: Sophia saw the lush contours of a female's thighs and hips, swelling into bountiful fesses, and all of them a shining ebony black; between the thighs rose a massive dark shaft and two pendulous balls very far beneath. Sophia's hand flew to her mouth. It was the most immense baubo she could ever have imagined, a massive shaft of glistening flesh that seemed to contain all power and all authority in the world. Numbly, she obeyed, and bared herself for punishment, yet seeing no whip. Her thighs apart and head bent between her knees, she watched as the masked witch took a very long coil of golden wire and began to wind it very tightly around her shivering stiff organ, looping it again and again, until a thick golden baubo stood in front of her like the prow of a ship. Sophia swallowed as she understood what was to happen.

The witch took position behind Sophia's submitting body, and with a flurry of her robe, twisted so that the shaft of her baubo cracked across Sophia's naked buttocks with a force so surprising that Sophia almost cried out and lost balance. The stroke smarted abominably; the organ itself seemed as heavy as lead, and the golden stiffening added pain and tears to her flogging.

'Baubo and whip,' she crooned, 'they are the same, and throughout the history of mankind a firm woman has wielded a merciless whip. Boudicca herself whipped, and was whipped. The circle turns, and nothing is lost.'

As though by magic, the gust of air raised by the whipping tool ruffled the pages of the book; they danced like butterflies and came to rest at the very first page, a cracked flimsy thing whose twin illustrations were faded with age. There again was Queen Boudicca: in one tableau, she was flogged and, in the other, she flogged

228

the buttocks of a naked young man, his Roman tunic pegged over black fesses: a dark-skinned man! In both tableaux, she was proudly naked, and her face and sacred portion clearly outlined. Sophia recognised her own sacred portion; she recognised her own face. The witch laughed sweetly as her harsh organ smarted horribly on Sophia's shivering bare.

'It is the cycle,' she said. 'The river to the sea, the sea to the clouds, and thence to the river. The Queen to the maid, the maid to govern in her turn; the ship returns to its maker. Poor maid, you are better flogged by me than by Mr Lee, the Master who wants from you more than you know you possess. Yes, I know all – I know Miss Brace's mind. This, I believe, is yours, Sophia.'

From the folds of her robe she took the bark vessel that Sophia had fashioned and cast into the River Roding. 'It came to me, all the way to Shoeburyness,' said the witch. 'And you shall follow it.'

Tears welled in Sophia's eyes and, despite her awed recognition of her own boat, she had to choke back her sobs as the flogging seared her naked flesh. She lost count of the number of times the inexhaustible witch had lashed her; it must be nearly, or over, a hundred, she thought as her tender bare skin shuddered at each fresh whip.

Suddenly the whipping stopped; the witch commanded her to remain in position and, with a sobbing sigh, Sophia obeyed, trembling from head to toe and fearful of what new humiliation awaited. The golden wrapping of the witch's baubo had stung her more severely that the clean stroke of a smooth cane or whip; it was as though every strand of filament were a whip in itself, a flame that lanced her burning flesh to new heights of pain and – Sophia sighed again, in shame, for she realised that in the excitement of her distress, her heart beat with another joyous excitement that was not pain.

Her thighs were oily and wet: her fount had gushed with liquor at the horrid force of her chastisement, and the unfamiliar thrill of taking punishment not from a lifeless rod, but from the flesh of another's body. She watched through her tears as the witch slowly uncoiled the golden filament from her gleaming stiffness, its ebony glistening in the firelight like a sacred, primordial pillar. The balls still hung menacingly low, but less so, as it seemed the stiffness of the organ had drawn and tightened their sac. Ordering her to stay still, the witch lifted Sophia's garments over her head, and down her arm, leaving her naked. Despite the warmth of the fire, Sophia shivered, even as she felt the soft hand of her tormentor gently stroke her inflamed bare bottom.

'There is no beauty without pain, and no pain without beauty,' murmured the witch.

She began to weave the golden wire with rapid fingers, plaiting and looping it until she had fashioned a solid baubo from it, with the remainder of the filament hanging as long wires. She took the wires and began to loop them around Sophia's back and breasts – it was almost unbearably tight – and with her free hand began to roughly pull and rub Sophia's nipples. Sophia suppressed a groan of protest, and in truth, at this stern massage she found that her spine and damsel felt little shocks of pleasure, until her nipples stood stiff and firm as young pears, and the witch smiled. She took the thin filament and began to bind Sophia's nipples, very tightly and painfully, until her breasts wore two little cones, like beehives. The wires stretched up across her chin, and looped around her tongue, running down her chin to the trussed nipples – thus, with the most delicate of strands, depriving Sophia of speech.

'To cry out in ecstacy is to release some of the ecstacy,' whispered the witch. 'I want you to hold your joy within yourself, Sophia. My flogging has made you wet – you shall become wetter as I punish you further, until you will not know you had such liquor in your sweet portion.'

The golden filaments were finally attached to the woven baubo, and the witch now parted Sophia's naked buttocks – causing her to flinch at the rough handling of her tender flogged skin. Sophia felt the air on her anus and stretched furrow, and knew what was to come – she knew, too, that she wanted it, wanted to submit, and – oh! She could not but cry softly as the tip of the golden baubo penetrated her anus, did not stop, but thrust and thrust as Sophia fought to relax her flesh and admit the sweet invader. At last, she groaned as the baubo filled her; the witch tightened the wires around her waist and breasts, and said she was trussed like a fine bird.

Sophia knew that the witch had spoken truth; her fount was flowing more copiously than she had dreamed. She longed to submit utterly to the caresses and whips of this beguiling voice. She felt fingers on the swollen lips of her quim, parting them gently, and rubbing the soft wet pink inside. The witch murmured in satisfaction, and then Sophia felt the tip of her massive shaft's helmet, tickling the entrance to her Lady's place! She wanted to cry out in protest, that she was virgin, that she must await a fine true male, but her tongue depressor made her unable to do more than moan and gurgle helplessly.

As though guessing her thoughts, the witch told her that virginity must cease one day, and that to be a true Lady it was not enough for her sacred portion to taste whip; her fount must taste hot cream. The witch's long legs straddled Sophia's, cupping them, as a man might ride an ass; she felt the witch's belly leaning hard upon her back and the tops of her buttocks, and then, sliding gently, slowly, but mercilessly, the giant black flesh entered her Lady's place. Sophia felt her wet pink walls give way, struggling to relax and accommodate the monstrous, longed-for invader.

With her bum-muscle, she squeezed the golden baubo in her anus, and found that the same action squeezed the organ inside her, beckoning it deeper, and causing the witch to grunt with pleasure. Sophia squeezed again and again, as though milking the shaft for the cream that should spurt from those tight black balls, and at the same time felt the agonising, delicious tickle of the baubo that filled her stretched anus.

The witch paused in her progress, seeming to reach a barrier; she seemed to draw back her loins; then in one mighty thrust, the baubo sank right to the neck of Sophia's womb. Sophia felt a momentary pain, and then a feeling of utter bliss as she was filled to her brim in her two sacred holes. Her tongue wanted to cry out in her joy; she knew the witch was right, and the flood of pleasure was not spent in mere sounds, but travelled back down her spine to make her belly and fount tingle madly in their pleasure, and the oils of her ecstacy flood her fount-lips and thighs.

Her damsel tingled and throbbed as the witch began to thrust rhythmically within her, slamming the helmet of the baubo again and again against her tender womb-mouth, and at each thrust, Sophia squeezed her bum-muscle in time, feeling the shaft move faster and faster as her plateau came, and she milked the organ until the witch groaned and a hot jet of cream spurted gloriously inside Sophia. She imagined herself helpless in the embrace of her fierce, strong African prince – there was no resisting the demands of her belly and throbbing nubbin – she gave way, feeling herself shudder and a cry growl deep in her throat as her juices cascaded in the ecstacy of her spend.

'Oh! Oh! Oh!' she heard herself panting. 'Oh! Oooh . . .'

And when the calls of her ecstacy had died away, she heard noises, as though others were present. She looked up through eyes that were drenched not in tears, but in sweat, and saw a host of maids and Ladies: amongst them, Chaste, Felicity, Ransome and Bella; Miss Sassi, Miss Flye, Miss Letchford, Miss Duckett and Miss Tunney, and even Miss Wyvern. The room rang with their joyful applause.

Her whole body glowed with pleasure, as if she were entranced. Dimly, she felt the witch's flesh and the metal baubo withdrawn from her, and she was unharnessed, then seated by the fire, brought drink and food and wiped with scented cloths. It was more jellied eels – she thought they were quite nice, really – and Miss Letchford placed a crown of seashells upon her head.

'We shall call you Boudicca,' she said.

'Why?' said Sophia, in awed incomprehension.

'Why not?' said Miss Duckett cheerfully. 'And you must take that as your Name of Advantage, when you become a full Lady. Everything is a cycle. Your deflowering is part of your womanhood; your comportment under chastisement has been observed in my study – you know, the picture, and the centaur's winking bum-hole? – a rather naughty conceit of Mr Bucentaur's. Now you have been favourably examined by the Board, and so *soon*! – your kissing of the gunner's daughter shall complete you. I am so proud!'

Sophia looked round, wanting to hold and kiss her sweet witch – but she had gone! She felt very confused.

'But . . . I haven't been examined by the Board,' she said.

'To be examined by the Board,' said Miss Letchford, 'means to prove one's Lady's comportment under the sweetest punishment a Lady can take. It means to relinquish one's tender flower, the petal of one's innocence, and taste the male's sacred spend, the cream of life spurting inside the womb. And we are all proud of you, Sophia – this night, you have been examined by Mr Bucentaur in person.'

233

13

Kissing the Gunner's Daughter

Sophia's sleep was deep and contented, and after only a
few hours she felt fully refreshed for her ordeal. She was
served her breakfast alone, in bed; around her the other
maids squealed in delight as they vied with each other
to soil their costumes for Submission Day. Sophia
looked around, wondered how many were still virgin,
and how many of the others should remember their
surrender of virginity with such fondness. To have been
taken by a witch, who was Mr Bucentaur himself! She
regretted only not having seen his face, but assured
herself she would do so, when she reached Shoeburyness
as Governess of young men.

It was a certainty: kissing the gunner's daughter was
in some way her last test on her pathway to Governess.
She stroked her bottom under her nightie, feeling rather
smugly that her sacred portion contained secrets other
maids could only guess. The shock of seeing her own
face, her own fesses, on the person of long-gone Queen
Boudicca, unnerved and thrilled her. Was time a cycle,
as the witch – as Mr Bucentaur – had said? And if
Sophia was Queen Boudicca, did that make Mr Bucentaur Suetonius the Roman? And the other maids . . .
Oh, being a girl was confusing enough, without history
interfering!

Miss Duckett attended her, and helped her dress, for
Sophia too must be soiled for Submission Day, her

234

sluttish attire sublime in its impropriety. When the maids had gone to breakfast and assembly – which Sophia was excused – Miss Letchford and Miss Sassi came too. Sophia was ceremonially shaved by the Purser, who trimmed her tresses to a stern crop, and then fitted her naked fount with a perruque of quite enormous proportions, whose mink-hairs hung like matted jungle fronds along her furrows and down her thighs.

Sophia laughed in delight. 'Why, my mink is hairier than my head! I look like a bear,' she cried, 'or a she-wolf!'

'All your quim needs is teeth,' said Miss Letchford. 'Now, as for your knickers –'

'But I thought, on Submission Day, we shall be knickerless,' said Sophia.

'*These* shall be ripped from you when the time comes, maid,' said Miss Letchford, holding up a pair of ripped silken drawers whose white sheen was noticeably soiled. 'They are special – see?'

Sophia drew them over her thighs and fount, and realised that there was an artful slit with an embroidered edge, which left her fount-lips quite visible! The slit extended all the way across her furrow, so that she felt the cool air on her bum-hole, too.

'I have been wearing them myself,' said Miss Letchford proudly, as Miss Duckett gazed at her with some hint of resentment, 'and I assure you they have not been washed. A wonderful invention! Now, a maid can make commode without squatting, just like males!'

Sophia's robing continued, and more of her friends and Mistresses gathered as she donned tattered blouse, stained corselet, filthy stockings and scuffed unpolished shoes. Even Miss Wyvern was there, attired once more as the stern martinet, yet all frilly and girlish, as though butter should refuse to melt in her. She was being prepared for the sacrificial ordeal of chastisement, but

235

in a strange joy felt more like a Queen, and playfully said so.

'Queen Boudicca, I suppose,' said Miss Wyvern. 'You saw Mr Bucentaur's book, Sophia: what has been, and what shall be. You saw yourself in the past. You were Queen Boudicca, once!'

Chaste Marsh sniggered.

'And what is it, maid?' snapped Miss Wyvern. 'Do you want to feel the whip on your bold Essex backside?'

'No, Mistress,' muttered Chaste.

'Then speak! I promise you may do so – this once – without sanction.'

'It's just, Mistress, that every Essex maid knows – Oh, I mean no harm, Sophia – that Queen Boudicca is buried under platform seven of Liverpool Street Station!'

This caused laughter and dispute in equal proportions.

'Everyone knows it is platform three!' cried Felicity.

'Platform two!' cried Ransome.

'Well, I say it was platform seven,' retorted Chaste with some dignity, 'for many's the time, in my naughty days, that I sucked the baubo of the station-master on the track below that very platform and, after he had spurted in my mouth, he assured me it was so. And,' she added most seriously, 'we all know that the only time a male tells the truth is just after he has spurted.'

Sophia said that she did not like the thought of being buried under Liverpool Street Station, or indeed anywhere, and that she would rather they got on with her terrible chastisement, without trying to make an amusement of it.

'Well, Mistresses,' she cried boldly, 'who is to be the one brave enough to caress my sacred portion more terribly than she has ever been caressed?'

There was an awkward silence. Miss Tunney looked at Miss Duckett, who looked at Miss Letchford, who looked at Miss Sassi, and there was no love in their glances. It seemed that no one dared speak, so Sophia continued, 'You are strangely silent – is it a question of precedence? Miss Duckett, who is my rescuer; Miss Sassi, who guards my shaven locks; Miss Letchford, whose own locks I possess –'

'And my knickers,' interposed Miss Letchford.

'Perhaps you should *all* chastise my naked body,' said Sophia, feeling regal. 'And every maid too – then I shall feel I truly belong to Rodings.'

'But who shall deliver the first, and harshest, stroke?' said Miss Duckett quietly, her question diverting attention from the figure dressed in black, who appeared at the doorway to the dormitory. 'There must be a hierarchy, an order of precedence. I am sure Miss Brace and Mr Bucentaur have thought of it. I shall go and ask.'

'Mistresses, Preceptresses, and maids,' said Sophia, 'I know that there must be a hierarchy in my punishment, and I propose the matter be settled by contest.'

'You mean wrestling for you?' gasped Miss Sassi. 'But that will take all day, and there is only an hour to the ceremony of the gunner's daughter. And,' she added wryly, 'Miss Letchford is bound to win.'

'I believe the witch has taken care of it,' said Sophia, 'when she showed me the book last night.'

'You have still to see all of it,' said Miss Letchford sombrely. 'You have seen the past, but the future is still there for your perusal. She felt that *too* frightening.'

'The past shall suffice,' cried Sophia, 'and so shall the noble Essex tradition, a game of buggerball. That is how you shall fight for your privilege, Ladies: no rules, and no advantage! I am sure Miss Brace and the Board will approve.'

'Yes,' came the soft voice of Miss Brace, the woman in black, who approached to embrace Sophia, 'she certainly does approve. The Ladies and maids who have troubled themselves to attend Sophia's robing shall

237

compete for the privilege of attending to her – now, in this very chamber. Strip yourselves and prepare for contest, Ladies!'

Entranced, Sophia heard the soft rustle of clothing as maids and Ladies alike divested themslves of their carefully spoiled skirts, blouses, stockings and under-things, and stood deliciously naked like neophytes in adoration of Sophia herself. Even the heavy, full-breas-ted splendour of Miss Wyvern's muscled frame seemed to breathe power and desire: she was no longer the trussed and tethered raven, nor the fluffy little maid . . .

They all eyed her eagerly, as though, once more, she were to be the ball, and she murmured this to Miss Brace, whereupon Miss Sassi pointed out that they indeed had no ball, nor goal posts and nets, and that anyway Sophia's person was too precious to risk dam-age before the morning's public ceremony. Miss Letch-ford said that she had a better idea, and whispered it to Miss Brace, who smiled in approval and said the matter was agreeably settled. There was no time to select teams, which in buggerball tended to disintegrate more or less at once, so it would be every Lady for herself. And in the absence of goals and ball, the trophy would be the person of Sophia Derrière.

Miss Brace's face flushed, and now took on the lustful aspect of the maenad revellers down by the river, as she outlined the game. Sophia was to be pegged, her breasts, po and fount to be fully revealed, and she was to be strapped lightly between two bedframes by her wrists, her sacred portion facing the ceiling. The aim of the contest was to be the attainment of Sophia's body and her sacred places, and the application of tongue and finger to her nipples and holes, in order to bring her to a spend!

This was to be signalled by Sophia's crying out, and she was on her maid's honour to do so. The female whose tongue touched her damsel at the sacred moment

238

was deemed to have won the contest. After a consultation with Miss Letchford, it was agreed that to speed matters, a player could be forced to submit after a particularly effective or painful combat with another, thus thinning down the ranks of contestants. Kicking, twisting and and hair-pulling were permitted but, for the sake of seemly appearance at the ceremony, Miss Brace regretted that there was to be no gouging. There was a groan of disapproval, until the maids cheered as Chaste Marsh asked if kicking below the belt was all right, and received Miss Brace's answer that it was.

The two bedsteads were brought, and Sophia pegged and trussed, so that her body was almost naked, and the air played agreeably on her nates and quim. Her ankles were fastened between the head and foot of the frame, so that her thighs were spread very wide, and her anus and fount lips exposed open and defenceless. She was not uncomfortable, and found that by a slight twist of her neck she could watch the proceedings quite easily. The throng of naked maids lined up at the far end of the dormitory, and Sophia found herself already excited and moistening at the thought of naked females fighting for possession of her! At a signal from Miss Brace, the contest began and there was immediate pandemonium.

Although there were no formal teams, loose and temporary alliances soon became apparent, as the maids devoted themselves to a veritable orgy of squealing, kicking and twisting, the aim being for the strongest to weed out their less avid sisters before anyone even had a chance to approach Sophia. She saw that Chaste and Miss Letchford were both adept at forcing submissions from the squealing maids, pinioned by their arms or legs, kicked most indelicately, or having breasts and nipples pulled and squeezed in a passion that was lustful only of inflicting punishment.

Felicity seemed fond of clamping her opponents by the lips of their founts, which she would twist most horribly, or even thrusting her fingers or fist right inside her prey, trapping her and pummelling her into submission. Miss Duckett worked on the outside of the mêlée, peering over the flurry of arms and legs, breasts and bottoms, and methodically selecting a maid to make submit and clear her path to Sophia's body.

By the time Sophia felt the first touch of flesh on hers, the crowd had already diminished by two-thirds, as a throng of rueful maids dressed themselves again and consoled themselves with tales of unfairness and cruelty. Miss Brace gazed benignly, as though fondly recalling events of her own, or the long distant, past. Sophia was quite wet with excitement. She loved this game; she wanted to be won, and licked to a spend! She wondered if Queen Boudicca played buggerball; she wondered if Mr Bucentaur would not like to fight for her, and win her . . .

The unruly mob approached, and a group of tussling bodies locked in combat underneath her. It was as though all thought of being ladylike had for this intoxicated moment abandoned maid and Mistress alike, all savage with naked female fury. She noticed that Miss Duckett and Miss Letchford, Miss Wyvern and Miss Sassi, held back sagely, as though waiting for the ardour of the maids to abate, so that they could approach like graceful predators to drink the bounty of Sophia's juices.. The maids seemed dimly aware that the contest must go to the Mistresses in the end, and were more intent on scoring points by simply reaching Sophia and touching her, as though this act would gain them enough grace to retire. She jumped as she felt a hot, probing tongue stab at her quivering nubbin, and heard Chaste's voice moaning breathlessly that she must wet her, let her quim flow and spend all over her best friend . . .

Then her tongue was pulled away with an anguished squeal of 'Oh! My bubbies! Oh!' and her place was taken by another: Sophia thought it was Ransome, or perhaps Felicity, but could not be sure. As the struggle grew fiercer and blows were exchanged, the contest gradually became a free-for-all fight to settle grudges and exact revenge for cruel kicks to fount and breast, and reaching Sophia's own gaping fount-lips became of secondary importance. Those tongues that did reach her were able to enjoy a longer and longer licking, with lustful cries of encouragement or exasperation. 'Spend, my lovely!' or 'Spend, you slut, you filthy trollop!' and both of these were curiously exciting to Sophia's ears. She felt her fount gush with liquor, and started in delighted surprise when she felt a dual assault, with one tongue at her throbbing nubbin, and another poking a good inch inside her distended anus! She began to moan and writhe as she felt the liquor dripping from her swollen quim onto the faces of the eager supplicants at her altar.

Things began to slip from Miss Brace's tenuous control; the other maids of Rodings, hearing the commotion, arrived to see what was happening and, after a perfunctory request for permission, which Miss Brace was too excited to refuse, stripped themselves and joined in the fray. Word spread, and soon it seemed that every maid of Rodings was there, naked and fighting. Even Miss Lord and Miss Crouch arrived from Surgery to see what the fuss was and, after a pretence of disapproval, were soon as naked as the rest, biting and slapping the breasts and founts of their charges. Miss Wragge herself deigned to join, her comely figure trim and dignified but, as befitted her maturity, contented herself with the efficient submission of a few rowdy maids, and a swift, almost ceremonial, kiss of Sophia's tingling damsel, after which she graciously bowed to Miss Brace, and retired.

The spectacle of buggerball was quite enthralling, and Sophia realised why the witch, Mr Bucentaur, had said

241

it was good training for real life – in fact *was* real life. The original maids began to split into factions to repel the newcomers, whose competition they resented; the whole assembly seethed with settling of old scores. Miss Brace was stalwart in her insistence that a maid who submitted must leave the arena, and soon the number of wrestling females was reduced to a few, who began to wrestle one to one, in deadly earnest. Miss Duckett's attention was distracted by her old grudge against Miss Tunney, and the two seemed to have forgotten about Sophia as they writhed on the floor, their slippery bare bodies squirming as they wrestled with no holds barred, despite Miss Brace's prohibitions.

The combat of Miss Sassi with Miss Letchford revealed a hostility – or a pash? – which had evidently simmered long, while Miss Lord and Miss Crouch seemed to be settling some old grudge against Miss Wyvern by pulling her pendulous breasts and tweaking her big plum nipples most painfully, as though to pull her in two, while kicking her between her frantically squirming thighs.

Sophia wondered if Miss Wyvern's very girlish squeals of outraged protest were not for the most part theatrical; she could not believe the powerful Mistress would submit thus if she were not enjoying her thrashing. Miss Wyvern even managed to turn over, so that her buttocks and thighs were spread almost as wide as Sophia's own, and received a severe toe-lashing right on the swollen and exposed lips of her thick pink quim. Her wrigglings and squealing signified great distress, but she made only a token move to escape, and her cries seemed like cries of urging! Sophia was much distracted by this spectacle, even as she felt herself caressed by a thousand petals and borne nearer and nearer to the trembling wet spend she knew would engulf her.

At last, the throng of combatants retired hurt was a mass of yelling, cheering maids and Mistresses, embracing and clapping as the two remaining contestants fought over Sophia Derrière. They were Miss Duckett and Miss Letchford; their combat had no restraint, and no mercy. Sophia thought herself transported to the arenas of ancient Greece, or the gladiatorial arenas of Rome, where naked males fought beneath the gaze of swooning courtesans. Her fount flowed, now, with liquor unbidden by any caress. She knew that her spend could not be long; just the sight of the two magnificent naked females, one alabaster white and the other olive and raven-haired, would be enough to bring her to the ecstacy of her spasm.

But at last Miss Letchford had Miss Duckett down, twisting her arms most brutally, while viciously slapping her nipples and pounding her knee against Miss Duckett's open fount. Sophia saw that Miss Letchford's own fount, naked and shorn, glistened with her copious moisture, and that her nipples stood in the pride of complete erection. Time after time she urged Miss Duckett to submit, and time after time was refused. Her longing gaze met Sophia's.

'Tell her to submit, maid!' she cried out hoarsely. 'I must have you, it is I who must taste your juices!'

Numbly, Sophia shook her head; the contest must be fair. With an anguished howl, Miss Letchford cried that she could bear it no longer, and leapt from Miss Duckett's prone body, leaving her to writhe in anguish like a flapping fish. Miss Letchford's hand flew to her gleaming wet fount, and she began to diddle herself fiercely, as though her pink stiff damsel, quite visible between the fleshy folds of her quim, were an enemy or goddess to whom brutal sacrifice must be made.

She threw herself to the floor beneath Sophia's dripping quim, and Sophia felt her jaws clamp on to her Lady's place, the tongue feverishly licking and poking her stiff damsel, so hard that Sophia moaned aloud and her body began to shudder in spasms of uncontrollable pleasure. Miss Letchford's hands were busy at Sophia's dangling bubbies, taking the nipples between the thumb and index of each hand and squeezing them in intense passion, at the same time slapping the two heavy teats together to make a loud squelching crack.

'Oh, spend for me, my sweet Sophia, my Queen, spend for me!' she pleaded, moaning, her voice muffled and liquid amid the liquor that gushed unabated from Sophia's quim.

Sophia felt her deep voice vibrate all the way through her belly as she pleaded. Sophia knew she would spend, at any instant. Yet there was something that held her back, something she felt but did not know. She saw Miss Duckett rising to her feet, and watched as she leapt towards her. She imagined a further combat: that Miss Duckett would throw herself on Miss Letchford in another orgy of biting and kicking, but no. Miss Duckett's legs only were visible, as she positioned herself above Sophia's buttocks, and suddenly Sophia felt her hair caress her thighs, and her tongue penetrate the open hole of her anus with the sweetest and most ecstatic of ticklings.

Sophia cried aloud, and, as both Ladies tongued her, she was swept nearer and nearer her spend; she reached her plateau; then, hot pain seared her bare as Miss Duckett's palms cracked harshly on her exposed nates, both hands at once, one to each fesse. Her nose and lips against Sophia's furrow, she adroitly reached over her head to deliver the harshest and sweetest of bare spankings.

The spanking was as fast as a blur, the blows cracking like hailstones on her squirming hot bum, and after a flurry of at least twenty slaps, each stinging and crisp and sending shock waves of joy coursing through Sophia's writhing body, she gave way to herself and her spasm convulsed her. She felt her liquor flow over Miss Letchford's mouth and face, and heard her swallowing, as Miss Duckett continued to probe, her tongue to its full depth inside Sophia's bum-hole, and wriggling like a lovely soft fish, while her palms continued to crack against the squirming bare nates.

'Oh!' she cried, long and loud, 'Oh, I'm spending. Oh, my sweet lovely Mistress, I'm spending! Oooh . . .!'

She heard Miss Brace's voice. 'But by which Mistress, Sophia?' she said rather precisely. 'Miss Letchford's tongue, or Miss Duckett's palm? Who shall be the one to lead your chastisement? A chastisement may not be divided.'

Sophia longed for Miss Duckett to spank her for ever and ever – to whip her naked bottom, and make her flow with love until she was a molten pool of pain and ecstacy; at the same time she wanted to feel Miss Letchford's tongue deep inside her slit, while the firm fingers ruthlessly milked her teats of every drop of tingling joy.

'Oh,' she gasped, 'both Ladies shall chastise me, Mistress! I shall take my punishment twofold!'

'Are you ready, maid?' said Miss Letchford.

Sophia took a deep breath and nodded. Ahead of her stood the entire company of Rodings: sluttish maids, a rabble of torn blouses and stockings, some already bearing evidence of summary chastisement, but all arrayed in ordered ranks; Preceptresses with their dangling *fasces*, and haughty Mistresses in black finery. Sophia was pegged, her torn clothes around her shoulders: knickers, stockings, corset and stained chemise on full view, ready to be ripped from her.

Miss Duckett cuffed her wrists behind her back, while Miss Letchford fitted a scold's bridle on her head, its harsh iron brank around her her lips, forcing her tongue down and parting her jaws wide. Then she and Miss Duckett cracked their tools, Miss Duckett's a rustling *fasces*, Miss Letchford's a stern flail of many silver-tipped thongs. The small cortège, Miss Brace at its head, emerged into the bright sunlight of early summer. Sophia blinked at the light, and shuddered at the sight awaiting her: the giant cannon, its sullen iron shackles festooned with gay ribbons, and equipped with a harness to bind her for her kissing of the gunner's daughter. She felt mortified, suddenly, not at her captivity and impending flogging, but at the shame of having to wear a scold's bridle.

'In the old days, they used the cannon to fire shells at the Dutch,' said Miss Duckett merrily. 'But I think you shall stay on land, my dear. How I pity you! Yet how we all love you ... and envy you. Our Queen of pain, graced with the ultimate submission which all maids secretly crave.'

'First, the presentation to the House, and then the cleansing of water,' said Miss Letchford drily.

They made their way around the phalanx of maids, and at each step one of the senior Ladies ripped at her clothing – Miss Brace leading, with a slashing tear to her corselet which scratched Sophia's belly most uncomfortably. With one thrust, Miss Letchford divested her of the knickers she had so recently bestowed; sniffed them, made a face – to the titters of all – and tore them to shreds; Sophia hung her head in shame. At last she was completely naked, save for her gag and handcuffs, and followed the Ladies to the pond. A ducking-stool hung over the water, on the end of a pole like a seesaw, held by three drudges, who swivelled the stool round to the land, and curtseyed. Sophia, facing the crowd of excited maids, curtseyed to her spectators.

The ducking-stool was a curious but simple device, like the bar of a circus trapeze artist, with a rectangular framework above the seat. She was lifted and placed with the bar against the backs of her knees; then her calves were smartly bent around the bar, and her ankles bound to her wrists behind her. Further straps were

246

clamped painfully to her bare nipples and pinioned her torso upright in the frame, so that the merest shiver would cause her pinched breasts severe discomfort, along with a wide strap uncomfortably tight around her waist, which had the effect of discouraging her instinct to draw breath. She was firmly trussed to the ducking-stool and unable to move or, with hands bound behind her, lift an arm to defend herself. Miss Brace asked her if she were ready for her ordeal, and she nodded a firm yes, without hesitation – which to her pleasure brought a coo of admiration from the throng.

'It shall be one minute,' she said. 'No less – for your first ducking. The second shall be of ninety seconds, and the third two whole minutes. You know that you may shake your head at any time for it to stop. Your train ticket to London awaits you, if you desire. But – you know the awful consequences.'

She opened the brank of the scold's bridle for an instant, and placed a sliver of bread against Sophia's teeth before shutting it fast again. She explained that if Sophia bit through the bread, it would at once float to the surface, and be the signal for her immediate release.

Sophia nodded again in approbation of her ordeal, hiding her terror with an attempt to smile behind her gag. The drudges were amongst the most muscular of the poo-skivs, and now they stripped as naked as their victim and lifted heavy steel rods about three feet long. Miss Brace gave Sophia's fesses a last, lingering caress.

'What a lovely – what a supreme po!' she murmured.

Miss Letchford and Miss Duckett together took the end of the pole and swung Sophia out over the pond, which in her terror she thought a vast bottomless lake, although she knew it to be no more than ten feet deep. There was a creak of wood, and the pole started to move, to cheers from the crowd; with agonising slowness, the stool approached the pond's surface. Sophia could see the goldfish swimming in the clear depths which looked so inviting! She felt the cold water wet her legs, her fount and belly and breasts – she filled her lungs with air, and an instant later felt the water close over her head.

The water blurred her vision, but she could see her three chastisants plunge towards her, and feel the waves their bodies made. They took positions to her rear and front, and as though well-rehearsed, raised their rods as one, and began to flog her: one attending to her back, one to her fesses, and one to her bare breasts. They looked almost comical as the rods swung slowly through the water, but Sophia realised their slowness was an illusion of refracted light; in truth, the rods moved fast, and stung her silently and painfully, on her three tender places all at once. She was glad of her brank to bite: to cry out was unthinkable, and she must take care not to sever the precious bread and ask for mercy; she had to fight to restrain her gasps and conserve her precious lungfuls of air.

The blows came thick and fast and, at the end of an agonising minute, she was hoisted to the surface once more, where her joy at breathing in deep gulps quite distracted her from the smarting of her naked body. She faintly heard cheered congratulations, but concentrated on her breathing. She became aware that there were tears in her eyes and, without thinking, looked down to see that her giant mink-wig was still stuck firmly in place. It was – but she smiled at her silliness in worrying about such a trifle.

She smiled too as she realised that the smarting of the rods was fading quite quickly; that this punishment was more ceremonial than corrective. Therefore, when her perch moved again towards the waters, her heart did not beat quite so alarmingly. Now it was to be a minute and a half, and she knew that she could hold her breath without too much discomfort. But it was all she could do to hold back her giggles as the goldfish tickled her, swimming thoughtfully in and out of her mink and furrow, as though unaware of the lashes which descended on their hostess's naked flesh.

Even the strokes of the rod seemed only a distant irritation, now, although she could see from the contortions of her naked whippers and their rippling muscles that they were putting all their strength into the task. She was aware of a sea of faces at the pond's edge looking down into her sea, at this strange ballet of submission in which she was the principal dancer. She wanted to wave at all her friends. But then she wondered if they were cheering from love, or in glee at her humiliation. A scold, a wretch, flogged and bound underwater, unable even to cry out in pain!

The ninety seconds elapsed, and she was returned to the surface to regain her breath for the longer submission to come. By now she no longer cared. Bitter tears washed her cheeks – not at her discomfort, which she could easily master, but at the humiliation. She wanted to be returned to the depths, to join the goldfish, her only friends! And when she was reimmersed, she thankfully realised the true purpose of her shame: she was to pass through the vale of humiliation, and approach her fate strapped to the gun, with wisdom and pride and serenity in her heart. She would show them that a Queen could take the most shameful chastisement yet show the finest humility! And when her ordeal was finally over, and she was unbranked and unbound, and led dripping wet to the great cannon, for the nobler ordeal to come, the cheers were not of derision, but of admiration.

A leather cushion lay on the bare of the cannon; she was gently lifted with her belly on this support, so that her bottom and thighs were thrust high, even grotesquely, up in the air, their bold innocence beseeching the sternest flagellation. Her ankles and wrists were bound separately underneath the vast cylinder, forcing her legs and arms tightly against its cold bulk. She looked up and saw it stretch to the sky, to the very horizon, as though she were riding a huge baubo! And, to her shock, the thought gave her a little tickle in her belly – she felt her damsel press against the harsh grainy steel, and start to tingle as her fount spoke to her with shy droplets of moisture. She would be punished dry, but her excitement would bathe the gun.

The maids now formed a circle around her captive station: she would see the faces of her friends, and they would observe hers as she took her punishment. Miss Brace offered her a leather bit, and put a smaller cushion under her chin, explaining that as she thrashed under the pain of her flogging, she must not crack her chin on the metal.

Sophia shivered: she had known the flogging would be horrid, but this small chilling detail brought home to her just how much pain her helpless bared body was to take. Miss Brace announced briefly that Sophia was guilty of a terrible crime, that of proposing her own authority in place of the lawful Board of Rodings, that she accepted her punishment, and that her error was the result of momentary delusion, which her chastisement should cleanse. She sounded as if she were reading by rote, and Sophia knew that her purpose was deeper, that her punishment was a ritual purgation, a sacrifice and a blessing – just as the Board had orchestrated her blessing by the sacrifice of her maidenhood to Mr Bucentaur.

Still, despite the faces smiling encouragement, she felt very lonely and very helpless. Her straps bit her flesh; she saw Miss Duckett and Miss Letchford swish their implements in the air to test them, and felt awfully afraid. Both the *fasces* and the flail were much longer than the everyday ones she had seen. The rods of the *fasces*, and the flail's thongs, were polished like jewels. She inspected the watching faces, smiling of course, but still sombre and as fearful as her own. Some of the

Mistresses and Preceptresses stood behind her, out of her vision. Even so, there seemed to be one extra, a veiled Lady whose robe of golden sparkling stars was hidden behind a cluster of Preceptresses, yet stood unmistakably out among their black dresses. The Mistress clutched a leather book, like a large purse. Sophia looked at the piercing eyes, and started; behind the veil was dark skin – it must be Mr Bucentaur!

'Ready, Sophia?' said Miss Brace in a kind but sorrowful voice. 'You know you have volunteered to take double chastisement, to maintain the affection of both Ladies. It is a noble choice. Do you hold to it?'

Sophia nodded gravely.

'Very well. You shall be beaten on the buttocks first – including the backs of your thighs – then the shoulders, then the buttocks once more, and so on, alternating strokes between each chastisant.'

'How ... how many strokes must I take, then, Mistress?' asked Sophia, mumbling through her bit.

'Why, maid, this is a number thirteen punishment,' said Miss Brace. 'There is no limit, either in time or in quantity. You shall take as many as are given!'

She pushed the bit firmly into Sophia's mouth, gagging her, and signalled for the whipping to begin.

Sophia's still-wet body jumped sharply as the first strokes lashed her in quick succession; then, without a pause, there were two more strokes, and two more ... A deep moan welled from her throat, a moan of anguish and despair that seemed to fill her whole belly. Thereafter she was silent. The sun was high in the sky; as the whipping continued in hideous silence, she saw the sun start to go down with the passage of time. She had no knowledge nor care of time; all was irrelevant save for the pain that seared her naked body, more awful and more cruel than any flogging she had ever taken. Thought left her: the idea of dropping the bit she clenched so fiercely never occurred to her. There was only the sky, the sun, and an ocean of pain.

251

Three times she fainted; three times, in silence, she was wakened by a bucket of icy water, and given to drink. After her third faint, she heard Miss Brace order that the punishment should be complete in ten more strokes from each Lady. Ten more! It might have been a thousand more, so distant did the prospect of pain's ceasing seem to Sophia.

Suddenly, through dim, tear-blurred eyes, she saw a commotion, and heard voices: there was a harsh male voice, and one she recognised. She squinted through her pain and her heart leapt even more than at the whip-strokes: it was the horrid figure of her long-forgotten Master, Mr Lee! Vaguely, she heard him cry that he had tracked her down to this place, that Sophia Longshanks was his property, and he would claim her by the laws of England. There was protest and refusal; Sophia's whipping did not stop, but the rhythm of the strokes faltered. Mr Lee shrieked that he would not let a gaggle of silly females damage his property, and that if any resisted she should be spanked as severely as his bonded servant Sophia.

Then another, softer male voice interrupted, and said that this was Essex, and the laws that applied were of an older and truer England. It was Mr Bucentaur!

'You jackanapes!' cried Mr Lee. 'I have my deeds, my book, to prove it. What does a creature like you know of the laws of England?'

'We have our own book,' said Mr Bucentaur calmly, and showed his book at a distance to Mr Lee.

'What? Stuff and nonsense! Romans? Britons? Queen Boudicca? You are nothing but criminals, kidnappers!'

'Technically speaking, it is you who are Miss Sophia's property, sir,' said Mr Bucentaur, 'and all that is in the county of Essex, if we were to stretch the point. She can have you despatched with any torment she chooses to impose! However, your immediate departure, and promise to desist from further nuisance, will no doubt be satisfactory.'

Suddenly the whipping stopped. There were squeals from Miss Duckett and Miss Letchford. Sophia was confused, but heard Mr Lee cry for her to be released.

And then Mr Bucentaur's voice became a lion's roar. 'Sir, no gentleman strikes a Lady!'

Mr Bucentaur's sparkling robe was cast aside and, a naked black blur, he leapt from amongst the Ladies and pinioned Mr Lee to the ground. Mr Lee was strong, and resisted, so that for a few minutes the dust rose around the struggling naked body of Mr Bucentaur – witch, and Chairman of the Rodings Board! – and the villainous intruder. Despite her pain, Sophia thought the spectacle thrilling: two males, one gorgeously black and naked, struggling to possess her! Even in the confusion, she could see that Mr Bucentaur's baubo was as massive and exciting in its floppy state as when it had penetrated her in erection.

She wondered if the size of a male's baubo betokened savagery and prowess at fighting: certainly, in Mr Bucentaur's case it did, and it must betoken wisdom too, or how could he become such a beautiful witch and tender lover? Mr Bucentaur – her Mr Bucentaur – vigorously thrashed the intruder until his cries died to a whimper, and he was vanquished. Mr Bucentaur picked him up by the scruff of the neck, and dragged him to Sophia's side.

'The usurper is yours, Mistress,' he said. 'Command his fate.'

He called her Mistress!

'My punishment is not over,' she said weakly, but gathering a new strength with her excitement. 'There are four strokes to go. I . . . I was counting. I must take them.'

'Only four,' whispered Mr Bucentaur. 'You shall marvel when you hear, later, how many your poor noble bare has already taken. Your body glows like moon, sun and stars together, Mistress. But you shall have your four.'

With that, Mr Bucentaur spanked her four times in quick succession, with the lightest of taps, but letting his bare palm linger and stroke her naked bottom. His touch was cool and pure, and all the pain that seared her seemed to melt by magic at his touch.

'There!' he said with a chuckle. 'The punishment is at an end, and Sophia Derrière has kissed the gunner's daughter!'

To the tumultuous cheers of the whole House, Sophia was unbound, bathed and scented, and placed face down on a bed of goosedown, where her beaten body was anointed with healing unguents and swathed in the softest silk.

'What shall we do with the miscreant, Mistress?' said Miss Brace.

'You, too, call me Mistress,' said Sophia in wonderment. 'Mr Lee – well, the Preceptresses may whip him soundly with rod and *fasces*, then give him to my Rodings Riders to train. Chaste, you shall take charge of matters – ride him, and thrash him, and show him who is Mistress, and when you have had enough sport, cast him into the River Roding, and let him swim back to his den in Limehouse.'

Sophia was carried across the fields and over the stile, to the ale house, the Bargee's Rest. There, a feast awaited them; she was crowned with flowers and berries, and maids and Ladies danced at the pole for her. The pain of her flogging ebbed quickly with the soothing ointments; she was left with a glow of satisfied joy at her bravery, and the joy it gave to others. She watched the dancing and feasting, and Mr Bucentaur, robed again in his witch's costume, said that at last she might peruse the Long Book.

She looked, and saw punishments and trials and submissions of ages long past, and then wondered, for the closure of the book contained pictures with no date and no inscription. She saw maids and Ladies and males

254

naked, or in strange costumes, together at sport or
adoration of the river, or at chastisement, and all three
were often the same. And she saw herself! Now sump-
tuously arrayed in silks and brocaded satin, now magnificent in shining black leathers and gleaming silver
studs and chains, but always with whip or cane, and
always administering chastisement to a naked female or
male bottom. One of the male bottoms was full and
sweet as twin moons, and was ebony black.

'There is, you see, a vacancy for Governess at Shoeburyness,' said Mr Bucentaur, 'and the Board has
decided you must fill it, Mistress. Of course you will
have to start at the bottom, as it were.'

Sophia blurted joyfully that she agreed.

'Then we shall proceed there at once in your barge,'
said Mr Bucentaur. 'Your Royal Barge, that is, that has
plied the waters of the Roding ever since . . .'

Behind the trees, nestling in the water, Sophia saw a
glorious vessel, shaped as the magnificent curving hillocks of a naked female body, hung with crimson and
purple silks and pennants; her prow a carved, massive
naked female, brandishing a whip and a tricorn, her
buttocks and breasts proud and thrusting. It must be
Queen Boudicca!

'. . . shall I say, ever since your last visit?' whispered
the witch, Mr Bucentaur.

Every maid and Lady of Rodings was there to kiss
her and give their obeisance. The barge was ready to
cast off, when Miss Brace interrupted her farewell kisses
to tell Sophia that she had not yet chosen her Lady's
Name of Advantage, and must do so.

'I think there are no prizes for guessing what it is,' she
added coyly, glancing at the prow of Sophia's barge,
where the three drudges who had flogged her under the
water now awaited, dressed sweetly as maids of ancient
Troy, to guide her through the soft Essex air.

Sophia stood.

'I shall take my Name of Advantage,' she said solemnly to the hushed maenads, 'and it shall be a name whose beauty and wisdom has graced the world through all the centuries past, and all the centuries to come. The beauty of the female is the eternal principle, the beauty of her derrière the fruit and the sea and the spirit of all life. My Name of Advantage shall be my Name of Rescue . . . Sophia Derrière. And, advantaged as Sophia Derrière, it shall be my first task to right an old wrong, an old impropriety committed by one Lady against another. Miss Brace, you will please take the position. Make submission by bending over and raising your skirts, then lower your knickers and show your assembled Ladies your naked bottom.'

On the cushions of Sophia's barge lay the bright green rods of her new *fasces*. Sophia picked it up, and caressed the instrument with love. She had expected Miss Brace to bluster or protest, and was pleased that Miss Brace smiled wryly and did as she was told.

'So, Mistress Sophia,' she said, 'you have detected an impropriety in me, and I am to receive my just reward.'

'It is an unpaid debt, High Mistress,' said Sophia. 'I have observed your . . . your phrenology, Miss Brace, from a discreet maid's distance. I note a distressing bump. When I was admitted to House, you promised me a cup of cocoa on that first evening, yet I have still to receive it. I absolve you of the debt, but not of your correction.'

'Nor should I be absolved,' said Miss Brace. 'How the breeze tickles my bare! It has been such a long time . . .'

'Thirteen with my rods should tickle you most warmly, High Mistress,' said Sophia, lifting her flogging tool.

'Oh, Sophia,' said Miss Brace faintly, 'I don't think thirteen would warm me half enough.'

Miss Brace's trembling bare buttocks were well crimsoned with over thirty stroke of the rods before Sophia saw her shudder, and her belly flutter, and heard her

256

moan in pleasure as her naked thighs shone with her oily liquor. Sophia lowered her fasces, and stroked the squirming woman's bare nates, and kissed her, happy that she had brought the High Mistress of Rodings to a spend. Now she could embark.

Sophia lay on her cushions, and raised her *fasces*. The barge began its stately glide, taking Sophia, its Mistress, down the River Roding towards the sea.

Envoi

'My first day as Governess,' huffed Sophia, 'and already a miscreant for chastisement! How naughty males are!'

Secretly pleased, she glanced around her spacious study: the white walls and ceilings, the rosewood chairs and tables, the leather armchairs and sofas, the racks of canes and delicately carved baubos ...

'Come in,' she rapped at the nervous scratching on the door, then lowered her eyes to her paperwork. She was writing a memorandum indicating her extreme disapproval of pashes – unless (this was none-too-subtly hinted) they were directed at her own person.

Without looking up, she said, 'Whoever you are, cadet, you will please lower your breeches and take them off – knickers too, if you are wearing any, and show me your bared bottom, over the armchair by the fire. Spread your legs wide and stand on tiptoe until I am ready for you. I think I'll skin you nice and slowly with a good thirteen on the bare – I'm *sure* you've been a naughty boy – and, as I do that, you can tell me just how naughty you have been, and we shall discuss your further punishment. Make sure you fold your lovely uniform carefully, now. I shall inspect it later, and I hope it is spanking clean, for I abhor smuttiness in males – I mean, in all things.'

When she had finished with her papers, she put her pen away, reached for her cane – a stout four-foot yew

– and stood up. Before her stood, on tiptoe, the entirely nude body of the loveliest and most submissive male she could imagine. His massive baubo dangled tempting and devastating between his muscled thighs; his body was ebony dark; he was . . . her African prince!

The cadet looked up and smiled. 'Now you can see my face, Mistress.'

'Mr Bucentaur! I can see more . . . what . . . Oh!'

Quite overcome, she felt her belly and quim flutter. 'Where do you come from, sir?' she blurted. 'Are you an African prince, in truth? Tell me!'

'I am, as it happens, Mistress, and have committed many naughtinesses in my princely career. But I am afraid you shall have to beat the details out of my poor fesses, and it will take many visits to your study until I have told all.'

Sophia lifted her cane and swished the air, making him involuntarily clench his naked fesses.

'You are very bold, sir. To find *you* . . . here! Oh, how sweet and helpless your bare bum looks! How sweet it would look sheathed in my own frillies . . .! But first we must make a start on your correction, and have you well squirming.'

'I fought for you, Mistress, and now I shall have to learn to fight against you. I think I shall enjoy it. You have learnt that history is a cycle, Mistress Derrière – and that we must all start at the bottom.'

'That baubo of yours,' murmured Sophia, 'so strong and fleshy, so dark and hot and powerful . . . even now, it trembles, as though about to rise at the scent of my cane which shall lash you bare, young man. I think it a goddess who must be tamed indeed, for errors committed and misdeeds planned. Where has that goddess been, sir? In which silky wet founts has your baubo found a home?'

Sophia swished her cane in the air, a hair's breadth from Mr Bucentaur's quivering bare bum. 'Miss Brace?

259

Miss Letchford? Miss Duckett? Wyvern? Sassi? Even the maids . . . Chaste, Felicity, Susan . . .?'

The naked cadet nodded and sighed.

'Well!' exclaimed Sophia, her quim suddenly moist and hot at the thought of the beautiful baubo cleaving the Lady's places of her dearest friends. 'And you spied on me and Miss Duckett, didn't you? Through the hole in the painting?'

Mr Bucentaur nodded again.

'And what was your baubo doing then? Standing so firm and hard and dark as you watched us at our rites? I *know*, sir. You caressed her, made her spurt cream as you watched your Ladies writhe for you. And now it shall be you who writhe, sir, and you shall writhe for my lash not just today, but the next day, and all the days, until I decide you have been properly trained, and that your stiff baubo shall grace no Lady's body but my own! That my fount, and my fount alone, shall taste your sweet hot cream.'

The Governess brought down her arm; her cane whistled, and cracked against the male's naked buttocks; the young man jumped and his croup reddened and shivered. Mr Bucentaur's training had begun.

NEXUS BACKLIST

This information is correct at time of printing. For up-to-date information, please visit our website at www.nexus-books.co.uk

All books are priced at £5.99 unless another price is given.

Nexus books with a contemporary setting

ACCIDENTS WILL HAPPEN	Lucy Golden	☐
	ISBN 0 352 33596 3	
ANGEL	Lindsay Gordon	☐
	ISBN 0 352 33590 4	
BARE BEHIND	Penny Birch	☐
£6.99	ISBN 0 352 33721 4	
BEAST	Wendy Swanscombe	☐
	ISBN 0 352 33649 8	
THE BLACK FLAME	Lisette Ashton	☐
	ISBN 0 352 33668 4	
BROUGHT TO HEEL	Arabella Knight	☐
	ISBN 0 352 33508 4	
CAGED!	Yolanda Celbridge	☐
	ISBN 0 352 33650 1	
CANDY IN CAPTIVITY	Arabella Knight	☐
	ISBN 0 352 33495 9	
CAPTIVES OF THE PRIVATE HOUSE	Esme Ombreux	☐
	ISBN 0 352 33619 6	
CHERI CHASTISED	Yolanda Celbridge	☐
£6.99	ISBN 0 352 33707 9	
DANCE OF SUBMISSION	Lisette Ashton	☐
	ISBN 0 352 33450 9	
DIRTY LAUNDRY	Penny Birch	☐
£6.99	ISBN 0 352 33680 3	
DISCIPLINED SKIN	Wendy Swanscombe	☐
	ISBN 0 352 33541 6	

THE TORTURE CHAMBER   Lisette Ashton   ☐
ISBN 0 352 33530 0

UNIFORM DOLL   Penny Birch   ☐
£6.99   ISBN 0 352 33698 6

WHIP HAND   G. C. Scott   ☐
£6.99   ISBN 0 352 33694 3

THE YOUNG WIFE   Stephanie Calvin   ☐
ISBN 0 352 33502 5

Nexus books with Ancient and Fantasy settings

CAPTIVE   Aishling Morgan   ☐
ISBN 0 352 33585 8

DEEP BLUE   Aishling Morgan   ☐
ISBN 0 352 33600 5

DUNGEONS OF LIDIR   Aran Ashe   ☐
ISBN 0 352 33506 8

INNOCENT   Aishling Morgan   ☐
£6.99   ISBN 0 352 33699 4

MAIDEN   Aishling Morgan   ☐
ISBN 0 352 33466 5

NYMPHS OF DIONYSUS   Susan Tinoff   ☐
£4.99   ISBN 0 352 33150 X

PLEASURE TOY   Aishling Morgan   ☐
ISBN 0 352 33634 X

SLAVE MINES OF TORMUNIL   Aran Ashe   ☐
£6.99   ISBN 0 352 33695 1

THE SLAVE OF LIDIR   Aran Ashe   ☐
ISBN 0 352 33504 1

TIGER, TIGER   Aishling Morgan   ☐
ISBN 0 352 33455 X

Period

CONFESSION OF AN ENGLISH   Yolanda Celbridge   ☐
   SLAVE   ISBN 0 352 33433 9

THE MASTER OF CASTLELEIGH   Jacqueline Bellevois   ☐
ISBN 0 352 32644 7

PURITY   Aishling Morgan   ☐
ISBN 0 352 33510 6

VELVET SKIN   Aishling Morgan   ☐
ISBN 0 352 33660 9

Samplers and collections

NEW EROTICA 5	Various ISBN 0 352 33540 8	☐
EROTICON 1	Various ISBN 0 352 33593 9	☐
EROTICON 2	Various ISBN 0 352 33594 7	☐
EROTICON 3	Various ISBN 0 352 33597 1	☐
EROTICON 4	Various ISBN 0 352 33602 1	☐
THE NEXUS LETTERS	Various ISBN 0 352 33621 8	☐
SATURNALIA £7.99	ed. Paul Scott ISBN 0 352 33717 6	☐
MY SECRET GARDEN SHED £7.99	ed. Paul Scott ISBN 0 352 33725 7	☐

Nexus Classics

A new imprint dedicated to putting the finest works of erotic fiction back in print.

AMANDA IN THE PRIVATE HOUSE £6.99	Esme Ombreux ISBN 0 352 33705 2	☐
BAD PENNY	Penny Birch ISBN 0 352 33661 7	☐
BRAT £6.99	Penny Birch ISBN 0 352 33674 9	☐
DARK DELIGHTS £6.99	Maria del Rey ISBN 0 352 33667 6	☐
DARK DESIRES	Maria del Rey ISBN 0 352 33648 X	☐
DISPLAYS OF INNOCENTS £6.99	Lucy Golden ISBN 0 352 33679 X	☐
DISCIPLINE OF THE PRIVATE HOUSE £6.99	Esme Ombreux ISBN 0 352 33459 2	☐
EDEN UNVEILED	Maria del Rey ISBN 0 352 33542 4	☐

- - - - - - ✂ -

Please send me the books I have ticked above.

Name   ....

Address ....

         ....

         ....

         .... Post code....................

Send to: **Cash Sales, Nexus Books, Thames Wharf Studios, Rainville Road, London W6 9HA**

US customers: for prices and details of how to order books for delivery by mail, call 1-800-343-4499.

Please enclose a cheque or postal order, made payable to **Nexus Books Ltd**, to the value of the books you have ordered plus postage and packing costs as follows:
    UK and BFPO – £1.00 for the first book, 50p for each subsequent book.
    Overseas (including Republic of Ireland) – £2.00 for the first book, £1.00 for each subsequent book.

If you would prefer to pay by VISA, ACCESS/MASTERCARD, AMEX, DINERS CLUB or SWITCH, please write your card number and expiry date here:

....

Please allow up to 28 days for delivery.

Signature ....

Our privacy policy.

We will not disclose information you supply us to any other parties. We will not disclose any information which identifies you personally to any person without your express consent.

From time to time we may send out information about Nexus books and special offers. Please tick here if you do *not* wish to receive Nexus information.   ☐

- - - - - - ✂ -